DEEP
HINTS AND CLUES

NOVEL 1 IN THE SERIES
SCRAPBOOKS OF THE SOUL

MARILYN HAMMOND, PhD

EMPRESS
PUBLICATIONS
WWW.EMPRESSPUBLICATIONS.COM

SCRAPBOOKS OF THE SOUL

Explore the mesmerizing universe of **Scrapbooks of the Soul**, a compelling series of novels where fiction merges with profound inquiry. Each book is a rich mosaic, filled with diverse fictional characters who delve into the mysteries of the soul, sleeptime dreams, brain hemispheres, and the intersections of spirituality and science. Their dialogues, embellished with insightful footnotes, navigate through themes of whole-brain Christianity, and the intricacies of psychological, generational, and cultural healing.

These stories are more than narratives; they are a reflection on human experience, encompassing long-standing friendships, resilient relationships, and our struggle with life's opposites. The series offers a unique perspective, suggesting our reality is shaped by our perceptions and interpretations. Engage with **Scrapbooks of the Soul** to discover a world where each page mirrors the complexity of life and the varied interpretations that define our existence.

Novel #1 *Deep Hints and Clues*
Novel #2 *What Might We Know*
Novel #3 *An Empty Ache*
Novel #4 *Sit With It*
Novel #5 *Backyard Talk*
Novel #6 *Approach Boldly* (Plus Series Index)

Dedication

In loving gratitude for Jay's steadfast encouragement

Table of

Contents

Chapter One

What We See Is How We See

The morning sun was bright in Sandshell FL, as Dee Kendrick stood in the back yard this early summer day, glass of iced coffee in hand, enjoying her vegetable garden alongside the flower garden. Covid-19, the pandemic of nearly a year and a half was expected to lessen with the arrival of vaccinations and summer weather.

Dee, now past middle-age, had changed her name years ago. She'd been named Dempsey. This day in 2021, she was revisiting memories of the remarkable woman, Ann Dramm, who'd greatly influenced her. Ann was old enough to be Dee's mother. There were other friends, too, whose interests helped mold and shape Dee.

However, above all, there was Ann Dramm who'd inspired Dee. Ann, a part-time portrait artist from Stamford CT knew by the age of sixty that since her teen-years a religious impulse had been following her like a stray dog looking for a home. It was obvious to Ann she was greatly affected by three friends from Austin, TX—Beth, Gabby. Matti—who in casual, practical, personal and humorous ways easily talked about religion and related topics.

The three Texans were distinctly different. Beth was strawberry blonde in the first years, eventually turned a bit grey and then, back to solid strawberry blonde. The chemical fix looked just right on her. She was youthful, physically fit, and funny. Her humor was a delight, and if

Ann was to paint a portrait of Beth, her warmth as a people person and her clever wit would need to shine.

Gabby (Gabriela) was small, with olive skin, straight black hair and huge brown eyes with a look of forlornness. Not a people-person like Beth, Gabby had her own brand of humor and quick thinking alongside profound understanding. Over the years her hair scarcely turned grey. There were only random strands of grey which she did nothing to change. If painting a portrait of Gabby, her eyes would be the focus.

Matti, who Ann knew best, was least clear as a portrait. Rather than Matti's face dominating, it was her stately presence: body straightness, whether sitting, standing or walking she looked confident. A back injury as a high school cheerleader caused this appearance of confidence, or so Matti said. Peculiar how sometimes injury can become gain.

Matti's dark brown hair greyed and developed streaks of mahogany. She said she was becoming tri-color, like a dog. She didn't take herself seriously, though her interests were serious, intense, passionate. Revisiting these three Texas women Ann came to know them well. Beth, a Methodist, reared in east Texas. Gabby, a Catholic, raised in west Texas. Matti, an Episcopalian, grew up in central Texas. Texas is so big their childhood locations were reflected in their speech inflections.

Beth, a full-time volunteer with charities, was married to a stockbroker. They had two children. Gabby, a psychology professor at a local Catholic college, and her husband, an economics professor at the state university, had two children. Matti, a fulltime librarian at the university, was an independent thinker; a consistently independent personality who never married.

Ann Dramm recalled an earlier time, when seated with her three friends in a restaurant in Austin TX studying the lunch menu, Beth playfully instructed, "Remember ladies, it has been said, 'You are what you eat.'" To which Gabby replied, "A psychologist might say instead, 'You are what you think or feel.'" Whereupon Matti immediately offered, "I say, you are your hermeneutic habits," and the three Texans burst into laughter, while Ann remained an outsider to their humor.

Quickly, Beth and Gabby explained their amusement was the predictability of Matti's comment, and then they shared that though *hermeneutic* [her me nu/ tik] is not a household term, they were well acquainted with Matti's passion in how humans *interpret* themselves, others, and all of life. Yes, hermeneutics is about interpretation. Beth wrote the word *hermeneutic* on a napkin.

That day Ann learned *hermeneutic* is formed from the name Hermes in Greek mythology. Hermes had the complex task of delivering the messages of the gods to mortals, which meant he first had to interpret for himself what the gods were saying, and then translate the message in such a way that mortals could understand it.

Ann also learned that Matti was convinced all humans have the same complex task as Hermes; we are hermeneuts whether or not we want to be; for in the ordinariness of life, we always and everywhere infer, deduce, discern, decide, what our experiences "mean" or if they mean nothing, which is itself an interpretation. We have the immense opportunity and responsibility of interpreting what we encounter in our experiences, in our personality.

On one hand, our interpretations form a lot of who we are. On the other hand, who and what we are greatly influences our interpretations. What we see is largely a part of how we see. Our life is a scrapbook of our interpretations and the interpretations of others which affect us.

These facts about hermeneutics Ann learned that day in the restaurant, and knowing Matti as she did, she well understood Matti's conviction that we humans are largely formed by our hermeneutic habits. Ann knew Matti felt she had poorly interpreted her own needs, wants and longings when younger. Thus, Matti's hobby, her passion, her lifetime quest became uncovering the practical implications of how humans interpret themselves, their desires.

Ann would later learn that Matti's computer was filled with research gathered and thoughts processed about practical hermeneutics, which is, quite simply, profound personal awareness of oneself; not narcissism.

Chapter Two

Matti Dialed 911

Ann Dramm's trips to Texas and the influence of these three remarkable women formed an important chapter of her life, though she didn't know every detail of their everyday lives, simply dropping in on them periodically through thirty years crystallized into highlights, vignettes, sketches, patterns, portraits of each one. Over the years Ann often asked herself, "Why are these unlikely Texas friends so vital in my life? Why has this Texas connection remained open and important? Why do these Texas friendships beckon to me? What are they offering?"

Her relationship with Texas friends started when Ann came to know Matti from Austin in 1965 at the University of Connecticut when each needed someone to share living expenses; thus these two graduate students in their late twenties became apartment mates. Their time together was unforgettable.

Finishing her degree, Matti went back to Texas. The two former apartment mates stayed in touch, telephoning and then e-mailing, not constantly, but regularly. Their continuing relationship was enduring and perhaps unavoidable. They were bound together for the next thirty years.

Going to see Matti in Austin, Ann became friends with Beth and Gabby. Matti never went to visit Ann in Connecticut where Ann married and had the luxury of being a stay-at-home mother of two daughters, part-time portrait artist, and patron of the arts in the community.

Gradually, a tradition developed where every three or four years Ann would spend a few days with Matti the first weekend of December when Matti had an annual pre-Christmas party. Matti's first Saturday evening in December party was important to Matti and Ann understood why.

During Ann's Texas treks, she saw Beth and Gabby at the Christmas party and usually for lunch on Friday before the party. She remembered vividly the early morning telephone call from Beth who had never before telephoned her. Recognizing Beth's voice, Ann knew something was radically wrong and was told that Matti died the night before.

Ann learned that Matti spent the evening at her computer. A little after 9 p.m. she dialed 911, said "I'm ill," and gave her address. Her computer was "on" when paramedics arrived and found Matti dead at the age of 57. This woman Ann had known for more than thirty years died of a ruptured brain aneurysm.

Death was quick, family and friends were assured. Matti's life was not spectacular and yet it was. Those who knew her well felt she'd had a satisfying, meaningful, fulfilling life. To Ann, she became a woman of exceptional wisdom, who struggled mightily on many levels, including intense study, helping others with the topic of practical hermeneutics, a subject which had painfully found its way into her life.

Matti's name evolved from being named Margaret, changed to the elementary school girl Maggie, and finally to the college aunt Matti when her young niece could make the sound "t" easier than "g" and called her Matti instead of Maggie. The name Matti stuck. There was no "e" on the end of Matti because the six-year-old brother of the niece, wrote it without an "e," and Matti liked the way it looked. She loved her niece and nephew dearly. For the rest of her life she was known as Matti, though she never legally changed her name.

Would life have been different had she gone through life as Margaret or Maggie? Matti didn't spend time ruminating minor matters, for major concerns consumed her. In the outer world she came to have a predictable, staid life, while on the inside Matti was ever-changing into new patterns of understanding and new paths of questioning. This was her most distinctive characteristic to those who knew her well. However, there were other parts to Matti that only Ann Dramm knew.

Matti's undergraduate degree had been a major in business and a minor in medieval history—an eclectic combination, like Matti herself, who enjoyed ballet and baseball. She worked in investment banking for three years after graduating from college and three years was long enough for her to know she didn't want to continue that career path. Luckily, she saved money which helped her survive on a pittance wage in the library at the university when she decided to begin a master's degree in psychology.

Partway through the degree, she found psychology was not the love she thought it would be, and her disillusionment with psychology caused Matti to flounder for some while before she came to realize what most invigorated, stimulated, and satisfied her undying quest for learning were the books in the library. Much was to happen, enormous pain and struggle, before her passion for books focused on practical hermeneutics, which she found close to *phronesis* in Greek, practical wisdom; one might use the label *commonsense*.

After earning a master's degree in library science in Connecticut, Matti returned to the University of Texas to supervise students who worked part-time at the library, which kept her ever aware of the struggles of young adults; those on the verge of becoming young adults. She felt privileged to work with these students and could easily relate to their stresses: developing personal discipline, time-management, clarifying priorities, romantic entanglements, heartbreak, money problems. Matti had agonized with the same issues. Indeed, the pain from her late twenties remained with her always.

Chapter Three

Fearful, Lazy, Stupid

Matti remembered her own adolescence, when peer pressures seemed to drown out the powerful questions that were emerging within her: Who am I? Why am I here? What am I to do with my life? How can I answer these questions? To her, adolescence was an extraordinary breakthrough time of life, superficially dealt with in American culture. Her own adolescence was not traumatic, but it was inadequate in helping her know herself. She returned to this topic often.

At the age of 57, her death, Matti was an attractive woman who dressed in a tailored chic style. She'd started dressing that way as soon as she got to make clothes choices. She had a classic look about her. Of medium height, she looked taller because of her thinness and erect posture. Disliking nondescript hairstyles, her changing hair styles were always distinctive in some way.

She didn't enjoy shopping, because she didn't leisure-shop; she research-shopped, which means she didn't shop unless she was looking for something definite. And she didn't understand people who shopped just to be shopping; she never had time for that. Time drove Matti most of her life. Time and timelessness were important to her.

Yet, Matti always had time for family and friends, which was evident at her large funeral in the Episcopal church where she was an active member. It was the simple service Matti wanted, as she'd expressed in casual conversations over the years with the choir director who was a friend.

At the funeral, the Episcopal priest described Matti as a woman of "intelligent faith," and explained why he thought of her in this way. Matti told him she was convinced Jesus knew what he was talking about when he said if we seek, we find; knock, and a door opens. Matti was a seeker; she never stopped knocking and the door of understanding opened again and again. One of her gifts was asking questions. Certainly, anyone who knew Matti knew this. Ann commented on Matti's questing attitude and was told by Matti, "After I die, I don't want to be asked, 'Why, on earth, didn't you ask more questions?'"

Matti easily shared her religious experiences. Like the simple prayer she told Ann came to her and remained a favorite. The prayer was, "Please, God, help me not be fearful, lazy, or stupid." When Ann asked her why she thought the words "fearful, lazy, stupid," came instead of their more attractive opposites, "courageous, industrious, wise," she said she thought we often meet what needs development in our personality before we meet our abundance. "Besides," Matti concluded, "I like the starkness of fearful, lazy, stupid."

Later, Matti discovered the Jesuit aphorism: "Pray as though everything depends on God. Work as though everything depends on you," which she found more refined than her fearful-lazy-stupid prayer, though both are about needing God's grace alongside our efforts, she summarized.

Those who knew Matti best agreed that the priest's description of her as a woman of "intelligent faith" was appropriate.

Chapter Four

The Garden of Ego

Ann went to Texas for Matti's funeral and came home with a restless urgency to understand Matti's story anew. Matti was born into a stable, loving family, had a younger brother, her parents were ethical, civic-minded, altruistic Episcopalians, a prominent family in a mid-sized town in central Texas; her father, a regional manager in retail appliance sales, her mother an elementary school teacher. Matti was baptized when young and attended church regularly with her family until undergraduate years in Minnesota, where life was filled fully with living college life, while god, faith, church became unimportant. In her late twenties, Matti's need for God became critical.

There was a time when Matti was living in Austin after graduating from college in Minnesota and her difficulties came from several sources. First, there was an unpredictable romance with John, which lasted several years but finally died, leaving wrecked emotions that wouldn't go away. She was in love with John but never liked his personality. She didn't know what that was about. She dated wildly to ease the pain of the breakup, but, indeed, her dating only caused a great deal more pain.

The void and distress of the broken and chaotic relationship with John coincided with Matti's failed efforts to stop smoking, a habit she acquired as a college freshman when the dormitory wisdom was that smoking depressed the appetite for fattening dorm food. Matti had tried for several years to kick the smoking habit and felt she was making headway when the stress of the breakup with John and its aftermath made her need cigarettes even more.

She was accumulating debt after depleting her savings, and had only a small paycheck from part-time work in the library. She hid money problems from her parents, wanting desperately to be independent and provide for herself, but found herself digging a deeper financial pit each month.

And last, Matti had a dreadful fear that not continuing the master's program in psychology might be a mistake, yet increasingly she saw that the study of psychology was not what she thought it would be, and didn't want to continue. Disenchantment with psychology grew as she more clearly found the scientific paradigm not adequate to fully explore or express the personality or human existence, as she wanted to investigate it.

Despite high regard for science, its many contributions to humankind, and the rigorous hard work it entails, science became a kind of stranglehold on her, a hindrance, for she wanted to look at a bigger picture of life. Perhaps philosophy was the way for her to go, but she enrolled in no courses the spring semester.

In a quandary, feeling paralyzed, unable to find a sense of direction, she continued to work part time at the library, accumulate more debt, smoke while wanting to stop, and she could not stop missing ex-boyfriend John, despite frantically dating others.

Years later, she told Ann that alone in her apartment one evening, nearly out of her mind with turmoil, she partly "saw" and "felt" the faint impression of a human hand in the room, which she dismissed as a mere uncanny event, a result of her current neediness.

At about the same time, the song lyrics "He's Got the Whole World in His Hands," which had never been important to her, spontaneously came to mind. She disregarded this also. Years later she connected the song with the hand image and felt that a synchronicity had been working in her life, though she didn't discern it because of her concrete-thinking, reductive mindset at the time.

But then, despite her skeptical attitude, she did find it significant that a particular book crossed her path at the library which helped her stop smoking. The book mentioned smoking as a symbolic activity, which struck a chord with Matti. She began to play with the idea that inhaling while smoking is magnifying the normal process of breathing.

Breathing is taking in the breath of life itself, and many meditational practices regard attention to breathing critical in learning to meditate, to contemplate. Also, fire, so important in the survival of our ancient ancestors, and thus part of our own evolutionary story, is part of smoking. Matti began to connect the fire of the cigarette symbolically with enlightenment, insight, being able to "see."

It occurred to her that the burning bush of Moses in the bible was a revelatory breakthrough. She also understood that in alchemy, fire is vital in the effort to transform gross metal into gold. Translated psycho-spiritually, fire symbolizes transformation of the personality; the tongues of fire at Pentecost, for instance. She symbolically connected fire to the wisdom waiting for us when we are ready for it.

Many years later Matti was able to figuratively say that short-sighted understanding *goes up in smoke* (like smoking a cigarette) if we endure the flames of enlightenment which show us our limitations, shortcomings, incompleteness. To the degree that the dross of ego, which is "I" in Greek and Latin, is purged and purified, Eden (as in the Garden of Eden) is ignited within and we can walk and talk with God.

The Eden-Ego contrast lived in Matti throughout her mature adult years. She never doubted that nicotine was physically addicting. However, recognizing the symbolic gestures in smoking brought added strength to her efforts as she tried to quit.

One evening, after insights about smoking as a symbolic act, Matti was craving a cigarette, and in her desperation found herself inhaling the word "help" and exhaling the word "me." Continuing the breath-word activity at length, the craving lessened. Repeating the practice over the next few weeks and months whenever the craving returned, she was eventually able to kick the habit. Much later, she was amused to realize that "me" was exhaled, as if "me" was being replaced by a greater "help" which she inhaled.

She had been working at her computer on an essay contrasting Ego-Eden when paramedics arrived her final evening on earth. She believed we spend life on earth suspended, vacillating, being formed out of the tension between self-sufficiency and dependency on God; this is the vital pattern of our life.

From Matti's Computer
Ego vs Eden

The Garden of Eden was likely an oasis in a desert in the Middle East – its location now uncertain. To desert people, an oasis is "paradise" and the Hebrew story about Adam and Eve takes place in Eden (paradise) where Adam and Eve walk and talk with God. Why not regard Eden also as an ideal psychological "place," state of awareness, when a personality is in touch with the Divine.

Neuroscience is shedding light on brain functions during non-ordinary states of consciousness, such as meditation (contemplation), which I consider psychological-biological Garden of Eden spots in us.

The story of Eden concludes that when human-divine communication is broken, humans are left to struggle alone—in the Garden of Ego, one might say. Ego means "I" in Greek and Latin. In today's idiom it's my comfort zone—my frame of reference; a goldfish mentality. Ego is the limited awareness I have of myself and everything else and it is living by my own efforts.

Speaking metaphorically, in a personal Garden of Ego, thorns of old psychological wounds prick one with negative thoughts and fearful, despairing emotions. The Garden of Ego has seeds— potential—unable to sprout, choked-out by thistles, weeds— everyday worries and cares. In the Garden of Ego, there can be drought—the dryness of too little hope and joy. Religion, at its best, helps Ego find Eden. Too often, the platitudes of religion leave us with Ego alone, which can bring the companions of fear, guilt, shame, worry and dread; or on the flipside of Ego with prideful arrogance, which at its worst can be callous, brutal attitudes and behaviors.

An Ego-centered life is like the stress of a four-cylinder engine running on one cylinder. It's like the bulb in a flashlight unaware of the batteries that make it shine. It's like a toddler wanting to be and do more than it can. Ego-based living is anxiety-ridden. An Ego-driven personality is a kind of pre-packaged personality formed out of genetics, family dynamics, schooling, institutional and cultural traditions, language limitations, unconscious components. However, Ego at its best knows it longs for God, and at its best Ego wants creative answers to why we're alive, what we're about, what we can become and do.

Not asking these questions or having inadequate answers to them may be a large part of today's rampant depression—a kind of widespread Ego-exhaustion, which can become destructive acting-out. Today's addictions and compulsions, ideological fanaticisms, are misguided ways of trying to find Eden; trying to reconnect with bliss, joy, serenity, through sex, drugs, comfort foods, etc., or through rigid, simplistic ideologies. What humans deeply desire is uncovering the mystery of one's own personality and life in relationship with the creative Source and Sustenance of Life Itself.

As for her money problems, Matti received money from her parents as part of getting their assets in order, for her father was ailing. Though not wealthy, her parents were financially comfortable. The money Matti got that summer felt like a life raft to a drowning person. For the rest of her life and beyond, Matti gave money to those who needed it, so that they too might find the universe a caring place. She knew how cruel circumstances can be.

As Matti was preparing to enter the master's degree program in library science in Connecticut in the fall, Matti learned she was pregnant from a short fling with someone she scarcely knew. That's when Ann and Matti met. The year was 1965.

Chapter Five

Pregnancy

Matti went to Connecticut for graduate school and, though strangers, she and Ann ended up sharing not only an apartment, but Matti's pregnancy, labor, and delivery. Matti attended classes, was healthy throughout the pregnancy, and in the spring delivered a healthy baby girl she "gave away" (Matti's words, "to burn the reality into my being," she said). She then continued at the university, completing her master's degree in library science.

Later, during Ann's visits to Texas, the two of them often talked of the adoption. Matti could not let go of the "agonizing truth," again her words. She never told family or friends about her baby. It was her lifelong secret, a wound only God's grace could heal, she said. She believed that wound was the source of any strength she might possess, she told Ann the last time Ann saw her.

Matti came to be regarded as a woman of wisdom, though others did not know about the dark night of the soul which birthed it—the internal wrangling and deep loss of giving up the baby she'd held in her arms once, just once, which created a pain so wrenching she prayed she'd die. When she didn't die, she prayed to lose her mind so she wouldn't remember. That didn't happen either.

The rest of her life Matti second-guessed why she didn't keep the baby she called Mary. Women didn't do that so easily back then, she reasoned. Her reasoning didn't help much. It would take more than rational explanation to bring peace to her inner chaos.

Matti felt she'd been a coward; denying her parents knowing their granddaughter. But it wasn't so simple, for she also wanted to spare her parents. She'd felt like a trapped animal at the time and graduate school in the northeast was a readymade answer. She never considered abortion, not because she was a moral heroine, but because the solution of moving away for graduate study was already at hand, and she used it.

Very often she crumbled inside remembering the psychological neediness which led to the pregnancy. How could she have been so desperate, vulnerable and weak, unable to unhinge herself emotionally from John whose personality she never liked, and getting pregnant with someone she scarcely knew, who she never told about the pregnancy. Yes, he had the right to know he'd fathered a child. She assumed he wouldn't want an ongoing relationship with her forced on him. She didn't want to be anybody's pity-party.

Matti was a bundle of contradictions. She, who had a stable, loving childhood, how could she have been so conflicted? A confident child she'd been; bright, curious, independent. In retrospect she felt early adolescence was when her confident integrity began to be compromised. She didn't think it was her parents' fault. She blamed herself that an interior strength she had as a child began to erode in adolescence. Eventually she came to see that the broader culture lacked elements which she sorely needed growing up, for at the very time youth become capable of asking questions about existence, they are thrust into superficial conventionality that dissipates the questions.

Uncovering and restoring these cultural deficiencies became her lifetime avocation. When she began her work of passion she did not know the word hermeneutic, nor had she ever thought of the contrast between the Ego in us and the Eden part of us. By the time she died, she had some of her own terminology to talk about the art of reading and interpreting oneself, one's thoughts, emotions, desires, cravings, longings and yearnings; recognizing divine longing and presence in the personality.

By the time her life on earth ended, Matti discerned God as Unceasing Creative Wisdom. She came to regard the hand image and song lyrics as synchronicities, invitations of available help, which, had she been able to make that interpretation at the time of their happening she might not have needed so desperately the temporary comforts of a near stranger, Mary's father. Matti could undo nothing. She could only continue to learn from her experience. Matti took the secret of Mary to the grave. Daily, she prayed for Mary and the family that adopted her.

Matti updated information with the adoption agency so Mary could easily find her if she chose. That never happened and it hurt. Of course, Matti had "given Mary away" so why would the child search for her birth mother? That thought really hurt. As Matti grew older, she deeply regretted not telling her parents, though that would have carried its own difficulties. How would her precious niece and nephew have reacted?

A job was waiting for Matti in the library at the university in Austin after graduate school. Taking a baby home would have had complications. It was best to never tell anyone. Why burden anyone with her secret. She apologized to Ann for having to bear the secret. As for her not telling Beth and Gabby, she was ensconced in her secret by the time she met them. The secret was part of her identity. When Ann Dramm became a grandmother, Matti wondered if she was a grandmother.

Matti's inability to discern the hand-image and song lyrics as meaningful synchronicity caused Matti to remember something else. She told Ann that at the age of thirteen or so, seated alone on the back steps of the house her family lived in, she was thinking, feeling, wishing the grass would stop growing so she could catch-up. This, Matti later regarded as a youthful brush with timelessness, the eternal. She also came to see it as a clue about her ongoing struggle with time. She was a time-driven person, even as a child, because she was bright and had many interests; there wasn't time for all of them.

She wished she'd understood the grass incident earlier, before her late twenties when everything seemed urgent. If only she could have seen the hand of God in her life. Perhaps she could have appreciated the wisdom of the end of the dead end relationship with John. It was years before she began understanding her mixed feelings about John.

Chapter Six

Allusion Confusion

Overall, Matti learned to recognize synchronicity (the workings of divine grace) in her life; synchronicity as a kind of *right time*, when profoundly meaningful events fall into place; when there is a rhythm, flow, harmony, the proper beat. She found stress greatly lessened when she made time every day for quiet, as she could be easily derailed.

She came to understand a fulfilled life in terms of a pendulum, the oscillation between Ego and Eden, time and timelessness, the human and the divine, the human Jesus equally the divine Christ in whom time and timelessness intersect. He was increasingly the center of her existence. Ann's trips to Texas became more and more spiritual as Matti's spirituality matured, expanded, refined.

Matti's ideas about romance were troubled. She was convinced romance is a harsh way to find a life-partner. She considered "being-in-love" a strange mental/emotional state. She could not understand how one could fall into such a heightened state of being, recover from it and fall into the state again with another person. And why do so many people fall in love, marry, fall out of love and end up divorced?

After Mary's birth, Matti carefully and casually dated, but found that if someone thought they were in love with her and she didn't have the same feelings for the person, then the other person's *in-loveness* seemed strange indeed, something driven from within the other person and she was merely its object. "Being *in-love* is a pathological illusion," she declared to Ann. It seemed to Matti that we are seduced, entranced, snared, trapped and eventually disappointed by this mysterious romance illusion. As with all illusion, there is deceit and trickery involved. To Matti, romantic attraction was an illusion, a deception, a trick of some sort.

She still felt compelled to figure out how she could have been *in-love* with John whose personality she didn't even like. Eventually she began to understand she didn't love the person John, but was *in-love* with some of his qualities, traits, and characteristics.

She first saw John in an off-campus college hang-out when she was with friends. There was a small dance floor and he was dancing with someone. Matti fell instantly *in-love* with him. In her exuberance, she let her friends know of her new love object. It was through a friend that she met John at the same club a week or so later. It was likely her lively interest in him that led to his interest in her. Anyway, from the start, Matti was more intrigued by John than fond of him. She learned to dance for and with him. They were so good dancing together others stood aside to watch them on the dance floor. He fascinated her. She was caught in a trap of her own unintentional making. Over the next few years, she could not get out of the trap, though she dated other people at times when the relationship with John was shaky. He remained somehow magical to her.

Matti would one day be able to explain to Ann, "Exaggerated, emotionally-charged positive or negative reactions to people, events, things, tell us about our personality; but we can't be thickheaded. It takes subtlety and nuance to detect and connect interior reactions with exterior triggers."

Eventually, Matti understood that her instantaneous *in-love* reaction to John was more about dancing than it was about John. His rhythm, timing, had to do with *time*. John personified time, which had this unusual hold on Matti. She told Ann she knew it may sound abstract and farfetched, but had she realized John epitomized perfect timing, (synchronicity, divine grace), she could have saved both of them a lot of trouble.

Matti's conclusion that romantic love is pathological illusion was not to be her final word on romance. Rather, she would come to regard romance more accurately as *allusion*. Gabby talked about allusion with her psychology students: cravings, impulses, urges, inordinate attractions and aversions as hints or clues about vital aspects in the personality, in one's life. All people have longings and yearnings which can be misunderstood, mislived, as addictions, compulsions. Gabby created the term *allusion confusion* for her students to talk about misinterpreted longings.

Matti came to realize her attraction to John **alluded to** (were hints and clues) about something critical in her personality. However, lacking adequate discernment tools, unable to understand with subtlety what John represented, symbolized, Matti assumed incorrectly it was John himself who was the object of her affection, though she readily admitted she was not fond of his personality. It was his dancing that was a mirror reflecting her problematic relationship with time, timing, timelessness. His dancing mimicked, represented, symbolized *time* to Matti, but she didn't know that.

Gabby said, "Undiscerned symbols can become symptoms, physical or behavioral symptoms. Or turn the phrase around, and symptoms may be undiscerned symbols."

Gabby helped Matti understand allusion confusion with examples: Eating disorders can be thought of as *allusion confusion*. That is, eating physical food when it is psychological hungers that need to be fed and nourished. Hungry for friendship, hope, understanding, opportunity, or such, we might try to fill our emptiness, seek fulfillment, with food from the kitchen. Or, starved for attention, affection, purpose, worth, we may externalize the impulse and stop eating, as in anorexia. Alcoholics Anonymous shows that thirst for alcohol is actually Spiritual Thirst, which is what the Twelve Steps are about. Matti knew from experience that smoking cigarettes had an element of allusion confusion in the habit.

Gabby's allusion confusion opened a whole new horizon for Matti; a new way of interpreting events in both the inner world and outer world.

Chapter Seven

Gabby

Matti first met Gabby at an assisted-living facility where Gabby often visited her mother-in-law who was living in the skilled-nursing section. Gabby admired the clever, colorful displays on a large cork board in the social-TV-dining room. The board seemed to change frequently. Gabby complimented the staff on the artistic display and was told it was not their work but the creation of a woman named Matti.

One day Gabby came to see her mother-in-law, noticed a woman changing the display, stopped to praise her for the refreshing brightness of her creations and how the cork board did not become stale because it was changed often. Matti graciously accepted the compliments but said the display she was putting up just then was going to be up longer than she liked, as she was going out of town. Gabby offered to make changes on the board while Matti was gone. Two days later Gabby was at Matti's home picking up new pieces for the cork board. Thus began their friendship.

Gabby's life was a surprise to Gabby. She was of Mexican-American heritage, whose family had been on the U.S. side of the border for several generations. What came to surprise her is that added to the commonsense virtues of her frugal hardworking childhood were added interests in seemingly impractical (yet absolutely vital) symbol, allusion, metaphor. Nothing in her background prepared her for this. And yet that was not true.

Traditions, stories, folklore of her Hispanic heritage and the Catholicism of her youth were full of symbol, allusion, metaphor. No one ever told her that. Not directly. But indirectly she knew that at Mass the priest's vestments, the color of those vestments, the statues at church, the stained-glass windows, the crucifix, the liturgical year, incense, candles, the Eucharist, all *alluded* to the great mystery which life is and which death is. They are hints and clues about living and dying and Jesus the Christ is at the center of all this.

She had unknowingly grown up in a symbolic world. Jesus' parables about the kingdom of God, read at Mass, were metaphoric stories. Almost every word Jesus uttered, as recorded in the bible, is figurative, she later realized. Yes, allusion, symbol, and metaphor were part of her upbringing. She understood this when she was older.

Gabby remembered preparing for the sacrament of confirmation at age thirteen. When the day came she was disappointed, for nothing mystical, unusual, life-changing happened. She expected to experience something distinct, special, extraordinary, which didn't take place. She wondered if her parents and other relatives also wanted more than they got from church. Yet, she also sensed they were strengthened by what came to them through church, and she never stopped going to Mass.

Gabby never stopped wanting more; yearning and longing for more. Many years later she understood the yearning and longing for more on her confirmation day was special grace that would continue the rest of her life. It wasn't until her early thirties that symbol, metaphor and allusion began to unfold with meaning. Why hadn't such happened years earlier? Gabby had such a huge appetite for religious knowing that she lived with the disappointment of never having enough, always wanting more. Only after Matti's death did Gabby speak with Ann of these things.

Gabby shared that the sadness of her Hispanic ancestors whose lives had been bleak, difficult, marginal survival for too many generations, still lived in her. She discovered this during hypnotherapy sessions which she participated in as part of her psychological training, which came after putting herself through college, marrying, having two children, continuing her education until she had a doctorate in psychology.

In the hypnotherapy sessions the world of images opened to her and she began to pay attention to her sleeptime dream images. The theme of ancestry showed itself again and again. When Gabby and Matti met, Gabby had been keeping dream journals for some time.

Ann made a Texas visit when the world of dream images was new in Matti's life through Gabby, and though Matti confidently embraced new ideas, she deferred to Gabby when it came to images, metaphor and symbol, believing that Gabby was extraordinarily gifted with figurative understanding. Matti told Ann she felt superficial compared to Gabby. Over the years Ann saw Matti's curious, penetrating mind become increasingly figurative.

Gabby suffered from a kind of chronic fatigue for reasons that would later become clear and break Ann's heart, for Ann cherished Gabby.

Chapter Eight

Beth

And then there was Matti's friend Beth, who also became Ann's friend. Beth met Matti on a sidewalk near the university. One day, Beth stopped running and began walking alongside Matti, suggesting they formally meet each other since they shared the same sidewalk. Beth commented on the many books she often saw Matti carrying to and from campus. Uncharacteristically flippant, Matti replied, "Socrates said the unexamined life is not worth living." And Beth tossed back, "Maybe Socrates didn't know that an unlived life is not worth examining." Matti was impressed. The two became friends.

Beth's outgoing energy, her generous upbeat attitude, her wit, were in sharp contrast to Matti's more serious personality. Beth's life had been easy and then again, it wasn't. She grew up in east Texas, a descendant of oil riches. In her words, "We didn't have oodles of money because we were passionate and prolific Protestants. By my time too many heirs had divided the spoils. But my family did have more than two nickels to rub together at one time." She came to her marriage with money, and charismatic Thomas, her husband, knew how to woo clients in the stock business. They did well financially.

"Thomas can charm the pants off of anybody," Beth said one day when she and Ann lunched alone because neither Gabby or Matti could be with them. During that lunch Ann learned Beth's life indeed was not easy. Ann already knew about Beth's 30-year-old son's alcohol/prescribed medication overdose which was accidental or suicidal. That wasn't clear. But his alcoholism became clear. The family knew Wesley was called "Whiskey" by his buddies. They didn't know why. Only after the emergency room episode did some of the friends confirm what Beth and Thomas suspected: Wesley was an alcoholic. Wesley survived. Beth sought out Al-Anon, which became a mainstay in her life.

That day at lunch Beth told Ann of husband Thomas's amiable, attractive, appealing personality which so drew her to him, but that wasn't all there was to him. Mood swings started some years ago. The highs were too high and would last for months. With her irresistible humor Beth said to Ann, "I told you he could charm the pants off of anyone and he has done that more than once with his "female friends" since we've been married. When I found out, I thought I'd die. But I had to keep the marriage intact for the kids. I know that's a cliché, but for me it's a profound cliché," and looking-up, Beth seemed to ask the air itself, "Is 'profound cliché' incongruent?"

She continued, "Thomas can be fine for months and then fall into the clutches of mania again. I can feel his mania. It's swirling madness; palpable energy gone awry. A frenetic frenzy. Then depression begins and paralyzes him. He can go weeks or months scarcely able to get out of bed.

"Gabby and Matti know all of this," she told Ann. Then she paused, looked at her food as if trying to decide whether to say what she said next. "What they don't know, and what I don't want them to know, is that he nearly caused us to go bankrupt during one manic episode. Even my inheritance scarcely saved us. When the financial woes came crashing in, he fell into his worst depression. I couldn't leave him then because he was nearly dead with despair. It took years to dig out of that financial pit."

Then, Beth easily continued, "My volunteer work is a godsend. The hospital, the nonprofit boards I am on help keep me sane; and Al-Anon. My Higher Power is my anchor. I'm blessed, very blessed. Thomas is on a medication that is working. Wesley is doing OK. Our daughter Susan and family are fine. Matti and Gabby know everything except the financial stuff. I think I couldn't tell them out of loyalty to Thomas. Strange that I don't want them to know his greatest stupidity. I am protective of him. Maybe that's love, I'm not sure."

Ann felt invisible as Beth confided Thomas's "stupidity" to her. Others have told Ann she feels safe; a kind of invisible safeness, and she has suspected her invisibility allows portrait subjects to comfortably emerge and simply "be" while she paints their portrait.

Listening carefully to Beth, Ann noticed again Beth's endearing east Texas accent. Beth talked about how "chaaarmed" her life was despite difficulties. She exaggerated her east Texas talk, sensing Ann enjoyed it. Beth explained her "chaaarmed" life: "I have many God-moments when I'm jogging in the morning, and when I'm volunteering at the hospital. Last week a fellow in the jam-packed emergency area, waiting to see a doctor because two fingers had been cut off, gave his bed to a man brought in with a back injury. He said the other man with the back pain needed the bed more."

Beth could handle human drama. Her energy, spunk, vitality, humor, prevailed. She said, "Sometimes I feel a holy presence." The word *holy* startled Ann, who wasn't raised with religious words. Religion wasn't something her parents did, and Ann was like her parents.

In Matti's last will-and-testament Gabby was given Matti's computer to do with as she wanted. Beth was asked to be executor of a trust fund for charitable purposes. Ann was listed as the contact person at the adoption agency Matti used over thirty years ago, and Matti's biological daughter was to receive a sum of money; not a huge amount, but more than adequate to express caring.

Alone with Ann, Matti had outlined every detail of what she wanted done through the adoption agency for Mary the baby she "gave away," her own cruel phrase. Her will-and-testament in Texas had instructions about contacting Ann in Connecticut. Legally, everything was set in place in Connecticut without anyone in Texas knowing. Matti had everything ready for her own death. Did she have a premonition?

Chapter Nine

Metaphoric Discernment

Ann remembered a lunch when Matti, Gabby, and Beth were exceptionally lively. Together they produced a mixture of humor and seriousness: a barrage of puns, random associations, and insights. The topics that day could make a brain ache.

The word *desire* was used in a chance remark, which started a cascade of kooky connections; one strange response was that the word *desire* was formed from *de Sire* (the sire), that is, the male proclivity to sire, make, produce, hatch, spawn, procreate. And that it was Adam, phallic snake that he was, who seduced Eve, then blamed it on her, and they got kicked out of Eden.

The ladies concluded that since then, we've all had our troubles, especially in the areas of money, sex, and power, which the religious vows of poverty, chastity and obedience are to harness. Well, they concluded, the strategy wasn't working well for the Catholic Church with the problem of priest pedophilia which the church hierarchy tried covering-up with the power of secrecy, and then had to use money to pay off victims of the sex scandals. There you have it. Money, sex, power—the roots of human frailty and folly.

However absurdly the discussion on *desire* began, the buffoonery led to the tragic topic of priest pedophilia for Catholic Gabby, but also for Beth and Matti, for these women cared deeply about each other. Their conversation took a serious turn. Pedophilia became the conversation. Their ideas flowed.

Gabby said pedophilia is horrendously destructive allusion confusion, whereas Matti's romantic allusion confusion related to John/dancing as an allusion to time was a more neutral allusion confusion. Using hyperbole, "It's the difference between an unnoticeable scratch on one's skin and bleeding to death."

In pedophilia, psychological dynamics relating to childhood, childlikeness, or childish issues are mistakenly interpreted and mislived. Instead of psychologically embracing and becoming psychologically intimate with personal 'child-related' dilemmas in the personality, a pedophile literally, externally, embraces and becomes intimate with an actual child. Pedophilia is notoriously difficult to treat and conventional psychotherapy has little success dealing with it.

Beth reminded the group that regular psychotherapy can't do much for alcoholism either. Psychotherapy without Spirit doesn't offer much help. Grace is needed for healing. Beth added, "Everyone recognizes the need for grace so one can stop denying, stop lying to oneself and others. Alcoholics Anonymous recognizes the power in powerlessness, the limitations of human effort alone, without grace. Alcoholics often come from alcoholic families, and though it may not be your fault you're an alcoholic, only you can do something about it."

Gabby said pedophiles often say they were molested as children. In families where pedophilic behavior has been passed down generationally as conditioned, learned behavior, the first perpetrator's allusion confusion can be assumed to have started the chain reaction when instead of getting in touch with one's 'inner child,' the perpetrator got in touch with outer, real children in the family.

Beth asked the question, "Can a Twelve Step Program cure a pedophile?" And then answered her own question: "A Twelve Step Program doesn't *cure* anybody. An alcoholic never claims to be *cured*. However, anyone with an *unmanageable* problem can be helped if the person sincerely works the Twelve Step program."

Gabby observed: "The *anonymous* part of AA is important. Anonymously confessing sin is the idea of Catholic confession. However, confession and AA are both after-the-fact. We need a proactive approach; preventive understanding."

Bringing out-of-state-visitor Ann up-to-date with their provocative insights, the Texas three switched into a historical perspective with Matti leading the way: "As we've discovered, AA is the return of what began to be repressed five-hundred years ago in Europe when fourfold interpretation of the bible was substantially abandoned. The Church had until then largely interpreted scripture figuratively (allegorically) during its first 1,500 years, until a kind of constrictive literalism started to encroach and eventually dominate in the 16th century."

Matti continued, "Freud said the repressed always returns, whether in an individual or culture. And as we've found, AA is a secular grassroots return of this exponential, mostly forgotten way to interpret the bible. When you see old biblical fourfold interpretation adapted to today and put it alongside AA they are similar, for AA views alcoholism from four angles: the spiritual, moral, psychological, physical (biological sensitivity to liquor), and concludes that alcoholism is a thirst for intoxicating Spirit, not a thirst for drunkenness from alcoholic spirits. Alcoholism is an example of allusion confusion. Addiction and compulsion in general are allusion confusion."

Though often quiet in these animated conversations, Ann asked a question about how the AA paradigm would change if even one of the four angles was discarded and the answer was obvious: AA would be ruined if any one of the four exponents (interpretative viewpoints) fell by the wayside. Beth demonstrated the demise of AA with her hands, splaying palms down on the table, uttering "wrecked, kaput, nothing."

Gabby took the conversation into the topic of *metaphoric discernment* which she said U.S. culture lacks. Her examples demonstrated what she was talking about. "One might say 'you're a real doll,' 'you're barking up the wrong tree' or 'you're such a fox,' which doesn't mean another person is a toy doll or a barking dog or a fox. These are examples of *descriptive metaphor*, which is easily used daily.

"However, culturally we are strangers to *metaphoric discernment*, which is about interpretation, not description. Descriptive metaphor and metaphoric discernment are two sides of the same metaphoric coin. We need metaphoric discernment to uncover and understand emotions, moods, cravings, impulses and urges. Metaphoric discernment reveals what is going on in longings and yearnings so they do not become addictions and compulsions.

"For example, we use the term 'comfort foods' to indicate eating to soothe ourselves for reasons other than physical nutritional requirements. As we've talked about before, we may eat because we are hungry for friendship, for hope, for opportunity, for love. Eating kitchen food for psychological reasons is allusion confusion. Anorexia and bulimia, might be tied to being psychologically starved for worth, recognition, acceptance, or innumerable psychological reasons. This is allusion confusion."

The Texas women agreed that culture's tendency to literalism is limiting. For instance, they suggested that though some believe the New Testament second coming of Christ, the "rapture" (Greek *parousia*), is to be a cataclysmic external event, there is another more likely scenario which is that after Jesus' death, his Presence returned and continues to return to earth in each person who is internally *enraptured* in his Spirit. People may work side-by-side, one enraptured by the Spirit of God in Christ, (the Holy Spirit) while the other person is not. This is a more plausible second coming of Christ, with some being "left behind" psychologically, mentally, emotionally. One who is spiritually enraptured with the Christ has less need of a drug like *ecstasy,* or alcoholic *spirits*, the friends theorized, emphasizing the importance of these words.

These were some of the topics that day with the smart, bold Texas women. Ann felt she got much more from them than she gave to them. She could not know that in the future the conversation she experienced that lunchtime would be found intact, refined and greatly expanded, in Matti's computer. What Ann did know is that increasingly she was feeling invisible, vacant, emotionally dull. She wondered what was happening to her.

Chapter Ten

In a Goldfish Bowl

There was another Texas lunch Ann remembered when institutional religion was discussed. The Texas threesome, church goers themselves, talked about church as a matrix, a womb, a container of the numinous, the sacred, the divine. They often qualified their comments, by saying, "At its best, institutional religion is . . ."

They agreed institutional religion can be an obstacle to spirituality. The root word *religio* means *to bind*. Institutional religion can bind us to a hopeful, creative notion of Spirit, as well as to a restricted, restrictive outlook, even to destructive beliefs and actions tied to "God." Also, institutional religion can be merely second-hand religion because it is the compiled legacy of the religious experiences of others, often long ago.

That day talking about institutional religion, Matti said, "Humans probably get religion wrong as often as we get it right." Gabby expressed the opinion that organized religion sometimes inoculates humans against religious experience, and Beth, as always, claimed Al-Anon was the primary midwife of her adult spirituality, though she still attended the Methodist church.

Ann was once again fascinated with the commonsense lucidity of her Texas friends. That day the conclusion was that if religion does not penetrate the depths of the personality one lives an Ego-oriented religious life, which can be simplistic, inadequate, annoying in varying degrees. They decided humans long for more.

That day, psychology professor Gabby used a goldfish to explain the Ego part of human psychology: "A household goldfish in a goldfish bowl in a room has an extremely limited view of the house in which it lives. This is like the limited-Ego part of the personality, which is what **I** am aware of—**my** reality. Ego is not a thing but a state of consciousness; awareness compared to unawareness. Even if the goldfish hears noises and has inklings of happenings in other rooms of the house, it is acutely aware of only what happens in the room where it has been placed.

"The analogy highlights unknown, unconscious, unrealized, unlived aspects of me such as inherited tendencies, pre-language experiences, forgotten and repressed experiences, as well as potential waiting to be discovered, developed, and expressed; my unique contributions to life. With additional awareness our Ego matures, develops, grows." Thus spoke professor Gabby.

That day, the Texas Trio also spoke of *kenosis*, Greek for emptying the ego-personality to make room for the divine. Ann was impressed with their knowledge. Art had been her religion. Her parents were artists and she was much like them. The conversation then turned to finding one's niche in life; our talent, the contribution(s) which is ours to make.

Matti knew of a proverb from the Middle Ages which said there are two times in one's life (adolescence and mid-life) when one has a sense of what one might be and do. She said she knew as a young adolescent she wanted to come up with ideas that would help people. Then she forgot that desire for years, though by middle age she had gathered much information and began working on practical personal hermeneutics.

Beth remembered that in early adolescence she wanted to be a medical doctor and humorously suggested her volunteer work at a local hospital might yet qualify her to be a brain surgeon. Gabby said the word *soul* captivated her when young, though she didn't know precisely what it meant. Later she would find dreams were her path to the soul, which is *psyche* in Greek, as in the words psychology, psychiatry, psychotherapy. As she spoke, Ann came to understand Gabby's eyes as soulful; full of soul. Perhaps that is what Ann saw in Gabby's eyes.

One evening when Matti and Ann were alone Ann mentioned her impression of Gabby's eyes. "It's true," Matti agreed, "Gabby is hyper-intuitive; she lives close to the unseen of life."

Ann's last night alone with the Texas Trio was two years before Matti died. It was Thursday evening before Matti's Saturday evening Christmas party. Matti's upstairs home and the yard below were gorgeously ready for Saturday evening. The female friends laughed easily that evening which was made cozy by fireplace flames.

Ann made the unimportant comment that none of the Texans used their original names: Matti had been Margaret, Beth was christened Elizabeth, and Gabby was Gabriela. The discussion turned serious for a moment, discussing contrasts, incongruencies in the church of Gabby: Intellectual brilliance in some of its great minds who have been giants in western culture, compared with times of close-mindedness; an exclusive male hierarchy in "Holy *Mother* the Church."

Ann silently recalled that Matti named her baby Mary because of Christianity's Mary, Mother of Jesus. Matti considered herself Catholic—Anglican Catholic—and told Ann that politics, not theology, separated the Anglican church from the Roman church.

Gabby mentioned the words *apophatic* and *kataphatic* as different prayer experiences. These were new words to Beth who prayed when she jogged. Beth jokingly asked, "Is there 'jogaphatic' prayer?" Gabby deadpanned, as she crossed the room to use the bathroom, "For you, yes." Beth said, "Hurry back," which wasn't funny, but when Beth said it, it was hilarious. Minutes later when Gabby returned to her chair, Beth, using Texas twang, asked "Feel better, sister?"

That last evening of the four together was filled with foolishness. Low energy Gabby said she felt invigorated from the laughter and planned to go home and invigorate "Millie" (Milford, "Ford," her husband). Beth asked, "Would that invigoration be apophatic or kataphatic style?" which brought a round of guffaws; sly suggestions. Before leaving, Gabby did explain that apophatic is spiritual experience without images, words, or other content, whereas kataphatic is spiritual experience which includes images, concepts, words, symbols. Beth mouthed an overly serious, comedic "Oh."

This was the last time Ann would be together with the Texas Trio.

Chapter Eleven

Baseball Diamond

The evening of Matti's funeral, after the reception at the church, a small group gathered at Gabby's house. One of Matti's colleagues, Kenneth, a loud, provocative anatomy professor who knew Matti well, was there. The group talked around the kitchen table in Gabby's kitchen. Kenneth spoke in detail about aneurysms. He threw out a question about why God didn't heal that time bomb in Matti's head before it exploded. "Matti was a woman of faith, why didn't God heal her?"

Gabby answered his question with a question, "Perhaps God is more mystery than magic?" She immediately professed, "I don't know what I'm getting at." Beth was quieter than usual that evening. The past few days she'd spent time with Matti's brother Philip and his family, helping with details of the funeral. She was exhausted. Energetic Beth was human after all, Ann reassured herself. Pizza arrived and the conversation turned again to religion.

Kenneth shared, "I was raised Methodist, and if I went back to church, I'd probably go to a Methodist church, but there's so much that doesn't make sense to me. For instance, the Trinity. I saw the movie *Matrix*, and the character Trinity made me remember I never understood what the Christian Trinity was about."

Gabby said she and Matti decided the Trinity was about relatedness, but could not do much more with it, for they did not have enough theological background; did not know the nuances related to high and low Christology.

"Christology means?" Kenneth wanted to know.

"Low Christology means looking at Jesus from a human perspective, whereas High Christology is more from God's point of view, or something like that."

Kenneth responded forcefully, "Like humans can know God's point of view?! This is precisely my quarrel with church, institutional religion."

Then, surprisingly, Gabby's husband Ford, an economics professor at the university, entered the conversation. "Religions, like universities, are flawed but necessary. They give continuity to human effort, human history."

Kenneth was amused, "Well said, my friend, well said." Ann assumed he was agreeing that institutions of higher learning are flawed, having had his own tensions with college administrators and his contentious personality.

Ford had more to say, "A human lifespan is short and limited. Without institutional continuity each person, each generation, would, in a sense, have to reinvent the wheel."

Gabby seemed intrigued listening to her husband. Ann was surprised he was so forthcoming in a group. Yet he was a professor, she had to remind herself.

Ford continued: "For example, the Catholic church is an old institution, so old it has had time to make almost every kind of mistake, but it learns from its mistakes, which is why it is still around. If an institution or a corporation doesn't do that it dies out, ceases to exist. In my mind the staying power of the church is that it reforms itself from time to time. That is different from reinventing itself. The difference is that what it's about has remained the same through the centuries. It has not written a new mission statement, but rather implemented its mission sometimes more effectively, sometimes less effectively, sometimes almost counterproductively; but it always has had the same mission."

"Which is?" Kenneth pursued and Ford responded. "Its mission is to plumb, preserve, and promulgate what Jesus and His Spirit brought to earth and still offers humanity." "Which is?" Kenneth asked again.

Ford's mind was processing. He was an exacting speaker, not a quick processor. While he was formulating a response, Gabby looked at Ford, "I didn't know you were such an alliterative genius with your "p" words, plumb, preserve, promulgate."

Ford continued: "I'd say what Jesus brought to earth and continues to offer humanity is what Matti, Beth, Ann, and Gabby seem to have talked about for years: heightened consciousness about oneself which thus improves the human condition one person at a time. I believe the church has the same problem every person has that Matti expressed as living in the Garden of Eden versus living in the Garden of Ego, which is trying to listen to the Ultimate in the universe rather than lesser voices, such as the least evolved collective mindset of one's culture, or one's own egoistic concerns and view."

Everyone applauded. Beth said to Ford, "Your contrast of reform and reinvent is enlightening." "Very impressive," Kenneth added. Gabby was beaming. Ford really was a calculating, prognosticating person. Ann felt honored to be included in Ford's assessment.

Kenneth continued, "Speaking of impressive, at the reception today I found the former student in Matti's adolescent Sunday school class impressive." Yes, Ann had heard the 30ish-looking woman tell of her drug addiction in her twenties and how a remembered Sunday school teaching of Matti's when the student was in high school helped her overcome her battle with drugs.

The former student explained that Matti used the game of baseball with adolescents to explain a healthy personal hermeneutic, an abundant kind of interpretation, a way to interpret one's experiences with complexity and thus avoid allusion confusion. Matti's former student explained, "Matti's baseball game went like this: homeplate is the spiritual part of us, first base the physical part, second base the moral element, and third base the psychological aspect.

"Matti said that like the pitches thrown in baseball, we never know what life is going to throw at us, from the outer world or the inner world; our own personality. Matti emphasized the need to interpret events and happenings in our life from four perspectives: spiritual, physical, moral, psychological, which was a very old way to read the Bible." Matti's former student continued, "Matti's instruction didn't keep me from getting addicted in the first place, but her baseball analogy did help once I was in a Twelve Step program, for the Twelve Steps and the whole AA philosophy match what Matti taught."

Ann had heard the recollection of this woman at the reception and recognized that Matti's hermeneutic passion carried over into her church class for adolescents. Ann wanted to reveal that evening the secret of Matt's baby, which was the root of Matti's obsession with practical personal hermeneutics, but Ann said nothing.

The post-funeral friends helped tidy the eating area in Gabby's kitchen, and Beth suggested everyone return in six months, in December, for a nostalgic re-enactment of Matti's annual pre-Christmas party with just them; no other guests. The funeral evening ended a hard day, and had to close with plans to continue tradition and bonds of friendship beyond the loss of Matti.

Chapter Twelve

Christmas Lights

When December came, Ann was back in Austin, staying at Beth's house, which was decorated Christmas-beautiful, well-appointed, and, thankfully, not lost to bankruptcy years earlier. The regal home suggested money and good taste.

On Friday evening Beth went to the food market insisting Ann stay home, saying her guest must be exhausted from the flight and all the work she'd been doing for Beth, which was greatly exaggerated. And so, Beth's husband Thomas and Ann talked by the fireplace while Beth ran the errand. Thomas was an interesting conversationalist in this room elegantly alive with a lighted Christmas tree, other baubles, and a white Italian marble manger scene.

Thomas talked about how fortunate Beth was to have Gabby and Ann and to have had Matti. He said women form closer bonds with each other than men tend to do with male friends. He said Beth, Matti, and Gabby seemed to be on the same spiritual wave-length, and he once told Beth, "I know the God-stuff works for you, but I don't yet know how," and then realized he'd said two things at once: "I don't yet know how it works for you," and he implied, "I don't yet know how to do it myself."

He switched to saying he was on medication for depression. He didn't mention the mania. Said the medication revolutionized his life, though it could not make him enjoy being a stockbroker, though he kept on with the profession. He said he was too lazy or too mentally blocked to figure-out what he wanted out of life, despite knowing in college he wanted to be a journalist, and when that didn't easily work out, he got a degree in business and drifted into being a stockbroker. He explained he has a habit of taking the easy way out, the road of least resistance.

He returned to the topic of religion which he believed did little toward uplifting the disenfranchised and rejected peoples of the earth, because religion was too busy proselytizing and giving simplistic pronouncements to life's complex questions. The idea of "being saved" which Thomas heard often in his small home town in Texas, smacked of literal-minded, fanatical belief without understanding. He found this brand of Christianity, phony, simplistic, sometimes mean-spirited.

Thomas's thought was cut short when the garage door was heard. Beth was home and he went out to bring in sacks of groceries. Ann appreciated this man she'd scarcely known before that evening. Quite frankly, he seemed to be a person of more substance than she had expected. Talk of his depression made her wonder about herself; her gray moods were darkening.

The evening of the Christmas gathering without Matti was a chilly evening in Austin and the fireplace was welcome, not only for its warmth but also for its light which merged with Christmas lights and created an evening all aglow despite Matti's absence. This tiny group was festive despite Ann's personal despondency which she hid as best she could. There was anatomy professor Kenneth, Gabby and Ford, Beth and Thomas, and Ann.

Hors d'ouerves were lovely; creations of Beth. The meal was created and catered by a young couple who served the group invisibly throughout the meal. The evening felt European, Ann decided. There was no rushing. Indeed, time seemed to stand still. Topics changed as the group luxuriated with food and libation.

Uncharacteristically, Kenneth commented on the beauty of the house, the decorations. He agreed and launched into his dislike of the Christmas season for most of his adult life. In years past he thought his distaste stemmed from gift-exchanges that take so much time, energy, money or the blatant commercialism about something supposedly spiritual, or irritating traffic problems because of the season's shopping, or the frenzy of students ending a semester while getting ready for Christmas at the same time.

But none of this, he now knew, was the source of his annoyance with Christmas. Glancing at the nativity scene, he explained that his discomfort with the season was the unease he felt about a literal, biological virgin having a baby, not only in Christianity but other religions as well, and having this story passed down for centuries to the masses who accept it uncritically. The scientist in him rebelled at the foolishness of the story and the gullible herd-mentality acceptance of the story even today with widespread science.

Kenneth related how Matti and Gabby lessened his aggravation when they talked about Christian Mother Mary as a psycho-spiritual virgin. That is, as one who had not been *impregnated* with the Ego-driven matrixes of her day, but whose *conceptions (concepts)* about life were somehow pure, authentic, real, virginal. The idea of her own virginal conception says she didn't inherit a lot of psychospiritual junk (original sin) from her ancestors, and this accounted for her exceptional ability to be in touch with the divine. Mary's purity of personality was passed on to Jesus. Kenneth could accept the idea of a metaphoric, psycho-spiritual virginal birth and Christmas was no longer the irritant it used to be.

He credited Matti and Gabby for broadening his horizons beyond the five-sense world, beyond what can be quantified, validated, and replicated. Also, he said as he aged he found life is bigger than science, at least science in its present state, although scientific methodology continues to grow, refine, expand.

He was precise, saying, "I have come to realize many events are not repeatable, replicable. They happen once and that's it. For instance, this conversation will never happen again. Even if we try to replicate it, the next time will be different for we will already have been imprinted from this conversation. It's true, one cannot step into the same stream twice."

Kenneth changed topics, "Matti used her obsession with time to say she was too old for me; sly female not wanting to hurt my feelings while she basically closed the curtain on any romance," and he laughed in his usual, unrestrained way.

At the end of the truly enjoyable evening Kenneth's loud voice rose to goad Gabby into giving a metaphoric performance. He teased that his rigid personality enjoyed "the poetic, metaphoric, mystical whirrings of Gabby's brain." She first resisted and then appeased him with a metaphoric view of the Christmas decorations in the house and the season of Christmas.

"The Christmas lights represent en*light*enment, the consciousness, wisdom and compassion which entered the world two thousand years ago with the birth of Jesus. The first nativity scene happened eight-hundred years ago when St. Francis of Assisi used people and animals to celebrate the birth of commingling humanity and divinity in Jesus Christ.

"Animals in the nativity scene might represent the instinctive, stark simplicity and naturalness it takes to grow spiritually. An ox is an ox with all of its 'oxiness.' But when is a human being, being human? Who are we at our truest nature? What is going on with us in our inmost being?

"No room at the *inn*, can be the *inner world;* when a personality is too full of itself, egoistic, (prideful, the first sin) rather than humble. The Christmas stable is earthy. The word humility comes from Latin *humus*, which means earth, soil. We are humble when we are genuine, honest, real in the sense of being *down to earth* about our limitations, shortcomings, our need for psychological healing as well as our gifted potential. Overall, Christmas celebrates the ongoing lifetime birthings of Christ in us helping us realize our creative possibility in living a full life."

Gabby bowed, "Has my brain whirred enough for you?" Kenneth hugged her, laughing his loud laugh, "You may now take your brain home for a long winter's nap." It took a while for the group to part. There was painful awareness that Matti, the glue that bound the group together, was no longer physically with them. No one mentioned a future Matti-meeting.

Chapter Thirteen

Time IS

When Ann tumbled into bed that night, memories of Matti were dancing in her head. Matti and her pre-Christmas party which she labeled the *Advent Event,* had evolved out of the depression she experienced each Christmas season after Mary's birth, reminding her of the bleak, frigid Christmas when she was pregnant in Connecticut.

Matti told Ann, "After my time in Connecticut, I started dreading the Christmas season weeks beforehand at the sight of the Advent wreath and candles, though the priest at Mass said the roundness of the wreath symbolized the eternal, with no beginning or ending; the green wreath represented ongoing life, as evergreen trees and bushes remain green through every season. This didn't really help me.

"What did ease my pain somewhat were song lyrics that stirred in my head about there being a time for everything under heaven. I began to turn toward Christmas, not away from it as I had been doing. Christmas depression lessened when I had a small group of people in. The next year more guests and after that still more, with more decorations, more dedication to what was turning into a real event celebrating the people in my life and Life Itself.

"I began to recognize arrogance in my seasonal sadness. I couldn't forgive myself for giving my baby girl away; couldn't forgive myself for being flawed and limited. The pregnancy, birth, adoption should not have happened. I was a more *together* person than that. Realizing my self-righteousness, the symbols of Christmas began to awaken my five senses as when I was a child. The more childlike I became about Christmas, the more the symbol of the Christ child grew in me and I enjoyed the Christmas season."

Matti said she learned repeatedly that the universe is unendingly responsive to us when are attuned with it. Matti and Gabby together felt that eternal wisdom beckons humanity beyond the literal five-sense world through metaphor and symbol into truth. The literal five-sense world alludes to understanding beyond itself—to MORE—which metaphor and symbol uncover.

Matti ended her long soliloquy with a parable. To tell of *grace* she spoke of Jesus as an infinitely wealthy person who opened bank accounts for every person on earth. Each individual is required to withdraw money and use it well, combined with right intent, conscientious labor, honest endeavor (for which grace is also needed), or the money is of no help. Matti said this is how grace works. Grace needs our cooperation. Ann understood intuitively, deeply, what Matti was saying that night of the past.

Next morning after the post-Matti pre-Christmas party, Gabby met Beth and Ann at a restaurant for brunch before Beth took Ann to the airport. The three laughed at how much food they had consumed together over the years. Ann was overcome with how deeply she cared for these two women she may never see again, and clumsily tried to express her feelings. The soon-to-part friends joked and laughed lest they cry. Gabby brought something for the other two.

Gabby pulled from a folder, copies of a document she found recently in Matti's computer. An early riser, Gabby said she typically went to Matti's computer with her morning mind before her well-known fatigue cobwebs began setting in by noon. Gabby said it would take a great deal of time to go through all of Matti's writings. The document in hand was written several months before Matti died. Beth and Ann silently read their copies as Gabby softly read aloud.

From Matti's Computer

Time IS . . . Time is a gift whereby we savor life moment-by-moment. Time is a burden when life hangs heavy and we must endure. Time is a commodity: "Make good use of your time . . . Don't waste time . . . Time is money." Time creates anxiety when there doesn't seem to be enough of it. Time is the constant flow of past, present, future —endless flux. This is chronological time (*chronos* in Greek).

There is another kind of time, (*kairos* in Greek) which has to do with timing, the right time, synchronicity. I pray that I may die at the right time. A part of me has always longed for something beyond chronological time, just as when I was young wanting the grass to stop growing so I could catch up. There is nostalgia, a homesickness inside me that yearns for what is eternal.

And so I pray for death to come at the *right time*, for then, the prospect of death is not frightening, but seems instead, another unfolding of Life. Praying for death at the right time is comforting.

Have I answered the questions so important to me about who I am and why I'm here? Yes and no. The answers aren't as important as the questions, which have kept me seeking and searching. Yes, searching to continue my life. And the years have been livable; much more than livable. My life has been meaningful and enjoyable. I am deeply, deeply grateful. Yet, I long for death to pretense.

Gabby and Beth questioned, *death to pretense*? "Matti was not pretentious. That doesn't make sense. The writing is unfinished and therefore not clear." Ann remained quiet, knowing Matti ended with a sentence that said everything; Matti wanted to die to the pretense, to the secret about her baby."

To hope to die at the *right time*? This was brilliant all three women agreed. To desire death at the *right time*, they surmised, could bring comfort while still alive. And then, to yearn for what is eternal? To want to go beyond time? Ann was quiet as this was feverishly discussed between Gabby and Beth. Ann had her own feverishness inside.

In recent times Ann had begun yearning for something more than life as she has known it. Was this longing what Matti was talking about? Desire for the eternal, the infinite? Perhaps she needed to become a questioner like Matti to find what she wanted.

"**Time IS . . .**" Gabby and Beth suspected this was an incomplete title. Noticing the capitalization of IS, Beth mentioned the bible's great "I AM WHO AM" Moses heard when he wanted to know God's name. *ISness* and *AMness* are about time. "Is, are, was, were, will be, and such tell of time," Beth and Gabby concluded.

The three women knew Matti believed time was the stuff of life, for she acutely *felt* time, was bedeviled by the passage of time. Matti had told Ann that a part of her looked forward to death convinced that on the other side she would know about her Mary, the girl's personality and her adoptive parents.

As brunch ended, the good-byes were less wrenching than might have been, for they had talked too long, and now Beth and Ann would need to rush to the airport to make Ann's flight. Quickly, Gabby gave each Beth and Ann a folder "with a few more of Matti's writings." There was no mention of meeting again. Walking quickly to the cars, the three friends were surprised realizing they'd been hermeneutically hoodwinked; tricked into *interpreting* Matti's document this morning, for interpretation of practical experience was, after all, Matti's passion. Gabby and Ann had a quick good-bye embrace. Time had sneaked up on the friends; Beth must race Ann to the airport.

Chapter Fourteen

Interpreting Exponentially

Beth concentrated on driving, while Ann was a second set of eyes spotting airport exits. Airport traffic was dense and tense. Once at the correct airport terminal entry, Ann exited the car at the curb with bags in hands, nodding a kiss to Beth this slightly chilly morning, careful to not drop the folder Gabby gave her with Matti's writings.

Almost late for the flight, Ann was greatly relieved to have boarded the plane. She was anxious to get home to the security of husband Mel, their house, their life together. On this perhaps last weekend in Texas ever, she thought of the secret she carried for so long about Matti's Mary.

There was a part of that secret which she shared with no other person, not even Matti or Mel. This secret was the question whether she and Mel should have adopted Mary, for they were engaged to be engaged at the time Mary was born and briefly discussed adoption. But their life together was just beginning. The future felt uncertain. As time for the birth approached, the idea of their adopting the baby faded away.

Ann did hold Mary in her arms briefly as she was with Matti at the birth and asked a nurse if she could hold the baby. She had never forgotten the experience. Perhaps Ann would now search for adoptive Mary to see how her life had fared. What would Mel think of Ann seeking to find the person who had been Matti's baby? And how would Ann's and Mel's daughters Rachel and Sarah react? The questions made Ann feel anxious.

Adopted Mary was thirty-one now. What if her life has been tragic? Ann would then live with the guilt that they should have adopted her. What if Ann's intrusion into Mary's life would be bothersome to her and her family? Ann didn't want that, though in her increasingly cull restlessness, she didn't know what she wanted.

Seated on the plane, Ann flipped through the pages in the folder Gabby gave her, noticed familiar phrases, and was filled with nostalgia reading the ideas of her friends, which had been fine-tuned by Matti. The Texas Trio had been phenomenal in Ann's development. A most exceptional door had opened and stayed open for years.

Ann brought to mind Gabby, knowing about the very old fourfold way of reading the bible, which she and Matti tweaked, making the old fourfold format usable in today's world, which clicked with Beth's experience in Al-Anon and the main assumptions of Alcoholics Anonymous. Though fourfold exegesis had been abandoned, it seems to have reappeared centuries later as the philosophical foundation of AA.

Ann recalled the friends discussing pedophilia as undiscerned psychological symbols becoming behavioral symptoms: instead of "getting-in-touch" with child-issues psychologically, offenders incorrectly and destructively *get-in-touch* with actual children. Instead of dealing with <u>childhood</u> issues which need healing, or <u>childish</u> personality areas, immaturities in need of growth and development, or to realize their own lost mystical <u>childlike</u> enthusiasm for Life and Love, they literally reach-out, embrace, and mis-live these psychological cynamics in a physical climax with actual children. This is allusion confusion, which is not simply a catchy term, but one with profoundly practical consequences.

Gabby had come up with the term *allusion confusion* and its antidote, *metaphoric discernment*, to help her psychology students understand addiction and compulsion. Symbols in the personality *allude*; they are hints and clues about important dynamics. Metaphor means *to carry beyond or across* in Greek. Indeed, metaphors carry us beyond or across our current way of understanding to new awareness, insight and discernment.

Gabby was in touch with two facets of metaphor: (1) descriptive metaphor (2) metaphoric discernment.

(1) Descriptive metaphor expresses what has already been discerned. For example, If I tell you about "a forty-year-old man who is still tied to his mother's apron strings," I am saying he is overly dependent on his mother, not that the strings of an apron she is wearing are tied to his clothing or body. I have already discerned his unhealthy dependence.

(2) Metaphoric discernment is a hermeneutic tool. For example, we may eat because we are hungry for understanding, friendship, opportunity, for love. Eating kitchen food for psychological reasons is allusion confusion. Anorexia and bulimia, might be tied to being psychologically starved for innumerable psychological reasons. This is allusion confusion.

Alcoholics Anonymous readily understands that drinking alcoholic "spirits," an old name for alcohol, is a substitute for quenching one's thirst for Spirit. Alcoholism, compulsive gambling, compulsive shopping, using sex or drugs to inadequately relieve psychological distress can all be regarded as allusion confusion. The confusion in these examples is giving physical answers to psychological, ethical, spiritual questions and dilemmas, though it is also possible to incorrectly live other combinations of the fourfold hermeneutic, such as giving spiritual answers when physical answers are correct. Subtlety and nuance are required to interpret, to discern.

Ann knew what her friends had put together and she summarized in her own mind: *Human beings have thoughts, emotions, mental pictures, urges, impulses, desires, longings and yearnings which deal with us if we don't know how to deal with them, using an exponential mindset, which includes physical reality, psychological reality, moral reality, spiritual reality.*

For over a thousand years, Christianity read the bible exponentially. Today, Alcoholics Anonymous reads the human situation exponentially, with spiritual matters in seven of its Twelve Steps; moral concerns in four of its Steps; psychological factors are assumed in Step One and throughout AA literature; and the physical is in AA's interpretation of alcoholism as disease.

Exhaustion overtook Ann, she closed the folder and dozed-off until she heard the flight attendant announce seats and tables need to be in locked upright positions before landing. When the airplane landed, Ann telephoned Mel. He would be waiting in the car at the curb after she telephoned she had her luggage. Mel got out of the car, and put her luggage in the trunk.

Chapter Fifteen

Registered-Mail

In the car, they hugged and Ann exaggerated, "Good to see you again," as she'd been gone such a short time, and Mel answered with overstatement, "Great to be with you, my long gone love." This was their affectionate humor.

As he always did after a Texas weekend, Mel asked about her trip, and nearer the house, he turned into a café with their favorite clam chowder; a homecoming gift; "A most thoughtful gift," Ann told him, as they enjoyed hot food so satisfying this very chilly afternoon which had already turned dark. Ann was engrossed with the lovely warmth of such a cozy familiar place full of appetizing smells, favorite food and her husband of many years, and yet she felt somehow vacant.

Once home, Ann climbed the fanciful staircase into her glassed tower art studio, all architect Mel's brainchild. Everything was as she left it only days ago, including the chemical smells. She had recently become interested in painting a self-portrait. The idea had never before appealed to her. Should her turning-gray hair in the portrait cascade around her shoulders or be pulled back as she often wore it?

If the Texas Trio in the old days knew of her self-portrait idea, there would have been a discussion about the significance of a *self*-portrait; a portrayal, concretizing, embodiment, a revealing of her *self*! The group would have tossed the topic about and around. Ann knew with regret that now with Matti gone, that kind of group dynamic was also gone.

Ann descended the unique staircase and walked to the den where Mel had TV muted. She sat next to him wondering what they were going to watch on television. He handed her a registered-mail envelope addressed to her. It was from the adoption agency Matti used those many years ago. Mel said the letter came Saturday, which was almost exactly six months after Matti's death.

Ann's surprise and shock were apparent to Mel, for she simply stared at the address. He gently took the envelope, opened it with a letter opener and handed it back to Ann who took the letter out and read that Julia Montel, (Matti's Mary) was wanting to meet Ann. Through the adoption agency, Julia's letter told about Julia's intense turmoil after receiving money from Matti's will, which finally resulted in Julia wanting to meet Ann, who read the words again and again.

In his usual, calm, clear sighted way, Mel observed: "The thirty year saga continues." Ann knew his words were true, and felt anxious as she did on the airplane; a mixture of dread and delight. Matti's biological daughter, Julia Montel, was entering Ann's life.

Chapter Sixteen

Julia Montel

After receiving Julia's letter, Ann wrote to Julia who lived in Clarksdale KS, saying she was eager to meet her. Ann did not elaborate that she was as eager as she could be in her increasingly depleted state. Depression was creeping up on Ann, partly because she hadn't done enough with her life. That was her self-diagnosis.

In a week, Julia telephoned, and Ann forced herself to make plans for Julia's arrival several weeks following. In the meantime, Ann exerted herself and obtained pictures of young Matti through Beth who got copies from Matti's brother Philip and family. Ann told Beth she wanted them for herself: a new deception in the saga; though maybe not a total deception. It was true Ann did want pictures of Matti, as she had none, not one. This was before cameras in cell phones. Her times in Texas didn't include picture taking, the friends were always too busy talking.

And then the day, the important late morning hour arrived, and Julia Montel from Clarksdale KS was at Ann's door. Ann's first glimpse of Julia, upon opening the door told Ann that Julia did not look like Matti. But two hours later, as Julia walked out of the family room to the door, ending their time together, Ann saw Julia's confident, dignified, distinctive walk and then knew it wasn't Matti's cheerleading accident that made her walk in so stately a way. It must have been genetics.

Otherwise, Julia didn't look like Matti, for Julia's hair was nearly blonde, but mostly very light brown with golden highlights. She was about the same height as Matti. Her face had softer features. Overall, Julia gave the impression of an ultra-feminine woman, almost a porcelain or angelic type, a demeanor different from Matti's career woman image. Julia looked mellow, not intense like Matti. Julia wore little or no lipstick and needed no foundation on her cherubic face which had its own just-right coloration coordinated with extraordinary light blue eyes.

After Ann took Julia's coat and asked the usual questions about the flight, she offered tea, coffee, finger sandwiches, fruits and cheeses, on the table in front of the sofa. Ann had planned everything carefully, aware of her limited energy. On this cold gray late morning, settled in the cozy family room with the warmth and glow of the large fireplace and several lamps, Ann didn't know whether to ask about Julia's life or begin telling her about Matti.

In Ann's grayish state, she did neither; she shared how she came to know Matti, and stumbled into her memories of Julia's birth, though her recollection of that tiny face was dim and newborns are hard to describe anyway. Ann did not tell Julia that holding her tiny body in her arms for a few moments had stayed with her all these years. Ann found herself telling of Matti's anguished crying; so intense Ann feared Matti might hemorrhage to death, not knowing if such was biologically feasible. Ann told Julia how she asked the nurse "to hold you when the nurse took you from Matti's arms."

Ann told Julia more of Matti's desperation than planned. What Ann had rehearsed in her mind was first showing Julia Matti's pictures, which were still new and fascinating to Ann, too, and making comments on Matti's interests and personality. But what came to pass after sharing the pictures with Julia was Matti's bitter emotional suffering. Perhaps Ann's own depressive suffering at the moment was mixed with her storytelling.

Ann told Julia she was Mary to Matti, and mentioned the religious significance of the name Mary for Episcopalian Matti. Julia understood about Jesus' mother Mary, having been raised Catholic, Julia Connelly, in a family of Irish heritage.

Ann knew from brief telephone conversations planning Julia's visit to Stamford, that Julia grew up in Kansas City, the oldest of three girls and that her parents were teachers in different schools; her father a high school basketball coach who taught health classes, while her mother was a high school biology teacher. Ann also knew that Julia was a psychiatric nurse and her husband worked in his family's furniture store in Clarksdale KS, population 7000, in southeastern Kansas, and they had no children.

Ann told Julia that Matti confided she prayed for "Mary and her family daily" and looked forward to one day meeting them *on the other side of earthly existence.* Ann noticed Julia inhaled noticeably, but she otherwise appeared emotionless.

Julia told Ann more about her family. She was eldest with two other sisters who were not adopted, and she grew up nearly forgetting she was adopted. Her parents were great parents. "Matti's prayers for me and my family were answered and continue to be answered," calling her birth mother "Matti" for the first time.

Their two hours together passed quickly and the cab Julia arranged to return was outside to take her to the airport, a flight back to Kansas City, and then an hour's drive to Clarksdale KS. Two hours together was not nearly enough time but it was a prudent way to begin an unknown venture for both Ann and Julia, and more than enough to exhaust Ann's limited energy supply. Julia took home with her copies of pictures Beth sent and copies of Matti's documents thus far harvested from Matti's computer, which Ann felt sure would give Julia a sense of who Matti was.

Not many days later Ann received a lovely thank you note from Julia saying she hoped the two would meet again not far down the road. Ann was pleased and wrote back saying how meaningful their time together had been for her. But then, Ann heard no more from Julia as weeks turned into months. Ann did not take full notice of how much time passed, for a shock entered Ann's life.

Chapter

Seventeen

Tragedies and Depression

Beth telephoned Ann to say Gabby died. It would be learned that Gabby's death was a genetic heart defect, likely the cause of her chronic, fragile energy level. Ann grieved deeply, for while she had a long dramatic secret with Matti, and great admiration, respect and fondness for Beth's humor and wonderful openness, it was Gabby who stole Ann's heart with her metaphoric wisdom, diligence beyond fatigue; Gabby's soulful eyes.

In Ann's increasing state of depressive-fatigue Mel and Ann decided it was best for Ann not to attend Gabby's funeral. Beth was frightfully distressed. Ann plunged into additional unrelenting sadness. Gabby was gone.

Precious Gabby had had an ongoing concern about the superficiality of this country. She spoke of phantasies. She would remind her friends that sometimes in psychology <u>phantasies with a *ph*</u> can be regarded as distinct from fantasies. The *ph* type are spontaneous, uninvited, and have a mind of their own, whereas <u>fantasies with an *f*</u> are formed by humans willfully and purposely, as in daydreams. Matti wrote about phantasies.

Matti used her energy to put into a computer what Gabby did not have the energy to put into writing.

The teacher in Gabby urged her three friends to pay attention to phantasies whether they arrive as feelings, moods, mental images, thoughts, cravings, yearnings, longings, sleeptime dreams, or such. In phantasies the soul shows itself; the phantasmagoria of the soul is where we really live, Gabby explained.

Gabby spoke of *angst,* a German word close to *anxiety.* Gabby regarded *angst* a combination of fear and real or unreal guilt; a deadly duo which is the paralysis one feels in depression. *Angst* can have its way with us if we try to live on our own disconnected from the Ultimate in the Universe, Gabby had said. Gabby was, indeed, connected to the Ultimate.

Despite psychotherapy, *angst* in Ann grew with Gabby's death, along with meeting Julia and then not hearing from her again. Combined, these events escalated the emotional grayness. Ann's feelings of failure grew. As a portrait artist Ann never made much money. Perhaps she was afraid to market myself and risk trying to be successful and so her art work remained a hobby and she let word-of-mouth be her only advertising. Never having to provide for herself, she likely couldn't have done so, she fretted.

She felt dependent, weak, not a very talented person. Despite her laments, Ann and Mel's two daughters turned out well: Rachel became an architect in her father's firm; Sarah, a divorce lawyer. Both were married with two children.

Ann told herself to be real about the part Mel played in all this: he was the breadwinner and they were thus able to pay someone to clean house and help in other ways. In this scathing review of herself Ann decided she had always been a marginal cook. Further, she was regarded a patron of the arts because of Mel's generosity with his hard-earned money.

Matti and Gabby were gone. Ann's life was winding down, too, and she hadn't done much with it. She must have offended Julia and botched a relationship she wanted to continue. These were her energy-sapping thoughts. Ann began seeing a psychotherapist.

But then, Julia came back into Ann's life. First with a note explaining Julia had not been in touch because a car accident tragically killed Julia's husband's cousin's husband, a high school government teacher, father of a two-year-old daughter. Julia was busy helping the young widow Connie, Marc's cousin. Ann sent a note of condolence to Julia and husband Marc.

Then, again Ann heard no more from Julia. Another note arrived saying Julia's husband Marc's family, the Montel family, had two more tragedies. After the automobile accident, Marc's grandfather died and a short while later, Marc's father died unexpectedly from complications following routine surgery.

Again, Ann sent a note acknowledging with regret the difficulties of Julia and family. However, Ann began to wonder if what Julia was saying was true. There was something surreal about so much tragedy. Was Julia wanting to avoid Ann? If so, Julia might have simply stopped all communication. Ann continued in therapy and later realized the hiatus from Julia coincided with a time of solitude needed in Ann's own healing.

Chapter Eighteen

Giovanni Montelbano

Eventually, Ann would learn about the Montel family in Clarksdale and their prominent furniture store. Marc's grandfather who recently died, his mother's father, was Giovanni Montelbano, who came from Italy as a young man and eventually chanced upon a small furniture store in Kansas about to go into bankruptcy. With savings from jobs in New York and Ohio as Giovanni moved west in search of his "specific opportunity," he bought the fledgling store at a bankrupt price and built a large and stable establishment; the best business in Clarksdale KS .

Giovanni Montelbano was an adaptable man, fiercely adaptable, which meant he fiercely resisted change but changed with ferocity if it seemed expedient. He changed his name to John Montel. The sign on the store front would have cost more with the extra letters in Montelbano. Besides, it was good for business to Americanize. His store became Montel Furniture. And the name of one daughter changed, too.

Julia's husband, Marc's mother, Rosina, became Rose. Her younger sister Sophia, remained Sophia. Maria, John's shy, retiring, frail wife stayed Maria, because she insisted. She was the one person who could dissuade John—sometimes. Rose had the zeal and energy of her father. Sophia was meek like her mother. Rose took over the family store, married and had two sons. Marc was the younger son.

Sophia married, became full time wife and mother of daughter Connie, and did not work in the furniture store though she was part owner and received a yearly bonus "for doing nothing" Rose easily reminded others. The high school teacher who died in the car crash was Zan, husband of Sophia's daughter, Connie.

Why did Marc have the name Montel if it was his mother's family name? Because Rose was persuasive was the first answer given, but then there was more information; complicated information. Marc's father's parents (Marc's paternal grandparents) divorced. The mother remarried and her new husband adopted Marc's father who was given his stepfather's family name, so Marc's father didn't have his original family name anyway.

And then, because of the furniture store, Marc's mother Rose kept the name Montel when she married. Grandpa Montel wanted Rose's children to have the store name. Good for business, he said. Grandpa Montel was proud of Marco and his brother Stefan, the Montel boys, the sons grandpa Montel never had.

Julia told Ann the family dynamics of the Montel family were complex. Julia said grandpa Montel as an eccentric whose animated body language and spliced Italian-English helped him survive. With intelligent intuitions about people and situations, he knew how to get what he wanted. But he had heart, too, lots of heart. "Love lasts," he often said and the hearer was left to interpret his meaning. If asked what he meant, he would simply shrug and repeat "love lasts," seeming to enjoy the ambiguity his words generated. "I learn hard," he also often said which left others not knowing whether he meant he learned the hard way, or that what he learned left a lasting, *hard* impression on him. Maybe both.

The story was that Italian Giovanni Montelbano fell in love with Maria from a neighboring village in Italy when he was seventeen and she was thirteen. He waited for her to "grow up," and then asked Maria if she would marry him and when she said "yes" he asked her father who said "yes." She was fifteen and he was nineteen. Once the wedding was over, he announced the newlyweds were moving to America on money he shrewdly saved (and perhaps pilfered) plus what he had after selling his few livestock and two wagons he had built.

Maria cried, her parents cried, his family cried, but Giovanni had a plan and it came to pass. The newlyweds arrived in America with only a few coins, but he was a hard worker, shrewd, charming, and Maria was a quiet type who offended no one as she cleaned houses of the wealthy, through contacts he made. The first years were hard, very hard. Thank God no babies came. Giovanni, a man of passion, was always worried about that. Each month he was relieved when there was no sign of a baby. They therefore had time for work and saving money.

Then they moved to Ohio because when Giovanni heard the phrase, 'Go west, young man, go west' it had meaning for him, for he was a man of hunches. In Ohio he worked in a furniture store and was not one hundred percent honest with his employer or customers and got fired. He told that story often and ended with "I learn hard, I learn hard."

Once again he followed a hunch when a few days after losing his job a fellow Italian immigrant told him of cousins who were doing well in the rolling hills of southeastern Kansas. Maybe Giovanni could be a farmer, he knew how to farm. He took Maria and money and headed west where he immediately found work in a furniture store again, and did not become a farmer. At the store he hung a sign over his desk, written large in his own hand: "No cheating. Honesty is best policy. Cheating bad for business." Whether this was to remind himself, others, or both, he never said.

But he'd cheated on Maria, too. Early in the marriage he "like American women and they like me," and Maria found out. "She cry, cry, cry, morning and night, on her knees praying and crying. It break my heart. I say never again, Maria, never again. A little pleasure not worth so much pain. Never again I cheat Maria." He told these stories on himself as lessons to his family, the family assumed. His forthright open honesty was disarming to others and largely his genius as a salesman.

Sunday Mass attendance was sporadic for grandpa Montel when he was young and chose instead to mess around at the store as an excuse. Maria was religiously steadfast and as grandpa got older he went to church with her every Sunday. Again, he "learn hard that Sabbath is smart. Rest one day and work better other six days. Smart idea. One day for God, six for man. Good plan."

Through the years, Ann learned a great deal about the Montel family and their enduring furniture store.

Chapter Nineteen

Ann Dramm's Childhood

Meanwhile, Ann's therapist, husband Mel and their daughters, agreed with Ann that spending time with Beth might be helpful for Ann. Her depression was lessening with continued medication, talk-therapy, relating with her dreams, and Ann knew she needed to be with Beth. Ann telephoned Beth in Austin asking if she would come to New York City for theatre, museums, and to just spend time together. Death had cut their foursome in half. Beth was eager to meet Ann in NYC.

The two met in the city, but from the beginning, theatre and museums they had planned for themselves felt like imposters. What they both wanted was conversation. And soon after settling into their hotel room, Ann divulged the secret she'd kept all those years about Matti's baby, and then meeting that baby, Julia Montel.

Quick-minded Beth realized . . . that's why Matti was interested in teens and their religious training . . . she thought she could save them from her kind of sorrow? And her passion for hermeneutics, interpretation; she'd misinterpreted her emotions, her needs? She spurned Kenneth though she may have cared about him. She latched onto Gabby's *allusion confusion* and *metaphoric discernment* which helped get boyfriend John out of her system. Death to pretense; the reason for the annual pre-Christmas party; Beth's head was swirling.

And then, Ann told Beth about her depression, therapy, and what had been uncovered. Ann spoke frankly, "I'm not outwardly bizarre, but I have fragile spots inside. Always have had. My family situation with my parents was unusual."

Beth responded, "You've never talked much about yourself. In all these years you listened and entered into what was going on, but didn't talk about your parents, friends, and such. I know you're an only child, but that's about it. How self-centered of the Texas Trio to indulge our concerns and ignore what was going on with you. Only now do I see that."

Ann shared easily, "I likely diverted you away from discussing me. I learned in grade school to do that, just as I learned to be a compliant, congenial person so I didn't reveal myself, my life at home. You're thinking molestation or something really awful, aren't you. It's nothing like that. My parents were wonderful in all the important ways. They loved me, they were home a lot, they shared their abundant creativity with me. They just couldn't keep house."

"Poor housekeeping was their shortcoming?" Beth was mystified and amused.

Ann elaborated, "Yes. We lived downtown in Bridgeport, Connecticut, above several retail stores. Our upstairs apartment was huge—like a warehouse. My parents moved there when they first married and stayed until they were old and ill, when they came to live with me, Mel and our daughters.

"My father was a free-lance illustrator. He drew advertisements, catalogs, travel brochures, children's books. This was before computers and graphic arts as we know them today. He could draw anything. My mother was a script writer for her own show. She was her own Chautauqua circuit. She would research a historical woman, write a script, make a costume, play the accordion, and present her one woman act for women's groups, schools, whoever asked her and paid her. I was often her audience as she worked on a performance. She'd ask my opinion which made me feel important and grown-up.

"Our warehouse apartment was roughed-in but not finished with proper walls. We had two large bedrooms, a bathroom, a kitchen area, and all the rest was open space. One side was for my father and his work and the other for my mother and her work. Both areas were filled with stacks, piles, heaps of papers, boxes, books, completed projects, works in progress.

"The positive side of this is that my parents were home a lot. I had many interesting things to play with. I learned by watching them work. We were a cohesive unit. The negative is that meals, clean clothes, paying bills, were random, chaotic, and seemed to visit us as surprises. An adult was needed to run the household.

"I never had a friend to our warehouse, because I noticed in other homes I went to for Brownie Scouts, Girls Scouts, birthday parties, and the like, that people lived differently. I became a tentative person, a watcher, observing how others ate at a table together, and did things we didn't do. No one else's house looked like ours.

"I grew up with music in the warehouse, parents talking about what they were working on. Poetry, art, raw creativity was in our house all day, every day. My parents were voracious readers and read extensively to me. During our makeshift meals they discussed what they were reading. By the time I was seven or so, I would put a haphazard meal together for the three of us if I was getting hungry and they were so into their work that cigarettes and coffee were their substitutes for food."

"Were they healthy?" Beth asked.

"Reasonably healthy, until emphysema and lung cancer about age sixty."

"But there was always enough money?"

"It seemed so. Bills didn't get paid because they got lost in a stack. I remember a time or two there were tax problems because my parents forgot. I'd say we had money for everything we needed, though as free-lancers money was sporadic. My impression is that their talents were sufficient and that they made adequate money. It's just that we lived so differently from others that I became a constant observer to learn how to do ordinary things. I was tentative about myself, guarded, while remaining congenial and compliant."

"Were you miserable?"

"Oh, no. Socially uncomfortable, but not miserable. Our warehouse was a cocoon of sorts. I felt loved, secure, safe, creatively stimulated. My parents were fun. And we had stacks of canned food, nonperishables of all sorts. They were food hoarders, probably because of the Great Depression. We just had no one to fix meals, until I could do that.

"We had a washing machine, a clothes line in one corner, and an ironing board. There were piles of clothes, some needing to be washed, some clean. Before leaving the house one had to choose clothes from a clean pile, iron them, and be on your way looking presentable.

"My parents were night owls. I had an alarm clock, and from second grade on, got myself up, ate cereal, dressed myself. One of them got my clothes ready the night before so they could sleep in. Then when I was ready to go to school, I awakened them and one took me to school. They picked me up on time in the afternoon.

"They were diligent parents, loving, fun, thoughtful. Noticing I had no siblings, I came to wonder if I was an accident. But that wasn't important, for they were good parents, just deplorable with housekeeping, bill paying, and things like that. Sometimes I felt like I was their parent."

Beth exclaimed, "Oh, my. How exhausting it must have been for you."

"Exhausting? I don't remember that. Mostly I remember it was the tentative, observing unsureness; a circumspect feeling anytime I wasn't in 'the warehouse.' "The warehouse" is what the three of us called our living quarters. Together, we sometimes laughed about our messy home. Occasionally there was friction, annoyance, anger, blaming, because something couldn't be found, or something important was left undone."

Beth questioned, "Did you have friends?"

"Yes, always. Because I was congenial, and also talented. I could draw and write. I was in plays, musicals, wrote skits. Classmates and teachers throughout my school years admired what I could do."

"And throughout grade school and high school no friend came to your house?"

"They knew we lived downtown, which was unusual. I simply told them about my parents working at home and said they were messy artists. No one pushed to come there. I dated only a bit in high school and made arrangements to be picked up at a friend's home or I confined the guy to the small alcove inside the door of the building before the long stairs that led to our apartment. In that entry space I put pictures and a small table with a mirror above it. I figured people would look at themselves in the mirror, after they rang the doorbell at the foot of the staircase. I cleverly helped distract them from going upstairs. This was my youthful reasoning. It worked, I thought."

"Did you take Mel there?"

"Not for some time. I was in my late twenties when I met him. I first asked my parents to come meet him. My parents had the savvy to buy basic, classic clothes. They had few clothes but wore them well when necessary. They drove to meet Mel. The four of us had a fine weekend together, which made me believe Mel and I might have a future.

"And so, after thoroughly schooling Mel about my parents' living conditions, I took him there. He knew what to expect. He didn't jump out a window or break up with me. I appreciated his patient acceptance. It became the fulcrum of our relationship, in a way. I was grateful he accepted me and wanted to be with me despite the glaring limitations of my parents. He had a high regard for me being able to respect my parents despite their inabilities.

"He said if I was capable of accepting and loving my parents despite their imperfections, he felt I would be able to put up with him. Mel is a wonderful person. His acceptance of my family was fortification against my reticence, my fragility. He made me feel stronger inside."

Other than Mel, only Ann's therapist knew this much about Ann. It felt freeing, healing, to share with Beth.

"Your parents had no religious background?"

"I feel my parents didn't tend to religious matters because their creativity was fulfilling to them. This may sound strange, but their work was all-consuming. I believe the inspirations that were their livelihood fed them spiritually. They were filled with what people look for: meaningful, satisfying purpose. They were the most fortunate people in that sense, but they paid a price for total dedication to creativity. So far as I know, no letters, birthday, anniversary, holiday cards were sent to anybody. I didn't even know the date of my parents' wedding anniversary. Yet my birthday was celebrated from my earliest memories. I remember one birthday when I was maybe six: pink balloons tied to the back of a kitchen chair, a cupcake for each of us from the bakery down the block, a burning candle in my cupcake, contents of the cluttered kitchen table moved to one end of the table so the three of us could eat a meal prepared by my parents. A poem, or a sketch, or a funny something was made especially for me."

Beth seemed awe-struck by what Ann was saying. Beth didn't comment; just looked at Ann, through Ann. Beth's silence stirred Ann's fragility. Concluding that Beth found Ann's family too bizarre, Ann wished she hadn't told Beth. *Secretive is better than blabbing,* something scolded inside. Ann couldn't speak; she said nothing more.

Chapter Twenty

Cade's Death

Beth's mouth quivered. Beth was overwhelmed by what Ann shared. Beth sputtered, "That's beautiful." She choked, then recovered enough to say. "Unconventional parents who loved you in their own unconventional way. My upbringing was socially acceptable in every way, which I sometimes lament." But why was Beth teary?

Ann's mind and feelings were back at the warehouse of her youth. The warehouse had such a hold on her that whenever she talked of it at length or thought of it intensely, her mind and feelings stayed stuck there. Ann didn't yet know the full hold it had on her.

Beth explained her present tears, "Sorry I'm weepy. I'm thinking of kids and their parents in general but specifically of our neighbors whose fifteen-year-old son, Cade, was found dead a week ago from autoerotic asphyxiation, combining masturbation with a near-death experience. He died before he could undo the contraption he'd rigged up around his neck. I went to the funeral. Dear God, what sorrow."

Beth continued, "Cade was a good kid, a typical teenager. His parents found him dead on his bed on Sunday when they tried to wake him up for church. The door to his room was locked. When they couldn't rouse him, his father somehow opened the door. Cade's computer and cell phone showed where he was getting information and reinforcement for this deadly game of thrill.

"I can't get over the tragedy of it all and I feel angry about our nation's obsession with sex. We're very adolescent about sex. You'd think we invented it and can't get over ourselves for doing so.

"I've gone online and found that older people also die from autoerotic near-death activities and certainly that's regrettable, but it's the young who really tug at my heart. We are a sex-crazed culture and I am fearful for the young. I understand Matti's concern for adolescents. Maybe if we could all achieve constant orgasm, we'd finally be happy."

Beth was agitated, "We're more than genitals. Matti's metaphorical baseball diamond and the fourfold paradigm tells us this. We teach safe sex so one doesn't get a sexually transmitted disease or there is no pregnancy, but where does one go for a condom of the heart? Adolescence is a tough time with raging hormones, immature brains, peer pressure. I cannot let go of Cade's death, the suffering of his parents, a culture steeped in vapid sex. I want to rescue youth from the brainwashing that sex is life's ultimate satisfaction. Oh, the pain of losing a child. Our son Wesley's near-death will always be with me."

Beth wanted to shake herself out of the deep sorrow she was in, and asked, "When you were suffering with depression, specifically what was your breakthrough?"

Ann told her there wasn't one absolute breakthrough, but a series of them. She described the afternoon she attended with Mel a funeral for a friend and colleague of Mel's, and noticed the stained-glass windows in the church. She told how the stained glass flooded her eyes, her mind and imagination with radiant, dazzling, all-pervasive, translucent, uninterrupted, gleaming swirls of luminosity. The colors made her know she was not dead inside.

Ann explained further, "Today, color is manufactured. All kinds of fantastic colors surround us all seasons of the year. In former times, for the most part, only wealthy or powerful people had much color in fabrics or objects, and these were cherished. Houses, furnishings, homespun fabrics were mostly neutral, natural colors. Can you imagine how special the stained-glass windows of cathedrals were to eyes that saw far fewer colors than we do, especially in the winter months in Northern Europe. I believe we are somewhat desensitized to color because we have so much of it."

Beth blurted, "Ann, you know so much. I am sorry, sorry we didn't let you speak those times you came to Texas. How self-absorbed we were."

Ann corrected, "You didn't keep me from speaking, from sharing. I did that to myself. I covered my insecurities with compliant congeniality. The good thing is I became a listener. The not so good thing is that covering my insecurities eventually led to depression. My therapist helps me walk through what I've been covering up. It takes energy to gloss things over, to sit on top of smoldering feelings of inadequacy and failure. When I ran out of the energy it took to conceal troublesome, uncomfortable emotions, those life-sucking emotions were all I had left, and I was a despairing human being."

Beth had to know more. "Your childhood insecurities I understand, but your adult life, your marriage, daughters, grandchildren, being a portrait artist, a wonderful friend. Where's the failure?"

Ann told Beth, "Fresh out of college, I got a job teaching middle school art classes. Being an only child in the rarefied environment with my parents, combined perhaps with my own basic temperament, I was massively unprepared for middle school students—too fragile for them. I knew this the first day of class but couldn't bear to quit, so I forced myself to suffer day by day through the school year.

"I worked into the night, on weekends—should have taught another year to use what I developed, but the thought of another year was unthinkable. I failed miserably. To this day I am drawn to articles on adolescence because a part of me is still trying to figure out how much a failure I was. Was it the age of the kids, the way they were raised, or me? I gravitate to information that might shed light on this question."

Beth, apologized again, "I'm impressed with your knowledge and again regretful for the many years your wisdom was buried by chatter of the Texas trio."

Ann adjusted Beth's viewpoint, "But I learned much from the trio: your civic generosity, personal strength, and commitment to family. Matti's intense, questioning ideas. Gabby's metaphoric, symbolic insights. The three of you are luminaries in my life. My teachers. Being with you, Matti, and Gabby, your candid discussions helped lessen my spiritual lethargy. Also, Matti's and Gabby's deaths were awakenings.

These close friends dying, magnified death. I had largely ignored the inevitability of my death."

Beth observed further, "And your therapist? I'm so accustomed to the ways of Al-Anon, any other therapy seems alien."

Ann tried to explain, "My therapist helped me deal with dreams, and introduced me to drawing mandalas, which opened my soul. I can't say it much better than that."

Beth complimented, "I must say you seem a more complete version of who you have always been. That is, more lovable than before, which I would not have thought possible. What is this mandala thing?"

Ann shared, "Mandala in Sanskrit means *magic or sacred circle*, and I feel I began to touch the potential sacred within as I drew mandalas. The rose windows of Gothic cathedrals are mandalas." Ann reached inside her wallet where she had six photos of her mandalas. Beth ooohed and aaahed, "You say your friends in Texas were your luminaries? You've got to be kidding! These are extraordinary." Beth asked more questions about Ann's mandalas. Her amazement was astonishing. (Please see a mandala on the cover of this book).

Ann reacted, "Someday, I hope you will see my many mandalas in person. I've created quite a number." The two friends talked at length about the possibility of Beth someday visiting Ann in Connecticut. At the moment, Beth wanted to be reminded how Ann met Mel.

Chapter Twenty-One

Meeting Mel

Ann explained, "When I was in graduate school, a flat tire introduced Mel and me. On a cold winter day, ready to get into my car and leave campus, I heard a male voice, 'You've got a flat tire.' Since others were walking in the parking lot, I felt safe even if he was an axe murderer out to kill this innocent graduate student, so I walked to the back of the car and yes, the tire was flat.

"Mel asked if I had a spare. I hadn't a clue. He laughed, unlocked the trunk and the spare was flat also. He said he would take the spare to a gas station to be filled with air. Sensing I was suspicious of his kindness, he said he'd get his car a few rows away in faculty parking. He emphasized he was temporary faculty, teaching in the school of architecture as a graduate assistant. When he came round to pick me up, there was a faculty sticker on the windshield and I went with him to get the tire fixed. And the rest is history."

"You were living with Matti at the time?" Beth queried.

"Yes, and coping with the reality that Matti was pregnant, beginning to physically show the pregnancy, going to adopt the baby away. I felt like an accomplice."

Beth had another question, "She didn't tell you she was pregnant when she moved in?"

"She didn't."

Beth pushed further, "Tricky of her. Did that make you angry?"

"Not really. A compliant person assumes the other person knows what she is doing. Mel and I briefly discussed adopting the baby, though when we became engaged, we weren't quite ready for marriage, our future was uncertain, the timing was wrong. He was leaving the university to build his own firm. For many years I silently wondered if Matti's baby shouldn't have been our baby. However, since meeting Julia, knowing her adoptive parents are solid people, and she's had a fine life, that quandary has resolved itself."

"I'd love to meet her someday," Beth offered.

"You likely will. I never felt I would again meet that tiny newborn I held in my arms for a few brief moments, but meeting her has been one of the extraordinary happenings of my life. She's easy to like."

Beth backtracked, "You taught middle-school students before you went to graduate school?"

Ann summarized, "Yes, I quit after one year of teaching, then worked three years in an upscale dress shop, painting portraits and living in an apartment over the store until I realized my world was too small, whereupon I left that situation and enrolled in graduate school humanities with no clear idea what I'd do next."

Beth appreciated this new, bolder version of Ann no longer burdened by Matti's secret, or the secret of growing-up in a warehouse. Beth now also knew Ann ached to know why she had no known grandparents, aunts and uncles. This obviously was a secret Ann wanted to uncover.

After the weekend in NYC with Beth, Ann telephoned Kenneth. After all, he'd been rebuffed romantically by Matti because of "the baby secret." It might be soothing for him to know the source of that rejection. On the telephone, he seemed stunned, calm, uttering "Hmmm," and other reflex words. Mostly he was silent, until the end when he said, as if summing up, "Well, that's surprising. Would never have guessed. Matti gave me a cock 'n bull story about why our relationship would never go anyplace because she was too old for me. It didn't make much sense to me. I figured it was a way to dump me."

Ann explained that Matti told Ann she had too much baggage because of the baby secret to be seriously involved with anyone. Ann told Kenneth, "I believe you were simply on the receiving end of that part of her life." "Interesting, interesting," he commented.

Not long after telling Kenneth about Matti's baby, Ann received an e-mail from Julia telling that she and a colleague, her mentor, Lenore, a psychiatrist about Ann's age, were planning to attend a conference on behavioral medicine at Yale University. Julia was proposing lunch with Ann on the campus in New Haven and then Ann would spend time with Lenore while Julia attended an afternoon session. It was a tidy plan.

Chapter Twenty-Two

Telling About Marc

Weeks later, Ann met Julia on the Yale campus looking bright, scrubbed, wonderfully feminine. Her glowing qualities seem heightened. Quickly Julia told Ann she was pregnant. And then they were talking about Marc. Julia mentioned his thoughtfulness and sensitivity. Having seen Marc only in photos, Ann remarked in earnest jest, "Someone as handsome as Marc shouldn't have so many good traits. That's too much for one person."

Julia responded, "He's remarkable. He really is. But our marriage has not been easy. I'd say it's been complicated from day one. At times I thought it would all end in divorce. You remember stories about Grandpa Montel. Marc grew up with strange family dynamics. Our marriage has been hanging by a thread more than once though neither of us wanted divorce. And we both want children, have always wanted children. We knew this before we married.

"Marc's father Ben was a good father. Marc says his father was at every school event, most particularly athletic events and Marc was and is an exceptionally fine athlete. Marc's mother Rose was always at the store. Rose was married to the store. I believe her husband Ben and their two sons were like her stepchildren. When Marc was in college his father telephoned and visited Marc more than Rose did. She had to be at the store; concerned about the store.

"And there wasn't much hugging or touching whereas my family is huggy and we easily, regularly say we love each other. My parents were loving and affectionate in front of me and my sisters when we were growing up. We are a touchy, close clan. Marc's family isn't.

"Here I am blubbering all of this to you. But I don't burden my family with these details. They love Marc. Marc is easily likeable, loveable; a gem. I couldn't ask for a better husband in almost every way. But a sexless marriage is strangely unsatisfactory, at least when you're young. And we've had sexual problems.

"Marc's brother Stefan moved to Chicago out of college. I feel he didn't want to get trapped in the store. Marc was left to carry on the family legacy with the store. He says he doesn't feel trapped, seems to enjoy the store, which probably makes it harder for him to sift and sort through the unhealthy patterns in his family.

"Marc's father Ben was a man who did not complain. He adapted. He was trained as a lawyer and started a legal practice in Clarksdale after he and Rose married, but Rose was adamant he was indispensable to the welfare of the family business, so he gave up law and joined the family enterprise. Ah, the "family enterprise!" Though I admit the family enterprise makes for financial security.

"I always liked Marc's father Ben. He had a dignity about him. He was dapper in appearance. Customers were impressed with this man of presence who helped them find what they wanted. He wasn't a sales person. He listened, he adapted himself to what they were looking for and helped them find it. Marc says his father sold loads more than his mother, because he acquiesced to the needs of the customer. Whereas Marc's mother Rose tried to be like grandpa Montel and convince customers that something would work well for them, but she wasn't grandpa Montel and her tactics weren't as successful as she would like to believe.

"I believe Marc has a wariness, a fear of the feminine. He's experienced the feminine as treacherous, somewhat unreliable, maybe untrustworthy."

Ann had a question, "Why is grandpa Montel always "grandpa Montel" not merely grandpa? Julia shook her head indicating another unbelievable dimension of the family. "Get this, grandma Montel was never "grandma Montel." She was always Maria. Even to the grandchildren she was Maria. I noticed this when I first came into the family and asked Marc about it. He said he didn't know why, that's just how it had always been."

Julia added, "Marc more and more easily views his family dynamics as a mixed bag of healthy and unhealthy. And I tell him that's true for everyone, while he says he thinks his family history might be more mixed than usual. I'm not sure that's true. I try and dispel that notion, because in psychotherapy I've seen people almost compete to come from the most dysfunctional family.

"Marc doesn't feel comfortable seeing a local therapist because of my connection to the behavioral center outside Clarkdale. He went to a therapist in Kansas City for a while, but the drive is time consuming. So, he's doing his own work now, sometimes asking my psychological views about his impressions. He's found an author or two whose ideas he finds valuable. And I'm pregnant, which obviously shows some kind of sexual healing is going on."

Ann found Julia almost too unfiltered in what she had just revealed about the Montel family, Marc, sex, and Ann wondered again, *What is it about me that allows people to say almost too much around me?*

Julia, apparently feeling she exposed too much, apologized to Ann, "Sorry I delivered such a barrage of personal information. I could say that's just how I am, and I think that's true. However, living in a small town makes me sometimes feel caged. And I don't share this with my parents or sisters, for they find Marc and his prominent family wonderful. And I don't say all of this to Lenore, my psychiatrist mentor whom you'll meet later—because of the small-town atmosphere, people knowing people in the community. Not that Lenore would ever say anything. It's just that a small community can feel restrictive about what to share with others."

Ann would be startled later by her own sharing with the psychiatrist, Lenore.

Chapter Twenty-Three

Psychiatrist Lenore

Ann was with Lenore while Julia dashed off to a symposium. The smallish psychiatrist Lenore had slightly wavy salt and pepper hair which fell into place with volume, body, and determination, appearing to require no fuss on her part. The kind of hair Ann wanted when she was younger.

Lenore was warmly approachable, as if she remained herself despite her profession. Horn-rimmed reading glasses attached to a silver chain around her neck, gracing her slight upper torso. Her brown eyes were quick, penetrating, as if little escaped her. She seemed grounded and hyper-alert at the same time; widening her eyes as if listening intently when another spoke with her. To Ann, Lenore portrayed feistiness mixed with a good heart.

Talking with Lenore that afternoon was noteworthy because Ann easily talked about herself, her depression which had been easing. Lenore's relaxed manner invited self-disclosure, or was Ann merely taking advantage of an off-duty psychiatrist; wanting the reactions of a therapist beyond her own? Ann wasn't sure of her own motivation. She only knew it was unlike her to want to talk so much about herself. Ann's misspent life became the topic.

Ann poured out her misgivings. Lenore said, "It's not too late to find your calling, if you feel you have missed it. In Christianity, the parable about those who arrive late in the day for work and are paid the same as those who came earlier and worked all day, is for me a comment about what maturity can bring to spirituality.

"Maturity is required for real understanding, for wisdom, which I believe is our highest calling. In our fast-changing culture, youth is admired, aging is devalued, which is incorrect, for experience is the seed in the garden of time where wisdom grows. Neither human credentials or academic degrees insure wisdom. Suffering may or may not bring it. Julia regards you as a woman of wisdom."

This stunned Ann. "Why would Julia say that?"

Lenore replied, "I'm guessing Julia senses you carried Matti's secret when it was too heavy for Matti to carry alone. Julia says you feel safe, she can talk with you."

"It's good to hear that. I so often feel like a failure."

"In a highly competitive culture," Lenore countered.

"My talents are mediocre."

"Compared to what or whom?" the psychiatrist asked.

"I've wasted my life."

"Waste as fecal matter is also fertilizer," Lenore observed.

Ann elaborated: "I've never wanted high profile success, but maybe I have been fearful, lazy, stupid, *(borrowing from Matti)*, or I've taken the easy path, the way of least resistance," *(as Beth's Thomas said).* I savor time alone. Painting is a solitary business. I serve my community in a limited way because I relish time alone. I am caught between enjoying being alone and feeling guilty about it."

Lenore offered, "Julia says she enjoys your availability, your lack of rushing. She has talked about how busy both her parents were with their teaching careers. She says she will be a stay at home mother; for when around you she feels like she's on vacation, without a schedule.

"That's a compliment, correct?" Ann asked.

"Julia speaks of you in complimentary ways." Lenore was not observing psychiatric confidentiality, Ann realized, as she relaxed even more, confident she and Lenore were two women having a conversation, not a psychiatric session. Ann felt free to be speculative with Lenore.

"Sometimes I feel as if my solitude would be enriched if I knew how to pray better. I know this sounds insane since I'm not a religious person in the usual sense. When Sarah, our youngest, told us that she and her husband were getting a divorce, I wished I knew how to pray.

"My husband is Jewish, we raised our daughters in the Jewish tradition, my dearest friends are Christian, so to be sure I am covering all the bases, I have at times prayed to the God of Abraham, Isaac, Jacob, Mary and Jesus. Actually, I don't know what I'm doing, but don't want my prayers to go awry."

Lenore smiled, "I don't know about prayers going awry, but as our population increases with older people, I do wonder how the world might change if the elderly, who have more free time, had the habit of prayer. As I treat older people with depression, I wonder whether their quality of life and life in general wouldn't improve greatly if they knew how to pray well. Praying is certainly better than fretting, regretting, waiting to die."

Ann responded, "Dying without having found my niche in life, is my worry now, as I compare myself to others." *Matti, had an inquisitive mind I can't begin to match. Gabby possessed metaphoric genius I don't have. Beth is a quick wit, and I'm not.*

Lenore's words soothed: "Comparison, competition, this is the downside of an exterior-oriented culture. Culturally, we believe our lives must be more than quietly special; they must be outwardly spectacular. Satisfying marriages, sane children and grandchildren, enduring friendships aren't enough. Everything must be high-profile and marketable. Perhaps we will grow-up, mature as a culture."

Lenore had an afterthought. "Maturity is not the same as tradition, which can be infantile, stuck in a stage of development. The defining mark of maturity is discernment: the ability to weigh, assess, conjecture from many angles, points of view, over time; it can be both speculative and grounded in experience."

Ann began thanking Lenore for the richness of their conversation, for Lenore could not know what she gave Ann during their short time together. Though there was more time to talk that day before Julia arrived back with them, Ann was filled with what had been said, and began asking Lenore about life in Clarksdale, what drew her to psychiatry, and such.

When Julia appeared, Ann thanked Lenore with sincere words and a hug, which was not routine or simple for Ann, having known Lenore such a short time. Ann hoped she didn't startle Lenore with her hug, but Lenore's gift of listening sprinkled with wise commentary felt exceptionally fine that day. Ann had to risk shocking Lenore with uncommon gratitude. She felt optimistic about finding her niche. Lenore had said, "Vocation, from the Latin word *vocare*, "to call," is to find one's unique contributions to life; what each person might be "called to," the need to develop God-given potential not merely for personal aggrandizement but for the edification of others. This is self-satisfying in every sense."

The idea energized Ann, who knew what it was like to lack energy.

Chapter Twenty-Four

The Maternity Center

Since Ann's brief encounter with psychiatrist Lenore on the Yale campus and Lenore's confidence that each person has unique contributions to give Life Itself, Ann seemed to have absorbed Lenore's conviction and was waiting for her contribution to reveal itself, which did happen.

A clue about being beckoned was validated in a telephone call from the president of the board of the local maternity and adoption home which had voted unanimously to officially ask Ann with her reputation as a gentle soul and an artist, to implement a program to help pregnant adolescents use art to deal with their pregnancy; whether to keep or adopt-out the baby, to learn about themselves as individuals. Ann was overjoyed.

The sufferings of her one-year middle-school teaching career might still bear fruit, for it was during that time of suffering that she developed a plethora of artistic approaches to help stave off the desperation of her failure and help quell the energies of the students. She had used the art projects with her grandchildren over the years, noticed their joy and delight when they were "artfully" engaged with their grandmother. Immediately and enthusiastically, Ann told the board president she would accept the honor of creating such a program.

Then, sitting in her favorite chair, in the quiet of the house, looking onto their backyard haven, filled with the hope of undoing her dismal teaching experience, joyful at the prospect of helping people like pregnant Matti and her infant with maternity and adoption, Ann was overcome with a sense of *synchronicity*—the feeling that Ultimate Presence was tenderly present in her life—bringing her background in liberal arts to fruition; one of her heart's desires was becoming fulfilled. Ann telephoned Mel who was obviously overjoyed for her.

She was consumed by plans for this opportunity of sharing with other volunteers and the pregnant adolescents, in a place where parenting classes, counseling and group sharing, academic tutoring, preparation to take a high school equivalency test, therapeutic art activities, could provide opportunities to make the months of pregnancy a time of life-altering change, discovering worth, talent, potential; connecting with an adolescent's own story, her own deep being.

Ann imagined residents drawing mandalas as she recalled what she learned about herself drawing mandalas. Her days and weeks were filled with plans, arrangements, meetings, organizing art projects. She was meeting lovely, talented, caring people ready to help make this a reality. She was busy, filled with energy and enthusiasm. The budget for art supplies was meagre, so Mel and Ann fattened the cow with financial gifts. There was a glow about life.

Much was happening. Creative projects at the maternity center ranged from magazine picture collages for some, to skillful painting with watercolor, oil, acrylic for others. Talents and interests in the groups varied, but this was not a problem, for Ann's own range was broad, from junior high art, to portrait painting, to drawing dreams and mandalas. Other volunteers brought more possibilities. There were no discipline problems, no student evaluations, no grades to be given. The girls tended to be immature, but not rowdy. Ann contrasted these young mothers-to-be with the maturity of Matti, a graduate student pregnant in her late twenties.

Week by week, some members were new in the group, others delivered their babies, signed the necessary adoption papers, left without the baby. A few took their babies "home." Her hope was that creative activities helped them awaken to their own wisdom and worth so they would not be inclined to have sex to keep a boyfriend; or want a baby with the intention of the baby loving the young parent; or getting pregnant because it was the thing to do amongst peers.

Happily, Ann found once the young mothers-to-be began to discover themselves through drawings, writing, and other activities, they became increasingly interested. She wanted the program to engage the fathers of the babies, but this was not yet possible.

At the maternity center, there were few secrets. Everyone knew what is going on with everyone else in this community of warmth; a safe place. Ann often thought of pregnant Matti and the two of them slogging on together, but they were considerably more mature, had more education, could assess the situation better.

The administration and staff at the center were helpful, friendly, accessible. A secretary, in passing conversation, said a speaker was needed for the next annual meeting. Julia came to mind because Julia was on Ann's mind constantly since Beth telephoned last week, with news of a new episode in the Matti story.

Chapter Twenty-Five

Cal Hanover

Beth's telephone story was that Matti's brother, Philip, recently telephoned Beth. Beth first met Philip helping with Matti's funeral, and then she contacted him to get pictures of Matti and family for Ann to share with Julia.

Philip told Beth he received a telephone call from a fellow looking for Matti. Philip told the man his sister had died and asked how the man knew his sister and how he knew to contact Philip.

The stranger said he and Matti dated and she often mentioned her young niece and nephew, her brother Philip's children, of whom she was especially fond. Philip told Beth: "He was able to get our telephone number because we're still in the same house with the same telephone number. He found us online. The fellow asked whether there was anyone in Austin he could talk with about Matti. Told him I couldn't think of anyone, but he gave me his telephone number in case I recalled someone later. I'm calling you in case you want to talk with him. You certainly did know Matti. Just want to let you know this fellow has telephoned looking for someone who knew Matti."

Beth was intrigued. The fellow might be John, whom Matti was in love with in her twenties.

"Is it a local telephone number?" Beth asked Matti's brother.

"No, not an Austin number," and he read the number to Beth.

"I didn't have to **ask** for the number!" Beth screeched to Ann on the telephone. I couldn't wait for Thomas to get home, and I attacked him with my plan in the garage, for I raced out there when I heard the garage door go up. Thomas wasn't impressed with my desire to contact the fellow. He had to warm to the idea. It took some convincing.

"Can't we meet him this evening if he's available?" Beth exaggerated that she begged like a child, and Thomas finally acquiesced, provided Beth query the fellow on the telephone before suggesting they meet him someplace.

Beth explained, "I wrote out questions, preparing for the conversation, but I blew it when a male voice answered the telephone. After he said, "Hello," I said "Are you John?"

"No, this is Cal Hanover." He sounded cautious.

Beth burst forth, "Did you know Matti Jones?"

His quick answer was, "Yes, and you knew her?"

"Yes." Beth carefully painted an impression, "My husband and I were close friends with her." "Emphasizing the husband word," Beth laughed, as she told Ann.

Cal inquired: "How did you get my telephone number?"

"Matti's brother Philip said you telephoned him."

"I did," and Cal's voice relaxed.

Beth thought, *Who is Cal?* disappointed he was not John. Cal explained he and Matti dated a short while before she left for graduate study in Connecticut, and she said she'd send her address and telephone number but never did. He tried to contact her through the University of Connecticut, and searched for a telephone number, but nothing came of his efforts.

His wife of many years died several years ago. He was in town this weekend visiting his brother and family. He'd always remembered Matti and wondered what happened to her, and so he called the number he had for her brother.

Beth realized, *This might be Julia's father.* "My husband and I would love to meet you. Matti was one of our dearest friends. We did a lot with her."

Beth laughed telling Ann how she over-emphasized her words to Cal Hanover.

"Are you free this evening," eager Beth inquired, as she couldn't wait

"I can be," came the answer.

"At six o'clock?"

"That will work."

Asking where he was staying, Beth suggested they meet at an upscale mall restaurant near his hotel. "One must be prudent in these matters in case he's a demented type," Beth laughed at herself and rambled to Ann, "I was a wreck; Thomas told me to calm down or the guy would think I'm psycho if I carry on like this. Thomas can be sane when I'm not."

Beth and Thomas met Cal that evening.

Chapter Twenty-Six

Julia's Speech

Beth told how she and Thomas arrived a bit early at the restaurant, gave their name to the hostess, said someone would be joining them, and then sat in the restaurant waiting area near the door. Before long, a very nice-looking gentleman, fair complexion, blondish or grayish hair, (in the restaurant light it was hard to tell), average height or a bit more, well proportioned, casual clothes, entered the door."

Before the hostess could seat them, they introduced themselves, shook hands. Beth related to Ann, "I followed the hostess, Cal was next, then Thomas. I felt awkward, unsteady, and excited."

"Ann, are you still there?" Beth checked, for Ann had been stone-silent on the telephone.

"I am," Ann replied like a robot in shock.

Beth unfolded the story for Ann bit by bit; every word and gesture she could remember, every detail. It seemed to Ann they'd exchanged enough information with Cal to last several mealtimes: Matti's interests, writings, travels, annual pre-Christmas party, church work with young teens, her independent spirit, no marriages or lengthy romances when they knew her.

Cal's wife died, they had no children, he was a county judge in Santa Fe, and then after much exchange of information, there were labored introductory phrases from Cal: "I may be very wrong . . . certainly don't want to offend you . . . please know I don't wish to be crass . . . but I've always wondered whether Matti was pregnant when she left for Connecticut."

Beth told Ann, "I wasn't prepared for this, and didn't know how to respond. My tongue was stuck to my teeth. Thomas had the good sense to say, "We didn't come to know her until after that; when she was back here working in the campus library after graduate school."

"She never mentioned anything to you?" the embarrassed man asked.

"She didn't," Thomas responded cleverly, truthfully.

Beth concluded the telephone conversation with Ann, "Cal Hanover seems a lovely person; insisted he pay the restaurant bill, and left his business card with us."

Reeling from Beth's information, Ann felt concern for Julia, and immediately decided not to tell her about her probable biological father because she was pregnant with baby number three. Julia didn't need this turmoil. Julia had told Ann how her identify was shaken when she received money from Matti's estate. For then, who Julia had been was temporarily challenged and the only family she ever wanted, her adoptive family, was disrupted in her mind.

Before telephoning Mel at work, Ann digested Beth's information about Cal Hanover. Did Matti ever say that name? she asked herself. Not that she remembered. She recalled Matti would sometimes tell Ann she didn't want shame or pity. Being a reticent person, Ann never asked Matti what she meant.

Ann assumed Matti didn't want to bring shame on her family and didn't want Ann or anyone else to pity her, which Ann didn't think she did. Now Ann wondered if Matti was saying she didn't want Cal to marry her out of pity and so she never told him, never gave him her address or telephone number. Matti was a fiercely independent person.

Was Cal inquiring now out of caring for Matti? having a childless marriage and therefore curious about being a father after all? mere suspicion that she was pregnant? or all of these?

Ann did not share Cal Hanover with Julia until sometime later when Julia was the main speaker at the annual meeting of the maternity-adoption center where Ann volunteered. Ann had approached the agency's director with an outline of Julia's story, and Julia was invited to speak at the annual meeting.

The day of the meeting arrived. Julia's speech was a tearjerker. Beautifully, smoothly, with intense feeling, Julia told her story, beginning with her parents and sisters in Kansas City, her education, career as a psychiatric nurse, marriage, motherhood. Baby Patrick was in the room with Marc, which added drama to Julia's talk about her own life which began as an unplanned baby. Marc and Patrick accompanied Julia on the trip because she was breastfeeding.

The attendees of the annual meeting were accustomed to adoption stories, but while Julia spoke it seemed the crowd was in a cocoon of emotions; as if primal elements related to their own birthing, their most basic primitive existence stirred. At least this was true for Ann who learned more about Julia's adoptive family. Julia did not say "My adoptive family." Never. She always said, "my family."

Nearing the end of her talk Julia related how being a mother herself, she believed she had reached a place of integration, a place of psychological maturity, where she can now say she has had three mothers: her adoptive mother Ellen, for whom she expressed much love. Then, her birth mother Matti, a responsible woman of intelligence and integrity. "My third mother is Ann Dramm who you know as the person who contributes her creative talent and time here at the center, and makes possible the stunning, inspiring art on the walls in these buildings. Ann, has been another mother to me. Because of her I am here today. And during the process of writing today's talk, new psychological healing has come to me.

"Ann held me in her arms minutes after I was born, and continues to hold me psychologically in ways that she likely does not even know. She carried my birth mother's secret about me for thirty years."

There is another secret about your probable biological father, you will learn tomorrow. Ann mentally observed.

Finished with her written words, or departing from what she was going to say, Julia pointedly scanned the audience, breathed deeply as if pacing herself, and with tears slowly rolling down her cheeks, "I am immensely grateful for being able to tell you my story; you, who are involved daily with the emotions connected with unplanned babies. I say thank you for inviting me to share with you. I feel my own story has become clearer to me by telling it to you. And, Ann, I thank you, so, so much." She put her hand over her heart and gestured to Ann, as if saying, "From my heart." The group stood to applaud. Ann doubted there was a dry eye, but since she couldn't see through her own tears, she couldn't be sure.

In the van, driving home from the meeting, the four adults were emotionally drained. Infant Patrick peacefully slept. Julia was wrung out. She, Marc and baby Patrick were staying in Grand Suite, an addition to the Dramm home when Ann's parents came to live at the end of their lives. Julia, Marc, baby Patrick, having arrived yesterday evening, would be leaving tomorrow on an early afternoon flight. It was a whirlwind trip. Julia, Marc, and Patrick had time alone in Grand Suite while Mel and Ann made ready the evening meal, with thoughts of Cal Hanover on their minds.

Tomorrow morning Julia would be told of her likely biological father.

Chapter Twenty-Seven

Julia's Biological Father

Sunday morning, Mel and Ann were up early with coffee and the Sunday newspaper. Soon Marc appeared in the kitchen, chipper in dress and mood. Patrick was with him, asleep after being breast fed. Julia was up in the night with Patrick and had gone back to bed for a few more winks. She asked for the others to please eat without her, and wanted to be forgiven for needing more sleep. Ann remembered the times of broken sleep with new babies and how dreadful sleep deprivation is. And Julia's speech yesterday was emotionally sapping.

Breakfast was ready. Mel and Ann were experts from cooking frequent brunches for their grandchildren and the grandchildren's parents. This morning they ate in the glassed sun room of the kitchen. Marc commented on the unique, cozy, rambling home, its sun rooms, screened porches, Ann's upstairs studio, the lovely and private Grand Suite the Montels were using.

Mel gave an overview of how the home had grown through the years, what had been added when and for what reason. Marc reiterated the outline of the original house showing he understood what it was like when Mel and Ann moved in many years ago, and Marc talked about plans to add onto their home in the future with three growing children.

As the men chatted, Ann thought about when Julia could be told about Cal Hanover. The end of breakfast this morning was the designated time Ann had discussed with Mel. That way Julia would have already eaten, would not have lost her appetite and been unable to eat, should that be her reaction. Julia needed food for the flight home. As a nursing mother she needed regular nutrition. Ann was sometimes overly practical, perhaps stemming from her less than practical upbringing in the 'warehouse.'

Mel was engaged with Marc about the furniture store, the nation's economy, the global economy, sports. Ann remained quietly concerned about when to tell Julia, as the time before taking them to the airport was not long away. And then it occurred to Ann that telling Marc now without Julia might be best of all. His already knowing might be a cushion for Julia.

And so, Ann began, not knowing what to say, "This seems as good a time as any to share some news with you, Marc. Julia's biological father has likely emerged." Later the three of them laughed at the brusqueness of Ann's introduction. "No need to delay," she defended herself, when Mel teased her later.

Ann shared everything she knew about Cal Hanover with Marc; the business card which Beth sent, as well as every detail of Beth's impressions about him, especially his looking like Julia. As Ann delivered the information, Marc was outwardly calm, quiet, but his dark eyes were intensely alive. He responded, "This will get to Julia. Preparing for yesterday's talk, she repeatedly said she felt her presentation was an opportunity, a milestone in coming to terms with what she has had to absorb these past few years about her existence, which she has said is her identity crisis, not of her own making, but what has been thrust upon her by the circumstances of her birth. She has been angry about that. Sometimes says, 'Your family has its own strangeness, but at least you know who the people are.' "I don't know how she'll react," Marc concluded.

Then, Marc asked Ann, "When did Beth tell you this?" Ann gave him the exact date and Ann explained why she hadn't told Julia sooner. Marc re-checked details, "So as far as Cal Hanover knows, he never fathered a child with Matti, correct?"

"That's correct," Ann confirmed.

Marc speculated, "Julia may never want to contact him. She'll anguish either way. Hanover is alive, which makes it harder than coming to grips with Matti. Our kids have another grandfather; I have another father-in-law." Marc laughed. "What if he wants to be close to Julia and the kids since he has no children from his marriage. Julia will suffer but she'll work through this. The longer I live with her, the more I see how strong she is. It's like she dissolves into the pain of a situation and works her way back to coping."

Ann had just refilled coffee cups when Julia appeared at the kitchen door, apologizing for being in her robe and for sleeping so long. Ann said she was pleased Julia felt comfortable enough to be in her robe, for Julia felt like another daughter, and Julia surely needed the sleep, Ann reassured.

Meanwhile, Ann was thinking about Julia's light hair, beautiful blue eyes, porcelain skin that always looks freshly scrubbed, like Beth's description of Cal, and how Julia was the only adult in the room who did not yet know this bombshell news, however, this was about to change.

Encouraging Julia to join everyone at the table and eat her breakfast while they continued with coffee and conversation, Julia took her place at the table where a cup of fruit was set. It took but minutes for Mel to ready her waffles and scramble eggs and Mel was soon back at the table where talk was going on about the children Benjamin and Kendal in Kansas with a high school age babysitter and Rose, Marc's mother. The parents made this double babysitting arrangement when out of town, for the children enjoyed the young babysitter, while Marc and Julia felt more comfortable knowing an adult was there, too.

Julia commented on the comfort of Grand Suite and intriguing configurations of the house overall now that she had come to know more of it. Ann complimented Mel, "The house mirrors the intriguing personality of the architect and lord of the manor," who bowed his head in lighthearted appreciation.

Julia mentioned their wanting to add to the home. Yes, Marc had already mentioned such. Julia was voting for a someday renovation similar to Ann's tower studio with spiral staircase, when the children were old enough to navigate the stairs. Such a room would add loftiness and connection to the wondrous Kansas sky, which Julia obviously found an exciting idea.

"Where the skies are not cloudy all day," Mel inserted from the song *Home on the Range,* whereupon Julia corrected from the song, "However, we no longer have roaming buffalo," which led to a brief discussion of the disappearance of the buffalo and protected herds today.

And then, in the same way Ann had announced Cal to Marc, Marc now said to Julia, "Julia, there is probably no better time than now to tell you something which may or may not be to your liking. Your biological father seems to have appeared on the scene."

Julia stared at him, puzzled, pained, unsure, "You're not serious." "Marc's serious," Ann reassured.

Having just finished eating, Julia twisted her napkin and looked anxiously at Marc. He asked Ann to relay details, saying he wanted to hear them again himself. Ann re-told everything.

Julia put her hand to her mouth, biting her lip. Her breathing was marked. She was being smashed again, taken down, down, before she could begin to float up. Ann knew how this worked, because it was her modus operandi, too. Marc moved closer to Julia and put his arm around her shoulders. He expected anguish, and she looked stricken, close to tears. As Ann finished relating everything she knew through Beth, Marc took Cal's business card from his shirt pocket and handed it to Julia.

Julia read: Cal Hanover, county judge, Santa Fe, etc. With a huge sigh, she surprisingly quipped, "I don't know what to say . . . except that . . . I've got way too many relatives who keep coming out of the woodwork like termites. I am indeed an identity crisis victim . . . Talk about identity theft, my identity keeps being stolen from me regularly. Surely Cal's the last surprise unless there's an anonymous sperm donor somewhere or Matti was a surrogate mother for someone."

Her offbeat comments brought relief to everyone at the table. Julia then spoke to baby Patrick asleep in Ann's arms, "Now, your multi-identity mother is going to take a shower while your extended family grandmother who is also your biological grandmother's friend, cares for you with help from your daddy, who really is your father."

Perhaps Julia had risen to the occasion. With hand on hip, head cocked to the side, looking at Marc, she asked not quite seriously, "How are we ever going to explain this to the kids?" At the doorway leaving the kitchen she said seriously, "Let's just forget Cal Hanover."

Chapter Twenty-Eight

Ann and Mel on a Walk

A few Sundays later, Mel suggested Ann and he go for a walk, which surprised Ann. They used to routinely take walks on weekends, but the habit had lapsed. However, a walk sounded good this coolish early autumn Sunday afternoon. Ann felt wistful, not wanting to stay in the house.

As they walked, Mel took Ann's hand, which brought comfort; the power of loving touch; the satisfaction of an old marriage. Today they walked to the neighborhood park, unlike times past when they sometimes walked a mile or two and ended at the park for a rest, a chat, before going home. Today they were wearing sweaters, enough for the light wind. It was a quiet day. No children were out and about. A few leaves were falling.

Ann was reminded what it was like to be depressed, and didn't want to go there again. She was not feeling depressed, but a reflective mood was in the air. They talked little as they walked, crunching the leaves on the pathway. Ann suspected Mel felt her mood. He may fear she was falling into depression again.

Ann began focusing on the tops of trees, their movement in the wind, pointing skyward, suggesting a high perspective, they seemed content swaying and dancing unnoticed, their graceful rhythms soothing, enchanting, not depending on human intervention or attention to continue. Ann was caught in reverie, *Eternal Creativity is like this. The Creative continues creating whether we notice or not.*

Mel, looking upwards, asked, "What are you looking at?" Ann told him she found the swaying treetops mesmerizing. He looked up for a bit but then seemed to want conversation. He wondered how Julia was coping with the news of Cal Hanover. Mel recalled Julia's jigsaw puzzle analogy she used as they drove to the airport.

Julia said she thought her identity, her story, was finally together and now learning about Cal it was as if the puzzle had been taken apart, thrown back into the box with new pieces added, and she must now work to put this new version of the puzzle together, which she couldn't do unless she met Cal and she was not sure she wanted to meet him because an ongoing relationship would have its own life, and she didn't know if she had time or energy for that.

"What a mess," Julia said offhandedly that day on the way to the airport, her earlier humorous resilience gone. Marc had soothed her, "The kids are OK, you're OK, we're OK,".

As Ann and Mel walked and talked this Sunday, "Marc's words seemed to reassure Julia," Ann commented.

"Everyone needs reassurance," Mel's voice tone startled Ann.

"Except you. You are Steady Eddy," Ann was somewhat flippant.

"I need reassurance, too," Mel's words were baffling.

"I don't understand," Ann declared.

Mel was forthright, "Your changing ideas about religion are unsettling. I don't know where they're going."

Ann had an answer, "Going? They're not going anywhere. This is just my growth, what I am learning. It's all about ME," hoping to change Mel's seriousness by exaggerating her self-absorption.

"You're not naïve, Ann. We both know religion can cause lots of trouble. The history of the world is fraught with religious strife," Mel was direct.

Ann was equally direct, "How does that affect us? We won't be fussing about how to raise the children, they're already grown, and they are in charge of raising their children. I'm not going to impose my experiences on you or them."

"Will you continue observing Jewish holidays?"

"Of course. Jesus was a Jew who observed Jewish holidays. There is no Christianity without Jewish history and tradition; you know this is my understanding. I feel you also know I often find humanity quibbling about centuries-old concerns; tiny, rigid issues. People make God out to be petty."

"And you are evolved beyond religious pettiness?" Mel asked.

Ann was not defensive, "I want to be. I hope to be. No, I'm not yet that evolved. Are you that evolved?"

"Probably not," Mel replied.

Ann continued, "Like Julia, my spiritual jigsaw puzzle keeps being torn apart with new pieces added. My understanding is challenged, stretched, and this will probably continue the rest of my life—if I'm fortunate. Like the treetops, something is always stirring inside whether I notice or not. Truly learned rabbis' questions, debates, pithy remarks, surely come from such interior stirrings, including those of Rabbi Jesus. I can't undo world history. I only know I must be true to my own stirrings."

Mel cleverly said, "I'll use Marc's line: 'Rachel and family are OK, Sarah and girls are remarkably OK under the circumstances, you're OK, we're OK,' right? At this moment, everyone seems to be OK."

"Correct, so long as you're OK," Ann added.

"I am," Mel said convincingly, but Ann wondered if they needed more talk. He said no more, and seemed satisfied for the moment.

As they sat on the park bench, the sky was changing. Clouds were gathering. They started home. The wind was stronger and colder as Ann put her arm through Mel's crooked arm, hand in pocket, and they headed for the warmth of home, hot tea and an early evening meal. Her thoughts were: *Strange how enjoyment, contentment, peace, need not be dissected or analyzed. However, disquiet, turmoil, agitation, require attention if we are to learn from them. They are our teachers. We learn from suffering. I dislike this fact of life.*

After the evening meal, Ann retreated to her tower studio needing to write poetry, or draw, or paint, to somehow embody her feelings. Thinking was inadequate, insufficient. Yet Ann kept on thinking.

Julia's humor helped her initially cope with news of Cal Hanover. Humor is powerful. I want to help Julia adapt to the idea of Cal, but she's gone, back to her life in Kansas, beset again with difficulties not of her making. I hurt for her.

And now I am stricken with empathy for Mel, too. Strong, dependable Mel. Taking my hand on the walk today is symbolic of what he has done all these years, beginning the day we met because of a flat tire. Mel, who suffered through my depression with me, caring only that I get better. I have callously, blindly, not understood how my increasing religious interest might seem to him. I must first make clear to myself the reconciliations between my Jewish outlook and my Jewish-Christian understanding, and then apologize to Mel for my self-absorption.

I know Mel and I looked elderly as we walked hand in hand, arm in arm today. We are in the sunset years of our life, we are running short on time. What's life for? What's living about? These remain ultimate questions.

Ann hadn't a clue that another chapter in Matti's story was about to come to pass.

Chapter Twenty-Nine

DNA?

Months later, a meeting between Julia and biological father Cal Hanover did take place at Beth's elegant home in Austin TX after much work on Beth's part, Julia's reluctance, and finally Julia's approval. Then, on poolside chairs at Beth's house one lovely summer evening, Marc Montel and Ann Dramm were enjoying dessert and commenting on the large cowboy boot design glistening at the bottom of the Texas-size swimming pool.

At the other end of the pool sat husbands Mel and Thomas with their desserts. Julia and Cal were in chairs midway at the side of the water. No one planned this scattered arrangement, but it was working well; better than earlier when the group was eating and talking around the dining room table. Not long into the meal, Beth sensed the awkwardness of the table arrangement. At the appropriate time, she announced dessert would be served poolside.

Julia had first resisted meeting Cal. But then curiosity won out. She wanted to see this man Beth said looked like Julia. She wanted to watch his mannerisms, hear his voice, check out genetic connections for herself, her children. She wanted to know whether Cal and Matti cared for each other, though she wasn't sure what difference that would make.

When Ann shook hands with Cal she saw immediately how much he and Julia looked alike. In planning this evening, Beth told Cal about Ann having been Matti's roommate at the time Julia was born. This evening, when she introduced Ann and Cal, she said only, "This is Ann from Connecticut." No more need be said. He knew Ann was the thirty-year secret-keeper. For Cal and Julia, there was a mere handshake, with everyone present, including his potential miniature biological heirs, his grandchildren. Cal had the aplomb to play his part well with no outward sign of anxiety. Bubbly Beth seemed to know how to make this unusual evening work.

There had been no hors d'oeuvres for that would have been too casual and this wasn't a typical socially casual evening. Beth immediately took cocktail orders which were set up and served in a most timely fashion by the caterers. The three Montel children would eat in the kitchen tended to by a neighboring teenager after first being introduced to a play room so they had something fun to look forward to after the meal.

Clever name cards the shape of Texas told everyone where to sit. Cal and Julia were seated opposite each other at the middle of the table. Beth struggled with the seating until she realized her plans may not be perfect, but random didn't seem ideal, either.

Plates were served by the caterers immediately after cocktails found their way to the table. Marc was seated closest to the kitchen in case the teenage babysitter needed help tending to the children Benjamin, Kendal, and Patrick.

Almost immediately after being seated, Julia courageously or nervously cracked the ice with Cal, "Do we look alike?" and he answered, "It seems we might." Comments around the table were in agreement. Julia carried it further, "Should there be DNA testing?" He responded, "Possibly, but why?" She tossed back, "Wouldn't it be weird to believe something that isn't so, when we don't have to; when we can be certain? Since the situation has come this far, I would like certainty."

Ann was amazed at Julia's directness. Later, Julia told Ann it was a mixture of fear and anger. Fear of having nothing to say to Cal; fear of awkward silences; and anger that she was again in the situation of learning about a biological parent, an anger that stayed in her though she tried to make it go away.

Perhaps sensing Julia's agitation Cal responded, "I'd like to know if a DNA check is warranted by knowing more about coincidences at the time you were born. Did my name ever come up?" He looked at Ann, who answered, "Not that I recall."

"No name was mentioned," Cal stated, being sure he understood correctly.

"Correct, so far as I can remember." Ann could have added that Matti spoke of John but never as the father of the baby. Matti was no longer pining for John and spoke of him mostly because she was amazed she had been so "in love" with someone whose personality she never liked.

Ann had entertained the possibility that Cal had been a romantic rebound person after John but she couldn't be sure of that. Ann was the first at the table to use Matti's name: "Matti did more than once say she didn't want shame or pity. It was clear to me that she didn't want shame to come to her family, and I thought she meant she didn't want me to pity her. In hindsight, she may have meant she didn't want the father of the baby to marry her out of pity."

Cal's light skin flushed, or so it seemed to Ann. "Perhaps that is why she did not contact me once she was settled in Connecticut." His forthrightness was disarming. It sent a signal that he wanted to resolve this mystery of many years.

Prior to this evening Ann had been racking her brain and asking Mel for any relevant Matti memories from so many years ago. Mel had none, for in his own words, "Matti's situation was not my priority at the time. You were." Ann did remember Matti saying in later years she thought the father of the child had a right to know he had fathered a child but that they'd had only a few dates and she didn't imagine he'd want to hear such news from her. Maybe she wasn't that explicit. Maybe she only said she didn't want contact with him and assumed he wouldn't want contact with her. Exact words from many years ago are not dependable, and so Ann mentioned none of this at the table.

Julia's face was markedly flushed and distressed. Ann saw Marc look at Julia furtively, as if he'd put his arm around her had they been seated together. Beth now wished she'd seated Julia and Marc together. A blanket of discomfort was ensconced around the table. Robotic motions of eating continued, but awkwardness is what everyone was really consuming; years of Cal's pain of wondering; Ann's role of secrecy and the question of whether Ann and Mel should have adopted the baby, and indeed, Julia's countless feelings. Beth's Serenity Prayer to start the meal, "to accept the things we cannot change" seemed to highlight rather than diminish the tension. Beth realized this now, too.

After Julia's blurts about looking alike and DNA, Cal picked up the excruciating task of making relevant conversation. "I was attracted to Matti because she was a bright person, intellectually independent. For me, it was love at first hearing, hearing her talk. She was the smartest female I'd met to that point, and I wanted to marry her on the spot and I told her that. I think I came on too strong too soon."

"Did you have one date, two?" Julia asked. "No, maybe a total of ten or twelve over several weeks before she left for Connecticut. Long enough to meet her niece and nephew who meant so much to her. Long enough to see her fret over her father whose health was not good. She was rather overly serious and so was I. I thought we were a perfect match. Even had the same kind of humor. But once I was convinced she'd forgotten about me, I went on with my life."

"Did you suspect she was pregnant?" Julia asked.

"Yes, that was a real possibility. Our time together was more than a little passionate to a God-fearing Baptist like myself. Later, when my wife and I couldn't have children and we went through the fertility tests which showed I was OK, I felt it was God's punishment. I've mostly gotten over it, but felt justly punished for years.

"We were going to adopt but my wife was not strong physically. We didn't want to adopt a child whose mother's health was not robust."

Beth sought to help with the conversation. "Did your wife die from her original medical difficulties?" "No, she died from breast cancer. She was an extraordinary woman and we had a beautiful life together. I couldn't have asked for more."

Was he saying that as bravado to minimize Matti's never contacting him? Perhaps it was the truth. Ann scrutinized every word. Cal asked about Julia's parents, her growing up. Beth had told him what she knew, but he was perhaps making table talk or wanting to hear it from Julia. It was a relief she could talk about her family, education, career, being a mother, life in Clarksdale. She scarcely got to eat, but did not have much appetite anyway.

Chapter Thirty

Julia and Cal Talk

While the group struggled through the stressful mealtime adventure, Beth concocted her plan for poolside dessert. Yes, they would eat dessert outside. There were groupings of chairs around the pool. Without effort, they gravitated two by two to separate areas: Mel and Thomas closest to the house, Marc and Ann at the far end, Cal and Julia midway. Beth served dessert, checking in on the babysitter and Montel children in the play room.

Marc and Ann talked but couldn't keep their eyes off of Julia and Cal as Marc answered Ann's questions about Rose his mother, Connie his widowed cousin, Lenore the psychiatrist. Thank heavens they had these people to chat about. Their talk stopped when they saw Julia dabbing her eyes with her napkin. They watched to be certain. Yes, she was crying. Marc leaned forward in his chair as if he might go to her. Julia recovered. And then, Cal and Julia were laughing.

Marc talked about Julia having been through so much since they'd been married. His family had crazy dynamics and so did he. "Julia could have cut and run. Thank God she hasn't. I'm grateful my screwed-up family knows how to sell furniture so she can stay home with the children." Ann felt exceptionally fond of Marc who was self-depreciating, probably like shrewd grandpa Montel. The evening's earlier tension had been lessened by the lovely backyard ambience, the pleasant weather, a feeling that mature adults were coping well.

"I love that cowboy boot mosaic at the bottom of the pool. It's incredible," Marc remarked.

"Isn't it, though," Ann agreed, and asked about Kansas eccentricity.

Marc said there is no such thing as Kansas eccentricity, no such a thing. "We are plain folk."

Ann did not yet know she would one day make a trip to Clarksdale, Kansas, home of Marc and Julia. Beth appeared poolside to pick up dessert dishes and offer tea, wine, or water. Cal used Beth's arrival on the scene to say it was time for him to leave. As if following a script, everyone ambled inside, while Beth invited Cal to the playroom on the pretext of his needing to see their Texas-size home toy store, but actually, so he could say good-bye to the children in a casual way.

After a few minutes of watching animated activity in the playroom, Cal said goodbye to Benjamin, Kendal, and Patrick, saying each name while shaking hands. Out of the playroom, after shaking hands and saying good-bye to everyone else, especially thanking Beth for making this evening possible, Julia and Cal engaged a handshake but then mutually, spontaneously, hugged. Ann wondered how Cal felt walking alone to his car. She felt he'd been through a lot.

Julia's report about what she and Cal talked about poolside was not lengthy because Patrick was clinging to his mother, fussy and whining, tired, needing a bath and bed. No one else could distract or appease the weary child. He wanted only his mother. And so, the Montels stayed but a short while before gathering the young ones into the rented van and were off to the hotel.

Julia summarized briefly before leaving, "I shed a few tears apologizing for my abrasive manner during the meal and then we laughed together that he felt like a fish out of water and was glad that I could at least muster up something, for he had found himself speechless, he said.

"He's likeable, enjoyable, easy to be with. I have the sense he is, indeed, a decent person. He said he would be pleased to stay in touch with me; DNA testing can be pursued if I want; but above all he does not want to disrupt my life in any way; he is grateful for this evening; yes, he thinks we share a strong physical resemblance; he is relieved to know

I have loving parents, for this mitigates his longtime concern for the welfare of a child he felt he likely fathered; he is overwhelmed that the opportunity for resolving his personal quandary about being irresponsible has come to pass; knowing that I have had a stable life is important to him; he is thankful that good people like my parents picked up the pieces of his impulsive, irresponsible, passionate behavior.

"We didn't talk about Matti except I told him I have her computer which Beth shipped to me after Gabby's death and I haven't done anything with it. Overall, he seems a sensitive, intelligent, conscientious, gracious man." Julia's face was flushed as she summarized; she was overwrought.

As Julia and Ann hugged goodbye, Julia asked with a mix of desperation and sarcasm, "Do you think details of my biological heritage have finally come full circle? Surely, there isn't more."

Seeking to sooth Julia, Ann replied, "For your sake, I hope there isn't more," while Ann's feelings were mixed. For she so wanted to know about her own biological heritage, her ancestors, family lineage beyond her parents, which was a lingering ache, a kind of homesickness in her for historical family, while Julia was jarred every time another piece of her unknown past caught up with her.

Yet, Ann did not judge Julia, for she was the daughter Mel and Ann didn't adopt, and Ann never quite forgot that, for then, Julia would have grown up knowing about Matti and the other way round. It was a link that did not happen.

It seemed to Ann that fate, destiny, divine providence, unexplainable grace, incomprehensible mystery, kept the door to her Texas friends open these many years culminating in this day, this unique moment when she alone was able to share with Cal and Julia that Matti was not a callous woman, but merely independent, perhaps to a fault. Matti's streak of independence might have been her greatest strength and also her weakness.

Matti's love of ideas such as practical hermeneutics, metaphoric discernment, allusion confusion, may never have been articulated by Matti had she become wife and hands-on mother. But so what? Were the writings from her computer supremely important after all? While Matti never stopped working on ideas, she also never stopped questioning whether it was best for her to have placed her newborn for adoption.

A week or so later, Ann telephoned Julia whose voice indicated a kind of relief that her biological mother might have cared for her biological father and not merely used him. However, Julia's voice also indicated indifference towards Matti. No matter how hard Julia tried, and she did try, Julia could not care deeply about Ann's friend Matti—not really. This remained Julia's reality at the moment; more time was needed for Julia to fully forgive Matti.

DNA showed Cal Hanover was Julia's biological father.

Chapter Thirty-One

Clarksdale, Kansas

Months passed. *Life is filled with twists and turns,* Ann Dramm reminded herself on a Monday morning flight from Stamford, CT, to the Kansas City airport where Julia Montel would pick her up. Ann reviewed the Kansas schedule in her mind: Julia would meet Ann at the airport, and they would travel an hour or so to Julia's home in Clarksdale, Kansas, where Ann's stay would include a short trip with Julia's mentor-friend, psychiatrist Lenore, whom Ann has met only once on the Yale campus.

Never in Ann's wildest imaginings did she ever plan a trip with Lenore. Ann kept asking herself during flight, *Why am I taking this ancestral trip with Lenore when I desperately want to know about my own ancestry?*

Also baffling, Ann's hard-working husband architect Mel encouraged Ann to take this unusual journey within a journey: a plan concocted by dear Beth. Was Mel merely following Beth's lead knowing that Beth had Ann's best interests at heart? Was Mel's work schedule so intense he no longer had time for trips with Ann?

Some months earlier Beth had driven from Austin to Dallas to socialize after hours with Julia and Lenore whilst they attended a psychological conference in Dallas. Ann was scheduled to be in Dallas as well, but then was forced to cancel the gig when she was stricken with a last-minute bout of stomach flu.

During Ann's absence in Dallas, people-planner Beth, introduced the idea of Ann's short jaunt with Lenore who merely mentioned preliminary plans to someday visit her grandparents' homestead in north central Kansas. Beth, aware that Ann knew nothing of her ancestry beyond her parents, felt this might somehow be interesting to Ann. *But why?* Ann kept asking herself on the flight. *Why did Beth promote Ann's trip with Lenore when she knew Ann wanted to know her own family's history?*

Whatever the answer to the question, Ann flew to Kansas City where Julia met her at the airport, and then nearly an hour later they were approaching Clarksdale, population 7,000, where Julia lived with husband Marc and three children. On the way to Clarksdale Ann absorbed the lovely rolling hills and trees of southeastern Kansas, and paid special attention noticing the rural landscape with neat farms, fences, cultivated fields, pastures with and without livestock — all familiar to Julia. Ann wanted to soak up Julia's world. The woman from Connecticut consciously observed the boundless Kansas sky, beautifully blue with only a few white pillow clouds floating high in fresh summertime air.

Ann was excited to experience the town of Clarksdale, but continued to feel reluctant about the trip with Lenore and halfway hoped it might yet be canceled. Though Ann found Lenore an exceptional person in their brief encounter on the Yale campus, she simply didn't know her well enough to share even a short trip.

Reticent Ann, not as reluctant as she once was to ask questions and voice opinions, did not here in the car share any of her secondary trip misgivings with Julia. Just now, Julia was reviewing Marc's family for Ann: his mother Rose, his brother Stefan. Julia told Ann they would first make a brief stop at the furniture store to say "hi" to Marc, Rose, uncle Ted married to Marc's aunt Sophia, parents of Connie, Marc's young widowed cousin. Ann told herself she must adjust her view of Clarksdale and its people from the way she has long imagined it to what her eyes would now tell her.

Meanwhile, Julia told Ann of her plan on the day of Ann's return to the K.C. airport, when the two of them would leave Clarksdale early and spend time with Julia's family in Kansas City before saying good-bye at the airport. Meeting Julia's family would be another momentously fascinating happening for Ann and would truly bring Julia's story full circle, though earlier Ann felt Julia meeting her biological father had completed the saga.

It remained obvious to Ann that Julia was not yet enthusiastic about Matti, though publicly acknowledging in the speech at the maternity center in Stamford, the maturity and responsibility of Matti who chose adoption when Julia was born. Ann intuitively felt Julia didn't want to be saddled with the bitter feeling, yet there it was, sitting in her personality, beyond her control.

Chapter Thirty-Two

Montel Furniture

And now, Clarksdale was slightly off in the distance to the southwest, nestled in rolling hills, momentarily in the shadow of a few fluffy clouds as if to accent the location of the town. Julia grew up in the Kansas City area but when she married Marc she also married Clarksdale and the prominent place his family had in the community because of the furniture store.

Turning off the highway onto a well-maintained asphalt road for three miles, there was a sign which read, "Clarksdale, population 7,000." Ann alertly observed her first impression which was that most of the town was in a flat valley, though a few houses spilled over into the low hills on each side of the valley.

They drove down a main street leading to the downtown area, and parked in front of the furniture store with its large sign, "Montel Furniture." Ann was quietly engrossed in what her eyes told her. Julia, energetically opening her car door, proclaimed, "We have arrived at famous Montel Furniture, U.S.A." Out of the car, onto the sidewalk, Julia opened the front door of the retail establishment which at first glance inside, until Ann's eyes adjusted from the bright sunlight, seemed to be merely a huge area filled with furniture, but then Ann noticed other doors leading into more areas and an area toward the back left corner. This was a larger business than Ann imagined.

The large entry area artfully displayed small settings of furniture, carpets, lamps, accessories. Other areas may look like a warehouse, but not this central showroom, which portrayed a sense of style; a place to happily lose one's self in opulent well-placed furnishings.

At the back of the store, a woman waved; Rose, Marc's mother. They met in the middle of the store. Julia took a picture of Ann and Rose together, and for the rest of Ann's Clarksdale trip Julia was to be a mindful photographer snapping photos, many photos Ann could share with Mel, for Julia was fond of Mel, gracious, accommodating, humorous Mel.

Marc suddenly appeared as if by magic. Julia explained how everyone working in the store has a monitor to track where everyone else is, whether in a loading dock or other areas annexed since grandpa Montel first acquired the store. Here was handsome Marc in his everyday workplace—and quite a large responsibility it appeared to be. Julia took another photo and another during this quick tour through the entire large complex.

Julia had explained in the car that the store serves a large geographic area of farms and tiny towns. The economic base of the entire area was agriculture and Clarksdale with its medical, retail, legal facilities, schools and churches, served the wider rural community.

Rose explained that her sister Sophia and widowed niece Connie were at a nearby café waiting for Julia, Ann, and Rose for lunch. Then, after meeting uncle Ted (Sophia's husband, Connie's father who had been in a mattress area with customers) Julia, Rose, and Ann began walking two blocks to the restaurant to meet Ted's wife and daughter.

Outside, Ann moved her sunglasses from atop her head to shade her eyes, as she surveyed the two-storied brick downtown area busy with cars and people, not with the feeling of being rushed, though once inside the restaurant, the atmosphere was bustling as customers were immediately seated and brought menu, glass of water, napkin and dinnerware. The luncheon menu was ample including vegetarian items, heart-healthy possibilities. There was also a buffet which Julia and the others recommended.

Conversation was easy in the large corner booth which seated five, as Julia's relatives-by-marriage knew her connection with Ann, and knew every time Ann and Julia had been together. Perhaps everyone knows a lot about everyone else in a town this size, Ann assumed. Julia said her children were at day camp. Connie's daughter was involved with summertime activities as well. Rose and Sophia spoke less than the younger women, until the store was mentioned and then Rose dominated the conversation.

Eventually, Rose said she needed to get back to the store and left by herself while Julia and Ann lingered a bit longer with Sophia and Connie. Ann noticed Sophia was more talkative after her sister Rose's departure.

Chapter Thirty-Three

Stefan

After lunch, Julia and Ann drove to a skilled-care medical facility in a residential neighborhood of ample well-kept yards. In the skilled-care facility Ann met Stefan, Marc's older brother, who was in a wheelchair. Stefan, pronounced "Steven or Stefan," was baptized Stefano Montel. Now fifty-four years old, looking pale and frail, much older than his years, oxygen flowing through a nose piece from a tank attached to the wheelchair. Diagnosis: COPD, chronic obstructive pulmonary disease.

"Life is a bitch. Pardon my language," Stefan said in a surprisingly strong voice. "It can be," Ann replied, uncertain what to say next. She was alone with Stefan in his room at Golden Acres nursing home in Clarksdale, because Julia, his sister-in-law, left the room seconds earlier after her cell phone rang and the summer day-camp nurse said young Patrick fell on the playground, skinned a knee, and was crying, crying inconsolably for his mother. Julia spoke on the telephone with Patrick who insisted she come to him, which she said she would do, for the day-camp area was in a park only blocks away. Knowing she'd return shortly, Julia asked if Ann would stay with Stefan, and Ann said "yes."

Ann learned about Stefan, who, as part of the prominent Montel furniture family, was voted most likely to succeed in his high school graduating class, played first string varsity football well enough to be missed when he was sidelined his senior year with a knee injury which had students flooding to the house, the whole town caring if and when he would return to the game, which was Friday night entertainment for the town, "This wholesome place surrounded by rich farmland," Stefan would cynically label Clarksdale for Ann.

Stefan, eldest son of Rose and Ben Montel, Marc's parents, was Julia's brother-in-law, much to her chagrin most of the time. Ann had already learned from Julia that Stefan alternately blamed his weak father Ben, his strong mother Rose, his persuasive grandfather Giovanni and, even his own name Stefan, for the way his life stalled, stammered, fell apart; his health, three marriages, two estranged children, job failures, financial desperation.

"Life is a bitch," Ann first concluded was a comment on Julia's having to rush out to care for young Patrick. Julia had told Ann, "Stefan pretends to like me, as I am the only member of the immediate Montel family he talks to, for with his mother and brother he is gruffly stubborn, sullen and pretends he can scarcely speak because of breathing problems."

Julia suggested Ann stay with Stefan to secretly test Stefan's amiability or defiance with a stranger. He was such a trickster with the family. Stefan graduated with a degree in business from the state university. He had a difficult personality, intact in some ways but stubbornly unyielding in other ways. Something in Stefan was broken.

In Julia's absence Ann learned that Stefan's "Life is a bitch," did not refer to Julia's unexpected interruption and duty, but was a summation of his own life. Though he sometimes spoke slowly with shortness of breath, he told Ann his story, emphasizing his tale of failure is close to its end. "The only thing I've succeeded at is failing," he said without emotion. Stefan's words startled Ann, as he sprinkled what he said with comments about dying, "My days are numbered . . . won't be here much longer . . . it's about over . . . when I check out."

Only weeks ago Stefan telephoned Marc and told of his poor health. Marc flew to Chicago and drove a rental car with Stefan and his few possessions back to Clarksdale and the hospital where Stefan was a patient for several days of tests before coming to the skilled-nursing facility.

Chicago is where Stefan lived since graduating from college, distancing himself from the family in Clarksdale, avoiding them almost completely for the past ten years, remaining connected only by a cell phone he rarely answered. The telephone bill was paid by Montel Furniture as were all of his bills in recent years. Stefan shared all of this with Ann.

Ann came to understand that Stefan hated the store, Clarksdale, and his family's status in Clarksdale. As the eldest grandson of grandpa Montel, the store was Stefan's by birthright, which he forfeited to his younger brother Marc who returned to Clarksdale after graduating from the state university. "Good, dependable, Marc," Stefan observed.

"The store ruled my family. Because of the reputation of the store I grew up feeling I was better than most people in this town. In college and Chicago, when I sensed others had more than me, I felt I was not as good as them. I do not know how to feel on par with people. I am always weighing, judging, calculating who has more, who has less. Even with my wives, their backgrounds. I suppose I do care about this town and the store, and always figured one day I'd come back and sure enough here I am; home to die."

He waited, "I don't want people coming to see me. I'm a recluse with the *No Visitors* sign on the door. Gossip. Little towns live on gossip. I don't want anyone gossiping about how bad I look. I'm sure the staff here carries their own stories about me out to their families and friends. That's enough. I don't need to be their sideshow freak."

Another lengthy pause, "Maybe I should have been a monk, hidden away in a monastery. But religion never did much for me. Rules, regulations, rituals aren't for me. I could have been a farmer. There are lots of prosperous farmers here. I could have married a local, raised my kids in the country, kept my independence away from the busy-bodies in town. But it's too late now . . . all water under the bridge . . . I had everything by small town standards."

Stefan, staring at the floor, closed his eyes and was quiet for a time. *Maybe he is dying?* Ann puzzled. But then he lifted his head, looked out the window, said nothing. Finally, "What's this life for anyhow? To be a slave to a store? My grandpa Montel was in love with it. He's a town legend. I probably am, too. A legendary failure. But everybody gets old, sick, dies."

He began rifling through the pockets of the handsome burgundy colored robe he was wearing, and then inside to a top pajama pocket. Watching him struggle Ann asked him if she could help him find something. He put his head back looking slightly amused, "Looking for cigarettes which I don't need because I've got a nicotine-patch on . . . old habit . . . married to cigarettes . . . better than any of my wives . . . cigarettes are a faithful companion."

Lost in thought, he returned to the present with a question for Ann, "Have you had a good life?"

Startled, she answered, "For the most part, yes."

"Which means?" he asked.

"More good than bad, I'd say," Ann decided to skip the part about her depression.

He answered his own question with another question, "Good, bad . . . what makes a good life?" He continued. "If a high school counselor, college advisor, or someone would have helped me find what I was interested in, things would have gone better. I seemed to know what I didn't want but not what I wanted. Never knew what I wanted . . ."

Silence again. And then, "About all that interests me now is sports on television. Thank God for that, even though I'm not a religious person. I have teams I follow religiously: college, professional. Which is kinda silly because sports aren't about anything lasting. Just a distraction. Sometimes I can't remember who won the World Series, the Super Bowl, or the Final Four last season."

There was a long pause. He began to search in his right-hand robe pocket again and perhaps remembered he didn't need a cigarette. He stopped the search. Then put his right arm across his chest and grasped his right arm with his left hand, as if embracing himself. He breathed deeply. Was he in pain? Stretching?

Then, arms in his lap, Stefan began talking, "I don't fear death. It will be a relief to be finished living. I'm not interested in an afterlife . . . why would anyone want to go on living . . . that is what hell is to me . . . I want death to be the end. They know I am to be cremated and my ashes buried by where we used to go fishing . . . me and my dad a few times . . . before Marc was born . . . I'm some years older than Marc. . . don't want anybody putting flowers on my grave, visiting my gravesite . . . I'll be happy to fade from memory . . . as if I never was."

Stefan spoke without emotion.

Chapter Thirty-Four

Abandoned Farmyard

Ann's cell phone rang in her purse. Julia was apologizing for how long she'd been gone. Patrick was fine. "I didn't mean to leave you with Stefan for such a long time." Ann assured Julia she was enjoying her time with Stefan; exaggerating her words for his listening benefit.

Julia's telephone call made Ann realize life in a Kansas town can be time-pressured like life in a city. Stefan had wheeled himself to one of the large corner windows and seemed contentedly engrossed with what was going on outside yet spoke to Ann about the interior of his room. "This room is sized for two residents, but I needed privacy and the family is paying double for me to have the room to myself. And they made it pleasant enough for me." He painstakingly pointed out the bed coverlet, window treatments, love seat, lamps, wall hangings, dark book case with upper shelves and lower cabinets, and other furnishings. "Montel Furniture knows elegance and good taste.

"Marc's the good son. He does everything right. He's had it easy. The store appeals to him. He easily conforms . . . his marriage works. The store was my enemy. The store swallowed up everyone's time. Maria and aunt Sophia raised me because my mother was always at the store.

"I don't want to be buried in the family plot which grandpa Montel bought. I want my ashes buried down by the creek . . . where I was happiest the few times my dad and I went fishing there. I want to be as alone as I've felt most of my life.

"I've wanted something I've never found. No career or marriage did it. I look out these windows and wonder if the people I see feel that way. Julia and Marc are too busy to even know if they want something they don't have. Some people just have it easy."

He rested a bit and then continued, "What they serve as food here doesn't have names . . . my taste buds may not recognize good food anymore . . . I don't look forward to anything . . . especially not meals." His breathing was labored. Ann wanted Julia to arrive. Perhaps Ann was agitating Stefan. He was quiet for a bit. Ann said nothing, and busied herself looking out a third window onto landscaped grounds, pleasant houses and yards across the street; cars parked at the facility.

Stefan inserted, "This probably looks like a nice enough setup to you. I should be grateful and would be grateful if I could be grateful, but there's just so much crap, pardon my language."

"What crap?" Ann asked simply to make conversation, and also a technique learned during her own therapy.

Stefan had ready answers: "The crap that life hands out . . . like my health . . . I'm 54 with terminal illnesses . . . oxygen twenty-four hours a day . . . too weak to walk . . . is that crap or what . . ."

"Crap?" Julia asked as she pushed open the almost closed door to the room and entered, bringing fresh air, it seemed. She added, "Remember, crap is fertilizer, even the crap of our lives."

Stefan countered, "Easy to say if you haven't had a lot of it dumped into your lap like I have."

Changing the subject, Julia asked, "Are you coming to eat with us tonight, Stefan?"

"Can't make it."

Julia corrected him, "You don't want to make it . . ."

Smart-aleck-quick he flung back, "That, too." He began looking through a sports magazine. Julia gave a report on Patrick and the summer-school staff's concern about his having hit his head. After a few minutes she edged toward the door and reminded, "Don't forget you're invited to eat with us this evening. Ann picked up her purse and walked to his wheelchair saying, "I'll remember our time together. It's been interesting," hoping to shake his hand. He continued looking down, flipping through the magazine as if Ann and Julia were no longer in the room.

Walking out of Golden Acres this afternoon pleasant June day in Clarksdale, Julia waved or said "hello" to several walking nearby. Once in the car she vented, "Stefan is so difficult . . . so exasperating . . . so impossible. He has not been to our house, or Rose's house where he grew up, or the store. Since coming here some weeks ago he was first in the hospital and then insisted on being driven straight here to Golden Acres. Marc has offered to drive him around town to see how it has changed. Stefan can't or won't do it.

"He refused to eat with us tonight yet he complains about the food he's getting. He's maddening." Julia continued her complaints against Stefan; apologized for her comments; explained she tries not to talk about him to Marc and Rose for they already carry a heavy load concerning Stefan.

Ann listened intently to Julia and paid no attention to her driving then suddenly realized they had traveled outside the town and were driving down a trail in a pasture to a hill. Julia explained, "This is where I sometimes go to experience the Kansas sky without interruption, which may put me in better shape for this evening with Rose."

They arrived at the foundation remains of a once farmyard. Ann gazed upwards, turning her body to view the expanse on this lovely time of day with no clouds, only blue sky.

Ann asked, "Do you come here often?"

Julia said, "This is my fourth time. Though I need to come here often since Stefan has come to town, to dissipate miseries I pick up from him. His wrestlings rub off on me; his insufferable smugness mixed with despair. I guess that's how I'd describe him. Not only who he is now because he is very ill, but I'm talking about who he has apparently been over the years. It's all mixed into one glob."

"I recently asked Stefan after he'd been endlessly complaining and moaning about his circumstances past, present, future, and I was annoyed with his pitying, ungrateful attitude, I asked him if he prays. He shot back,

'Good god, Julia, do you think you have the right to ask me anything you want just because my brother married you?' He can be such a pompous ass."

Julia, looking up to the Kansas sky, hands folded as if in prayer, she uttered, perhaps in jest, "Please forgive me."

Chapter Thirty-Five

Matti's Grandchildren

Entering Montels' lovely spacious home to the smell of food cooking and the sound of a video which Benjamin 8, Kendal 6, and Patrick 4 were watching, having carpooled home with a neighbor, relaxing after day camp, the part-time family cook was setting the dining table. The Montel home décor was quality chic, cozy, casual with just the right furniture and accessories.

Marc's attractive mother Rose, arrived shortly, who after a day at the store still looked impeccable, her thick black hair streaked with shades of gray swept back from her face and gathered in a bun. Modest gold loop earrings with diamond studs completed her look of sophistication, well-appointed make-up accented her olive complexion and dark eyes which sparkled when she smiled, which was often, displayed zest, enthusiasm, looking younger than her years.

Of slight build, medium height, with the overall appearance of a career type rather than a woman of the kitchen. "You have grown dear to my heart over the years," Rose exuded as she hugged Ann in the kitchen. "You are important to Julia, Marc, our whole family." Rose offered Ann wine, tea, water, a mixed drink, as if completely available to meet Ann's desires; years of dealing with customers at the store.

Julia has domestic help twice a week in this spacious home, and even then seemed more than busy with the children, their school and athletic activities, civic, family and friend functions. Ann fondly recalled to herself she was to meet Julia's family in Kansas City on the way to the airport and flight back to Connecticut in a few days. But then discomforting pangs invaded Ann's mind about the reality of her impending trip with Lenore. Tomorrow morning Lenore and Ann would begin heading northwest from Clarksdale.

What would Lenore and Ann talk about those hours together in the car? Ann fondly remembered their easy, meaningful conversation when they met on the Yale campus, but hours together in a car? The children were getting settled at the dining room table, after having been reminded to wash their hands. The dining room had floor to ceiling French windows and doors looking onto a rustic patio courtyard floored with large Tuscan-colored scored concrete, a floor fountain in the center, ferns edging the area, spidery ivy climbing the native stone walls, with a wide opening and a few feet off of the courtyard, a huge tree, surrounded by much sand and a play house. Young Kendal said she'd take Ann to see their sandpile and play house after they ate.

Throughout the meal Ann was fascinated by the Montel children. Ann had met them in Austin at Beth's house, but the Austin evening was so filled with Julia and biological father Cal being introduced that everything else was swept aside. The children did not look much like each other nor Matti or Cal for they were configurations of Nordic-looking Julia and Mediterranean-featured Marc.

Then, food on the table, everyone held hands as Benjamin said grace, words of gratitude for the food, and for everyone at the table, praying for friends and relatives, especially Uncle Stefan. It was a lively table with the children talking about Patrick's fall, his skinned knee, other day camp activities and campers, camp counselors. No adult talk, only interaction with the children.

Ann was aware of how incongruent it was enjoying this moment with Matti's grandchildren without Mel. She'd been wanting him to retire; he says he is not yet ready.

Benjamin asked about Ann's grandchildren and Ann gave details. There was talk about camp and more talk about the important sandpile.

After easy table chatter, dessert was served. Then the children were excused from the table whereupon Kendal reminded everyone it was her turn to blow out the candles and did so, then, putting her hand in Ann's hand saying she wanted to show Ann the sandpile. The small hand (of Matti's grandchild) in Ann's hand was poignant, surreal, indescribable.

Benjamin and Patrick accompanied Kendal and Ann to the sandpile where the three siblings competed to show-and-tell the guest everything about their toys and tools, many items large and small kept in containers in the playhouse. Ann was engrossed watching and listening until their daddy called them in for bath time reminding them of day camp tomorrow.

Then, in their pajamas the children ran into the den, kissed their mother, grandmother goodnight, and shook Ann's hand, as Marc had suggested. *Matti's grandchildren*, Ann continued to marvel. Marc then joined the women with a glass of wine.

Chapter Thirty-Six

Rose's Questions

"Was Stefan friendly this afternoon?" Rose directed politely at Ann. "Yes, I would say so. For a man on oxygen he spoke quite a bit," Ann answered, mindful to mention the oxygen, remembering he is sparse with words to Rose.

Rose wanted to know more, "Did he talk about dying?"

"A bit," Ann acknowledged.

Rose searched, "And he wants to be cremated and buried down by the creek?"

"Yes," Ann nodded.

Rose's list of questions was long, "He doesn't want his children notified?"

With a slight head shake, Ann reflected, "This was never mentioned."

Rose continued, "How he can be so stubborn about not wanting his children to know. As if they are the ones who have slighted him over the years. I don't bring the subject up anymore because he gets agitated. He said if they didn't care about him when he was healthy and available, why would they care now that he's a dying man. I should have gone around his back years ago and kept contact with them.

"We can still track them down, but Stefan's ire makes me hold back. He can be tyrannical. His kids didn't leave him, he left them. He sometimes understands backwards. Always angry at his family and this town when both offered whatever he could want. He can't stand too much truth and turns situations on their head when it suits him. He's here now, safe, with medical treatment. He has what he never wanted."

Rose was more candid than Ann expected.

Rose continued, "I wish he'd say yes to a funeral Mass and burial in the family plot. If we'd withheld these from him, then he'd want them . . . always contrary . . . never wants what is available . . . sad, sad . . .

"One day, maybe not in this lifetime, I hope to understand Stefan . . . what went wrong . . . he seemed to know what he didn't want but not what he wanted, so he's constantly dissatisfied . . . a life of dissatisfaction . . . a terrible way to live. Julia, what are the psychological words you use? I know you say labels don't heal anybody, but still . . ." Julia responded, "I probably used terms like self-absorbed, narcissistic, oppositional tendencies, perhaps borderline personality."

Julia's words didn't interest Rose afterall, who continued, "Maybe it's genetics. We don't know anything about my parents' people in Italy. And we know almost nothing about Ben's family. Ben's mother was OK. I knew some of her family and they seemed alright."

Rose had more questions for Ann: "Did Stefan reveal much of himself to you?"

Ann calmly recalled, "He said he wished a high school counselor or college advisor had helped him find what he wanted to do, because he never found what his interests were. He only knew what he didn't want to do."

Marc unexpectedly asked, "Did he name possible careers?"

Ann replied, "He said he didn't want to be a monk. He said he might have been a farmer."

Rose didn't pay much attention to this talk of careers. She wanted to know if she screwed up as a parent and asked, "Did he talk about his upbringing?"

Ann did not tell her he said he wanted to be buried by the creek because there were a few happy times fishing there with his father. Ann did not repeat that Maria and aunt Sophia took care of him because his mother was always at the store, or that he wanted remote burial because he'd felt alone all his life. To spare Rose, Ann did not say these things. Also, because Ann could not be sure they were genuinely felt remarks. Ann was now uncertain that anything Stefan said was rock-bottom real.

To Rose's very pointed question whether Stefan talked about his parents, Ann cautiously replied, "Not really. He did say, 'My family has never cut me off and they could have . . . maybe should have.'"

Finally Rose concluded, "I want Stefan to have his final wishes. I would not feel OK otherwise. I want him to find peace and giving him his final requests might help. The lives of the dead and the actions of the living may be more connected than we know. Isn't that why we Catholics are taught to pray for the dead? I want to honor what he wants."

"I agree" is all Marc said. Rose readied herself to leave and Marc walked her to her car.

Back in the house, Marc apologized for the evening's conversation being so exclusively about Stefan. Marc explained, "But he is dying, and none of us forget that for long. I've stopped looking for why Stefan is as he is. I figure something went wrong for him a long time ago and don't expect we'll ever know what. I feel sure he didn't one day decide to mess up his life. I don't think anybody decides to do such a thing. Not directly; maybe indirectly with bad choices.

"Julia and I talk about our kids and want to be aware of any help they might need, just in case there are genetic factors. I was surprised when mother tonight brought up her parents' relatives in Italy. The Italian side of the family has always been sacrosanct, which Grandpa Montel promoted."

Marc commented on Ann's day of travel, meeting the Montel clan, and surely she was exhausted. Ann noted, "You've worked all day in that huge furniture store. You must be tired."

Marc summarized, "Usually I'm pretty used up by day's end. Grandpa Montel often said it is good to work hard and go to bed tired. He was a quotably complex man and left his impact daily on the family."

Chapter Thirty-Seven

Lenore and the Children

Next morning around 8:00 Lenore, Julia's retired psychiatrist mentor, rang the doorbell. Benjamin opened the front door while Julia was fixing lunches, putting them in the children's back packs for another day at day camp. The children were eating breakfast. Marc was already at the store. Ann had eaten breakfast.

To Ann, this morning Lenore looked much the same with her salt and pepper au-natural hairstyle, her smallish body frame and spritely demeanor exuding a sense of well-being, perhaps even more bountiful after retiring from her position at the behavioral center. Ann again wished she could convince Mel of his need to retire and be with her.

Watching Lenore interact with the Montel children and Julia, Ann began feeling enthused about the trip and reminding herself to share with Lenore her personal lament on the Yale campus about not finding her calling in life was no longer true, for the maternity center in Stamford was proving a most satisfactory outlet for her interests and contributions. Ann remembered Lenore's words that day on the campus. "It's not too late to find your calling, if you feel you have missed it. In Christianity, the parable about those who arrive late in the day for work and are paid the same as those who came earlier and worked all day is for me a comment that it's never too late to discover what is important in life." Lenore's words had stayed with Ann. Lenore was now pursuing her own personal agenda; this trip to her grandparents' homestead.

Just then in the Montel house the dog Boots and cat Tiger were wanting in the house from the back yard and Patrick left his cereal to perform the manly door-duty and explained that the pets "pwobably" went potty outside and so now wanted inside.

Lenore noticed the bandage on Patrick's knee and asked him what happened. He said he fell and he "bleeded," looking down at the bandage while hoisting himself onto the chair to continue his breakfast, and saying more about the pets. He explained that sometimes the family does potty "patwol" to clean the back yard and sand pile. Benjamin added that sometimes the yard people clean the yard.

Patrick had more information while continuing with his cereal. Boots is named boots because he is all "wust" color except his white feet look like boots. Benjamin added that Tiger is named Tiger because she is marked with tiger stripes. He added that Tiger should be a name for a boy cat not a girl cat. Julia was smiling, obviously amused by her children; delighted with them — a prime reason she couldn't fathom adopting one away, which she had indicated to Ann at various times.

Perhaps not wanting to be outdone by her brothers at the table, Kendal told how they had to rake the sandpile to remove Tiger's litter because Tiger uses "our sandpile for her bathroom," Kendal giggled.

Julia moved the conversation away from potty-talk and observed Lenore's outfit of dark brown jeans, sage colored v-neck t-shirt with 3/4 length sleeves, and rustic dark brown leather sandals and Ann's khaki trousers and lightweight jacket, black t-shirt and oxford loafers made the ladies look dressed for a safari and asked the children if they knew what a safari was and then explained. She asked whether the children thought there would be lions and tigers where Ann and Lenore were going. The consensus was there aren't such in Kansas. And Julia gave a brief contrast between a photo-shoot safari and an old-fashioned gun-shoot safari. The children's faces grasped the significance of the gun-shoot scenario.

Lenore explained their safari will be a video-camera shoot of churches which were built by this one group of people, her ancestors. She said their trip would not be long; they will be back in Clarksdale in three evenings, after sleeping two nights on the farm of Lenore's cousin and his wife close to where Lenore's grandparents once lived. The house and farm buildings are now gone from the grandparents' place. The ladies would spend daytime traveling throughout the county videotaping the churches Lenore's ancestors helped build.

Julia mentioned for Lenore's understanding that yesterday she and Ann had been to the abandoned farm site for some sky-therapy. Julia used these words to obscure from the children her hostile reaction to seeing Stefan yesterday, which she knew was not merely her reaction but her overreaction. Yes, Julia knew this about herself but seemed unable to modify the emotional exaggeration in herself.

Breakfast was now past, backpacks gathered and children out the front door on the way to their mother's car in the driveway on this lovely early summer morning, when scores of bright tulips of all colors in this southside yard smartly accented the shrubbery behind them which outlined the painted white brick house with dark grey shutters. This corner home had a large, lovely landscaped front lawn with well-placed trees and bushes and a big back yard enclosed by an ivy-covered metal fence.

As Ann put her luggage in Lenore's vehicle she mentioned a chorus of birds in neighborhood trees, as if the birds were sending the ladies off on their journey, she said. Lenore was amused by the idea that even the birds knew about their trip and mentioned the birdsong to the Montel children who took notice of the morning melodies while buckling themselves into seat belts in their mother's car parked next to Lenore's car in the driveway, readying for their ride to day camp.

Just then, Julia came out of the house to her car and thrust her voice in the direction of Lenore's vehicle saying, "Tell Ann about my sandpile experience and plans, as I'll be meeting with the committee after I drop the children off at camp. Ann will applaud my efforts to de-tox myself in the sandpile."

The cars backed out of the driveway and drove off in opposite directions. Ann was engrossed with looking at yards, houses, everyday Clarksdale which was Julia's world. She wanted these impressions to go home to Connecticut with her to share with Mel. Lenore could sense Ann's temporary preoccupation and was quiet until outside of town headed west to Wichita. Then Lenore began explaining Julia's committee meeting today and efforts to "de-tox" herself in the children's sandpile.

Chapter Thirty-Eight

Julia's Sandpile Therapy

Lenore summarized for Ann, "Julia realizes she has toxic emotions she wants to deal with. Not many weeks ago, when the children were still in school, before summer vacation, Julia was plagued by particularly bitter feelings about her birth mother. She went outside to the children's large sandpile and began writing words in the sand with a stick. She slowly, deliberately, wrote her boldest, meanest descriptors of Matti: fraudulent, arrogant, insincere, self-centered. Julia sat in the sand surrounded by her verbal indictments of this woman, and remained seated that bright coolish day while becoming aware of the contrail of an airplane forming high in the clear sky.

"Mesmerized by the white streak developing while also dissipating at the far end of the heavenly trail, she decided to lie face up, hands behind her head, body in the grass, watching the atmospheric phenomenon transpire. It was the kind of earthy thing she had not done since a child. She remained on the ground, intimately aware of earth, sky, sand, grass, relative quiet of the moment, and her own being. Closing her eyes she remained awhile until Boots licked her face, when she sat up, smoothed away the harsh words she had etched in the sand and went into the house feeling better.

"The next day with children in school, Julia returned to their sandpile where she began making a tiny house with twigs and gathered stones to create a pathway and yard around the tiny twig house and made a ditch for a make-believe river. She found a tea set inside the children's play house and other items that fit the scene she was creating; animals, vehicles, green sprigs for trees and leaves stuck in the sand for bushes. Fully engaged creating, she then sat with what she made and realized she felt calm. Agitation and turbulence were not present in the moment. Something inside Julia was better.

"She realized she made *a place* for Matti to live. Julia made *accommodations* for this fact of her life. However, that was not the end of that day's story. She realized that knowing the joy of motherhood herself, and endless fascination with her own children, her birth mother had increasingly come to seem like a "real idiot" for having forfeited the delights of motherhood by giving her baby away.

"Julia recognized her rage for this bright woman whom people admired for intellect and wisdom while Julia was stuck in contempt for the same remarkable woman who was careless enough to get pregnant when birth control was becoming available, and then give away the baby she would grieve for the rest of her life, and be careful enough to keep this secret for as long as she lived, never letting Julia's biological father know; never contacting him; likely having used his affections to soothe her broken heart from another romance that hadn't worked out. These feelings were all jumbled together and they didn't go away just because Julia wanted them gone. Why was Julia so cynical about her birth mother? The emotions were convoluted.

"On the third consecutive day Julie took with her to the sandpile from the kitchen a plastic bag the sides she had cut open to flatten out, and a jug of water, for she wanted a body of water in the sandpile that wouldn't soak away. Putting the plastic in the sand and filling it with water she had a lake and then with heaps of sand created hills and even mountain ranges, and made forest areas out of twiglets lying about from last night's rain storm. She was creating like god created the earth and laughed at herself.

"Having finished her sand sculpture, she contemplated what she'd made: a pool of water like the waters of the unconscious, mountains and crevices like the heights and depths of emotions, woods like the "woulds" (the will) of the personality. She brought to life a simple version of the personality. And then what? She was stumped. What else? Was there more?

"She sat and waited for an insight or a question. She knew she could pull the plastic sheet out of the sand and the water would drain immediately, flatten down the heaps of sand and abolish the mountains, remove the twiglets with a rake and delete the forests she had made. But destroying the creation would not satisfy her.

"She sat in the sand and reflected on her three days in the sandpile. First day: the harsh words scratched in the sand, contrasted with the formation of the jet stream above brought different emotions, perspectives, viewpoints, comprehensions of the moment. She came to realize her birth mother was not merely foolhardy or wise; she was both foolhardy and wise and more. Truth has its subtleties and nuances, parameters, heights and depths of understanding.

"On the second day: She made a place for her birth mother in her life. As Julia's hands worked that day, she later metaphorically deduced she could "handle" the strengths and limitations of her biological mother. Julia could "handle" the circumstances of her birth. Actually there was nothing for Julia to "handle," except to live her life as it is today; just as she would soon pick-up her children at school.

"On this third day: The water, mountains, woods she created represent earthly existence which is made up of things, and things tell us about ourself. Creating things like meals and clean clothes and a ride home from school for her children is what Julia did. We are doing-beings and Matti "did the things" she thought best under the circumstances of her pregnancy. She did not personally reject newborn Julia, merely sought a way for both of them to thrive.

"Julia, picking up the children from school on her third day in the sandpile, was asked by Kendal why Julia was so happy. The child sensed a transformation in Julia, which convinced Julia something had changed in her.

"Julia's three days in the sand continued to speak to her. Her sandpile therapy was somewhat like sandplay or sandtray therapy in psychotherapy, but she wanted to develop something without sand.

"She experimented with her children and their friends, as well as her adult friends, having them create a scene on a sheet of white or colored paper using miniature objects she'd purchased and otherwise gathered. The individual would then share a story of the scene they'd created with the group. Julia felt sure she was onto something, an activity which she called 'Tiny Things' and proposed it as an activity for residents of Golden Acres where Stefan lived.

Lenore summarized for Ann, "This morning's meeting of Julia with a committee at Golden Acres is to propose 'Tiny Things' as an ongoing activity of residents with psychiatric nurse Julia as facilitator. She hopes Stefan will participate and feels sure he won't. Julia admires your creative work with the young women at the maternity center. She also remembers Matti provided a creative cork board at a senior center. Julia's project has deep roots in her."

Chapter Thirty-Nine

Lenore's Husband Dennis

Lenore was as easy to be with as Ann remembered. Lenore was saying, "This trip has so easily fallen into place and now we two grandmothers are on a pilgrimage. Thank you for saying 'yes' to doing this with me, being my traveling partner."

Ann suggested the need for a "pilgrimage" sign on the car the way sports fans do on the way to a game. Lenore suggested, "The sign could say *soul* pilgrimage, since that's what it's about, a soul journey for me." Ann added lightheartedly, "We can be soul sisters on a soul journey."

Lenore's relationship with soul was longstanding. She had become a psychiatrist which means soul-healer, "Growing up in Catholic elementary school the word soul was often used. Of course you could lose your soul, but more importantly the soul wanted and needed God and could know God in various ways and God was eternal, so our soul could know eternal *things*." Lenore laughed that she was becoming infected with Julia's 'things' as in figurines and miniatures which allude to emotional, mental, inner-world dynamics (things).

"In recent years I have come to regard soul as what today is known as right-brain-hemisphere qualities and I believe what we today know of

as left-hemisphere traits long ago Christian writers labeled intellect.
Sometimes authors spoke of intellect and soul, two distinct aspects of
being human."

Lenore had more to say about the word soul, "Soul also means the
non-material body. When someone dies the body does not decay
immediately. The corpse is still in the room but the soul is gone. The
corpse is not animated, no longer alive. The electro-chemical system has
shut down. Or, we say the immortal soul has left the earthly plane of
existence."

Ann remembered her initial fascination with Lenore, who seemed a
reincarnated Matti, which meant Lenore had a brain full of information
which she happily shared, not arrogantly, but enthusiastically. Like Matti,
Lenore was a woman of depth and practical clarity. She was clear about
what she wanted on this trip: "At my grandparents' place, I want to
experience sunset until the glow is gone. There's much I want to get in
touch with on this trip. Much of my married life I wanted to make a tour
visiting the *Churches of Ellis County*, imitating the *Bridges of Madison County*,"
she jested.

Ann asked, "You married immediately after you finished medical
training?" "Yes, soon after I moved to Clarksdale to be part of opening
the regional behavioral center, which people still call the psychiatric
hospital. As the town pharmacist, my husband Dennis was the town's
most eligible bachelor, and we met within weeks, maybe days, after I
arrived in town."

"And it was classic love at first sight?" Ann asked.

"Mutual attraction at first sight. The attraction, whatever it was, lasted
until he died. Dennis was slender, tall, greenish blue eyes, thick brown
hair with a reddish tint, he had the demeanor of a self-contained person.
His reputation when I arrived was that of a recluse, but Clarksdale folk
did not know he had acute rheumatic fever when young growing up in
Wichita, and the heart damage which followed left him with limited
stamina the rest of his life."

"You knew about his health problem from the beginning?"

"I did. He told me right off."

"Your medical background didn't warn you to stay away?"

"Not really. The comfort I felt with him in our first conversation overshadowed his health situation which was manageable and clearly, he knew how to deal with fatigue as a feature of daily life. When marriage became a topic the third time we were together; we didn't waste time; I automatically assumed marrying Dennis would require compromises because his limited stamina would always be there, but so would our symbiotic bond."

"You were married how long?"

"Thirty years and two months. Neither of us expected that longevity. His precarious health kept alive the possibility that he would die young and I believe increased our appreciation for being together. All relationships eventually end, but it's easy to forget and thus live lesser lives."

Lenore asked Ann how she met Mel, who told the story of how he rescued her when she had a flat tire. "And you've been married how long?"

"Forty three years."

"A long time in today's culture."

"A Jewish-Gentile marriage."

"Which can present difficulties . . ."

"Not for us, not really. As you may know, I have been a non-religious person until recent times. By then our daughters Rebecca and Sarah, who were raised Jewish and continue so today, were adults. We have had quite an easy time of it, religiously."

"Dennis and I were quite different Catholics. He was a traditionalist and found me peculiar. I maintained I was a natural searcher, an inquisitive seeker. He said I didn't know how to be spiritually content I disagreed with that assessment and still disagree with it."

Lenore continued, "I stuck to my view that before widespread education and the ever-increasing information explosion, traditional views were less challenged, but not now. Also, my personality does not passively accept authority. Any authority. There is a free spirit aspect to me that will not be denied. Sometimes he just shook his head at my spiritual speculations.

"I once used our different careers to make a point. I told him filling prescriptions requires rigorous fidelity to what is prescribed, but as a psychiatrist I must do the prescribing and deal with the people who take the medications and from these people I see the rough and tumble of life, the struggles of mind and body, and these complexities do not precisely fit a particular prescription or proscription. I don't know whether he was impressed with my analogy. We differed on these matters until the end."

"Is it troubling to realize your personal differences now?"

"No. Not really. That is just the way we were. It added stimulating disagreement. Dennis said I psychologized everything, including religion. And he was right. It's just that I don't think it's wrong to do so. I don't believe he found what I did wrong or objectionable, merely unusual or unnecessary.

"Not long after we were married, I told him that at about the age of ten or so I began feeling Jesus and I had a lot in common because Jesus talked about farming, crops, planting and harvesting, and I knew those same realities living in a rural area. Dennis looked at me in a quizzical way.

"Our religious differences remained vibrantly clear towards the end of his life when the idea of Jesus' mother Mary becoming recognized as co-redemptrix with her son was being tossed about in the Catholic Church. To Dennis this was a radically wrong-headed notion, whereas I embraced the idea. Co-redemptrix means Mary *with* Jesus: feminine and masculine aspects of the divine. I've worked with patients who couldn't relate to God as masculine, depending on their experience with their father. Biologically, we each have both female and male hormones. Psychologically, we have both male and female traits and qualities. How can we relate to a god who is totally male? Sometimes we need feminine tenderness, feminine wisdom, feminine strength. In my view, our culture is lopsided, too tilted towards masculine power, competition. We need gentler, more cooperative, collaborative strengths. Mary with Jesus is a kind of psychological-spiritual homeostasis. Dennis asked why make changes; the church has always included Mary, and he was correct about that."

Chapter Forty

San Francisco and Logan

As the two women traveled, the Kansas sky remained clear except for a few fluffy clouds. Ripening fields of wheat, pastures, grazing animals, cultivated fields, neat farms, continued to surround; a pastoral panoramic picture was everywhere.

Lenore told how harvest crews and their combines begin cutting wheat in early summer in south Texas, then work through the Oklahoma wheat fields, into Kansas and continue north through Nebraska and the Dakotas into Canada. The crews are contracted by farmers and free the farmers from investing in expensive combines that are needed only a few days each year. "It's a spectacular combination of harvest crews working at a pace that coincides with wheat ripening from south to north."

The wheat they were now passing was still several weeks from harvest, Lenore guessed. When ripe, the wheat fields would be waves of grain, oceans of gold, baking under hot sun, hence, the name "Golden Acres" where Stefan Montel was living and where Julia was presenting "Tiny Things" to a committee.

Ann asked, "Do you know Stefan?"

Lenore said, "I have never met him, and know him only through Julia, who as we know finds him problematic."

Ann tells, "I spent some time alone with him yesterday afternoon," and explained Patrick's playground fall and Julia leaving Ann with Stefan.

"Did you find Stefan difficult?"

Ann summed-up, "Not difficult, but strange; a mystery unto himself; an individual who perhaps never found what he wanted to do with his life, for he said, 'And now it's too late for me. Too late.'" Ann had certainly known that kind of disquiet.

Lenore commented, "Stefan was born into privilege, as I'm sure you know. Grandpa Montel was quite a character. I knew him only from buying furniture. Colorful, full of himself, a strong personality, irresistible salesman; he established quite a business."

Lenore knew Ann briefly toured the furniture store yesterday and then spent time with Stefan. "I'm not well acquainted with the Montel family. Working at the behavioral center left me somewhat detached from townsfolk and that's good. I enjoy anonymity. Growing up amongst wheat fields and the vast sky makes one feel anonymous and small, which some find frightening, but I embrace.

"For me, the experience of immensity is spiritual enhancement. The experience of endless expanse as a child makes it impossible for me now to not believe in a spiritual realm. A fellow once told me if he lived in Kansas he felt the monotony would either make him go mad or he would believe in God."

Ann was intrigued, "You've lived with wheat fields, cows, farming, the big sky, your entire life?"

"Except for three years in San Francisco, my medical residency, where the ocean and surrounding nature were wondrous. I loved it there."

"Why did you come back to Kansas?"

"It seemed the thing to do. The behavioral center was opening here just as I was finishing residency. I believe when doors open in life, we need to think seriously about walking through them. Staff at the behavioral center were interested in me, perhaps because of my Kansas background, feeling I could naturally relate to the lives of the patients. I felt comfortable with the job interviews I had at the behavioral center. And then when Dennis walked into my life almost immediately upon moving to Clarksdale. I knew I'd made the right decision."

"No concern you might be leaving your heart in San Francisco, as the song says."

"Strange you should say that. San Francisco has a strong emotional pull on me to this very day. Memories of San Francisco itself are enmeshed with memories of Logan. I was "in love" with Logan during the last part of my psychiatric residency in San Francisco. He was a resident in general surgery in another hospital, and he broke my heart, or perhaps we broke each other's heart. I'm not sure."

Chapter Forty-One

Logan's Parents

Lenore had little to say about Logan at first, but then was engrossed remembering, "From the beginning of our dating, I was in awe of Logan's interest in me, a small-town Kansas girl who went to medical school because a high school biology teacher became a mentor and secured a scholarship for me at her alma mater. She shaped my life, and part of my motivation for coming back to this part of the state after medical training may have been to honor her memory. And then I met Dennis and have been here since."

Wanting to change the subject away from Logan, or perhaps simply wanting Ann to know about "Kansas skyscrapers" which are wheat elevators, Lenore spoke at length about their purpose, as she pointed them out: "These unusual structures, jutting skyward, concrete skyscrapers, in small towns and large towns, are grain elevators, even in rural spots where there is no town."

Grain elevators were interesting but Ann was also interested in what else Lenore had to say about Logan, wanting to know more without being intrusive. Ann mentioned his name and Lenore responded.

"OK, back to Logan. He was urbane, confident, cocky in a nice way, a breath of fresh air who knew how to be carefree and leave the stress and strain of medical training behind if for only a few hours. I never stopped being flattered that he chose to be with me, so ours was probably an uneven match from the beginning.

"After dating some months, he asked me to go to Seattle, his home town, to meet his parents. Fixing our schedules took some doing, but then we were on a flight to Seattle. I remember thinking how extraordinarily favored I was to be spending so many hours with him, privileged to meet his parents, to be in the house in which he grew up. He had never talked much about his parents.

"My entire life as a resident took on an element of increased sanity because of Logan. He was a wholesome distraction from stress. He embellished my sense of being; it was the classic 'being in love' syndrome and our trip to Seattle was the best yet. I had wholehearted confidence in him, was thrilled to be with him, but at the back of my mind still wondered why he chose to be with me when he was so utterly fine. It wasn't that I didn't think I was fine, but he was finer," Lenore laughed.

"So here I was, a budding psychiatrist in the grip of this being-in-love thing. Sure, there had been romances before, but bigger unconscious forces were at work this time. A part of me often made that observation, even at the time. Always, I remained astonished that he chose me.

"In Seattle, after picking up a rental car at the airport, we arrived at his parents' home which was more than I expected; larger and more elegant in an obviously privileged neighborhood. I knew Logan came from money, but I hadn't expected this. After the relationship was over, I wondered if my 'love' wasn't partly because of the wonderful places we dined, the concerts we attended. Being with Logan was freedom from my constant penny-pinching as a poor psychiatric trainee.

"Anyway, it was late Friday afternoon when we went in the front door of his boyhood home and met his mother Doris; and later his neurosurgeon father Franklin not yet home from his medical practice.

"Doris was a charming woman; my first impression. We would be going to the country club for dinner that evening, she announced almost immediately, giving instructions on how to dress. It didn't take long for me to feel she was one of the most unnatural people I'd ever met; a fledgling actress reading a bad script. Nothing about her felt real.

"She offered drinks. Realized she'd forgotten to hug Logan, but then didn't do so. It seemed she could talk best by starting each sentence with her husband's name: 'Franklin says . . . Franklin believes . . . Franklin told me . . .' she went on, seemingly connected to her husband's brain. And finally this Franklin man came home.

"He seemed remote, stiff and stern. He shook hands with Logan and me as if we might be patients in for a dire consultation. He didn't ask about our flight or chat in any way. Rather he began talking with Logan about the latest in neurology, making clear that general surgery was inferior to neurology. He, too, seemed to be reading a script; a cold, uninteresting jumble of words.

"At dinner Franklin and Doris competed for the talking prize; nonstop verbiage on different topics. Hers, about clubs she belonged to, interspersed with 'Franklin says . . .' as if he wasn't sitting with us at the table. He never veered from medical talk, except for occasional harangues on the menu, food, food combinations, food service. People waved from afar but no one came near enough to say hello. Was this etiquette or avoidance?"

Lenore continued, "I ate little, though I'd been hungry. My appetite was crushed by the tension. I tried to notice Logan's reactions without appearing to do so. He's wearing a mask, too, I decided, though I could detect no emotion.

"After my longest evening ever, I went to bed somewhat hungry, too tense to sleep, in a lovely room decorated in soothing fine taste. *Poor, poor Logan. He grew up with these people. Oh, thank god, we'll be leaving soon. Will we talk about his parents on the flight back? We have to talk about them some time. But what if he is comfortable with the evening? Then it's all me. I'm weird.*

Chapter Forty-Two

Heartbreak over Logan

Lenore continued talking about Logan's parents, "On Saturday morning I teased only a bit of breakfast into my anxious stomach. We were again at the country club; not in the main dining area, but in the Locker Room, which served an opulent buffet breakfast after golf, tennis, handball, or swimming. Doris and I were at a table in the Locker Room waiting for Franklin and Logan to join us after finishing on the golf course.

"Doris talked nonstop driving from the house to the country club, and then as we sipped coffee (irritating my hollow stomach) waiting for "'our golfers," *No one can be this insufferably boring* I said to myself as she told me the names of interior decorators she'd hired for different rooms of the house and her current plans for remodeling and redecorating. She was hyper-animated.

"Trying to be polite I said something about decorating of which I had little interest or knowledge, and this seemed to encourage her into complimenting herself. She said, 'I told myself, Doris, you've done an exceptional thing with this window treatment.' I found her a strange woman. She never forgot to include Franklin, 'And I told Franklin . . . Franklin always says . . .'

"Finally, the oft-quoted Franklin and his son Logan appeared at our table. Then we went through a lovely buffet line. Back at the table my ailing stomach could handle only bits of food while Franklin gave a stroke-by-stroke report of the golf game, enhanced by Logan's remarks.

"Logan was no longer the Logan he had been. Doris and Franklin were rearranging my *in- loveness*. I was hoping that on the airplane Logan would explain his parents to me; explain how they bugged him; how he loved them despite their driving him, an only child, crazy. What if he didn't say what I wanted him to say? Our backgrounds were too different. I decided psychiatric training was making me hypercritical of people. I was unable to chat, socially immature, underdeveloped. I felt miserable.

"On the way to the airport, Logan gave me an extra tour of Seattle. He was the Logan I was again flattered to be with. On the plane I fell asleep almost immediately after a near sleepless night. He, too, fell asleep. Residents are chronically sleep-deprived.

"I didn't know then that we would never talk about that short time with his parents, which marked the undoing of our relationship. Or maybe it didn't.

"Some days later he said his parents enjoyed our being with them. He didn't say they enjoyed being with us. I scrutinized his every word. He innocently remarked that his mother teased she'd never expected to spend so many consecutive hours with a psychiatrist. I was offended while knowing I shouldn't be. Perhaps Doris was being humorous.

"Just then I was especially busy at the hospital. An important research project had ended, data was being reviewed, preliminary writing begun for an article to be published. Logan and I telephoned as usual, but the workload was such I felt I couldn't go out with him. I don't know what unconscious forces were at work in me, in our relationship, in the cosmos.

"I don't recall events of the next few weeks, but was astonished to learn by the grapevine that Logan was seen socially with someone else. We had not dated others since being with his parents. I felt wretched. With no cell phones in those days, telephone messages sometimes didn't get to the intended person. I've repressed details of that painful time. I only remember feeling that my world had fallen apart. I missed being with Logan, felt I was "in love" with him, though I didn't know whether it was a workable relationship with Franklin and Doris in the background. He had them in him genetically and environmentally. But to have such a fine son they had to be more intact than I observed. Perhaps I hadn't lived up to their expectations. Why did Logan invite me to Seattle? I concluded my critical observations of Doris and Franklin somehow compensated for my feelings of inadequacy. It continued to be a terrible time.

"My residency was winding down. I would occasionally get details about a Logan-spotting around town. Several times someone said Logan asked about me. Everything tore me apart, but I knew the relationship was over. I pretended to be *over* him, which wasn't true. Distracting myself by dating others helped, but the pain lingered. I didn't know I could hurt that much. I felt I'd been ripped-in-two and would never recover.

"The final months in San Francisco required I deal with where I would go to "practice" psychiatry. "Practice" is a peculiar word in this sense, but quite accurate. Learning that a regional psychiatric hospital was opening in Clarksdale, Kansas, I was intrigued. A part of me didn't want to go back to Kansas. Yet, the job listing continued to hold my attention. I interviewed, and I came to Clarksdale."

"And you never knew what happened to Logan?"

"I know how Logan's life ended. Not so long ago, an old friend from medical school who stayed in the San Francisco Bay area, e-mailed an obituary that San Francisco surgeon Logan Bradshaw, M.D., had fallen to his death in a rock climbing accident in Oregon. He was survived by his wife, two children and grandchildren. He was a respected surgeon and experienced rock climber.

"The news sent an emotional shock that riveted through me and stayed for days, weeks. I still feel sorrow; terrible sadness at the tragic loss of his life, for his widow and family. Logan is still part of me."

Chapter Forty-THree

Lenore's Ancestors

Lenore commented on how unusual it was for her to be telling her story when her profession is listening to patients' stories.

Ann asked, "Often stories of broken romantic relationships?"

"Often romance is involved."

Ann wanted to hear more of Lenore's personal story. "Though Logan's parents were not a match for you, you were comfortable with Dennis's parents?"

"Yes, certainly. Everything about our relationship and marriage was comfortable; Dennis being Catholic and I'm Catholic to the core. You'll see how Catholic my ancestors were. The whole Logan experience taught painfully valuable lessons. It made me a better psychiatrist. The hurt and confusion of the break-up made me a more humble person. As I've mentioned, the word 'psychiatry' has to do with soul healing. In the breakup with Logan I came to know my own fragility. Any psychiatric arrogance I had about the ease of overcoming emotional pain, wiping away confusion about desires and motives, having quick fixes for the hard lessons of life, oh, they were greatly modified.

"A lot of immature haughtiness and arrogance began to die at that time and I was reminded that Jesus said unless a wheat grain falls on the ground and dies, it remains only a single grain; but if it dies, it yields a rich harvest. Something that broke my heart would make me more able to help the wounded, hurting hearts that would come into my office." Ann shared, "I have certainly known myself as a fragile soul, as you know."

Lenore noted the land elevation increased as they went west, and explained that though one may not notice it, the land elevation gradually rises to the west, "Eventually culminating in the Rocky Mountains. Travelers often think of Kansas mostly as flat plains, and miss the increasing elevation." Going west on Interstate 70 there was an occasional abandoned farmhouse and Ann wondered what circumstances caused the site to be deserted

The two women were quiet at times as miles and scenery passed. Interstate driving can be a kind of monotony as it bypasses small towns, leaving only a road sign with a town's name, making it seem there are no towns.

As if reading Ann's thoughts, Lenore said, "The Interstates helped kill small towns." Ann agreed with the possibility and had a momentary desire to comprehend the disintegration of small town America. Wanting to see the tragedy as it evolved frame by frame, and mourn its loss as she felt a melancholy for this rich earth with endless sky, "Bread basket of the world. Kansas is the largest wheat producing state in the nation," Lenore was saying.

"Rural families sent their children to college and then the graduates couldn't come home for there were too few job opportunities to fulfill their dreams, use their skills, provide livelihoods. They moved to big cities and faraway lands. Those who stayed are hardy folk. Those who arrived and survived, like my ancestors, were strong, tough, determined, capable of handling hardship.

"The climate can be harsh. Severe winters, hot summers, relentless wind both summer and winter. The wheat thrives in the inhospitality of the climate, the richness of the soil. My ancestors knew how to adapt to unforgiving conditions with the richness of their religious faith. Yet I've had to learn that traits which help immigrants cope may need revision in subsequent generations.

"Anyway, we're on this nostalgic, soulful pilgrimage partly because I noticed I was dreaming about my grandparents' farmhouse in several dreams within a short time. I began to wonder what the farmhouse might psychologically symbolize about me. The actual farmhouse was knocked down years ago, the stone rubble lies in its basement, as we'll see.

"I began to concentrate, contemplate, ruminate, about the farmhouse and began writing what came to mind."

Chapter Forty-Four

Grandparents' Farmhouse Dream

Lenore put her hand into the large envelope between the bucket seats and retrieved a notebook which she opened to a particular page for Ann to read, while saying, "Remember, I'm speaking as if I'm the farmhouse." Ann read aloud what Lenore had written:

> *I am very old and strong with thick, thick walls. I have gone through the great depression. I have kept the family safe, warm, protected. I am largely unappreciated. There has been too little joy here. Though I know how to survive, I do not know how to thrive. Appreciate me; be impressed with the protection I give, with my ability to endure, to persevere, to stand alone.*

Lenore's writing continued:

These words tell me: the very thick walls have to do with a dense frame-of-reference; the basic construct(s) of my upbringing, which lives in me and probably always will — about how to live and how to die — German-Catholic, overly serious frugality, dutiful, hard working.

The "great depression" is the depression of the 30s coupled with dust storms, plus ancestral despair (great depression) in the family. - Some relatives have been severely, chronically depressed — probably why I became a psychiatrist.

"I am largely unappreciated" says to me I have not always appreciated the strong (but limited and limiting) ancestral frame-of-reference in which I was raised though it has protected me from cultural fads, fly-by-night crazes, or being swallowed by the collective mindset of the moment. The coping skills of the ancestors were rooted in religious faith — their basic frame of reference and mine, too, though I've remodeled and expanded what they passed on, but they provided a strong foundation and it's good for me to appreciate this, because I tend to be more aware of the limitations of the mindset in which I was raised rather than its strengths.

My grandparents' farmhouse, standing on a hill, withstanding the relentless wind of the Kansas prairie, symbolizes psychologically coping with winds of change, which translates into being able to adapt, change, grow, without being

Lenore noticed Ann finished reading, and said, "Turn the page; there's more."

In my imagination I create a new picture of the farmhouse: I replace the thick-walled farmhouse with a contemporary home with many, many windows. The word contemporary means belonging to the same period of time. The contemporary house represents my desire to live more fully in the moment, in the present, which means being free of fearful heaviness, despondency about life, which still lurks within. When young, I assumed this was normal. I saw and felt heaviness in my relatives and internalized it.

Many windows suggest psychological openness. Looking from the outside in, the windows are my desire to transform the unhealthy introversion of my ancestry into a creative inwardness free to explore and realize my own potential. Looking from the inside outward symbolizes wanting to meet the outer world without defensive clinging to old ways. That is, meeting the larger culture without fear or inferiority, which was present in my ancestors, as they kept their world small, speaking German, keeping the ways of the old country.

***

Ann reread *despondency, heaviness*. Knowing them well she asked, "Still today, do you often feel this way?"

Lenore responded, "Often? No. I'd say occasionally. Anxiety is part of living. But the despondency and heaviness I refer to is the trait of longsuffering melancholy, sadness, chronic depression. A generalized sorrow over generations. Ancestry is especially potent for me because both my mother and father have the same background, come from the same ethnic group."

Lenore suggested further: "My parents surely share common ancestors for their people lived in small villages for many generations, and so there was a limited gene pool. Living in the same locale for generations was common and the reason why "banns of matrimony," naming couples planning to marry, are still listed in Sunday bulletins. It was the Church's attempt to avoid marriages between close relatives.

"What is certain is that my parents had the same cultural, historical ancestry for many generations. Though I don't know how far back the sameness goes, it's documented from Germany in the middle 1700s when life was wretched because of prolonged war. In the midst of these hard times Catherine the Great of Russia, who was German by birth, offered free land to settlers who would move to Russia's Volga River region which was largely uninhabited.

"My mother's and father's people left the Rhineland part of Germany and after countless miles of bitter deprivations, sometimes walking, the survivors arrived at the Volga River to find no tools, nothing that had been promised by Catherine the Great's government.

"Too destitute to turn back, they sought refuge in caves struggling to survive a brutal climate, criminal bandits, and cruel nomads who resented the intrusion of the Germans and therefore pillaged, killed and kidnapped them.

"The Volga-Germans kept to themselves, endured crippling hardships for a hundred years on the Volga before the Russian government, disregarding Catherine's agreement for she was now dead, began to conscript the Germans into the Russian military. This was intolerable to the Germans, for they were German. Never, not ever, did they consider themselves Russian.

"Meanwhile, halfway around the world the U.S. Congress passed the Homestead Act of 1862 providing the transfer of up to 160 acres of unoccupied public land to homesteaders who complied with requirements, and this act of Congress was the catalyst which started Volga Germans coming to the plains of Kansas in 1875; to once more leave relatives and the life they'd established from scratch in Russia, to brutally till virgin prairie in Kansas. To start over again.

"And once again, creek bank holes, board tents, sodhouses became their refuge against a harsh climate. And as before, the survivors depended on their Catholic faith, family, frugality, hard work, and German customs just as they did on the Volga.

"German-Catholic traditions helped them physically survive two devastating migrations but the cruel circumstances generation after generation wounded the psyche, the soul. What I wrote about *too little joy, knowing how to survive but not thrive*, that is the heaviness, the despair of my heritage."

The last words visibly affected Lenore. Her voice cracked. "You see how close this is to my heart. There was sadness, still sadness in me, yet not my sadness. It is the sorrow of my ancestors embedded in my body at the molecular level, beyond conscious awareness. I know this is why I became a psychiatrist."

Ann remembered a conversation like this with Gabby and supposed it was the Catholicism of both Lenore's and Gabby's ancestors that helped them survive a marginal existence; the trials of living off the land, Gabby's on the plains of West Texas and Lenore's on the plains of Kansas. And then, both Lenore and Gabby chose careers in psychology.

Lenore continued, "I psychologize religion because I believe Jesus was talking about healthy psyche, peaceful soul, which was part of what he called the Kingdom of God or Heaven; something we experience as inner peace, hope, which we desire but is not always easy to find."

Ann was soon to find religion in a cellar.

Chapter Forty-Five

Homestead Destination

The two women were on the interstate one county away from their destination. The land had become flatter. Oil wells were pumping. Lenore talked about the wealth of the area. Rich in land, grain, cattle, oil. She had her cell phone and was contacting her cousin and his wife, letting them know the travelers' location.

Familiar with the area, Lenore recalled childhood memories. The early afternoon sky had a few clouds. A brisk wind rippled through vast fields of green-gold wheat ripening on its way to harvest. Lenore told of the anxiety of farmers at this time: anxious about rain which is not now good for the wheat; hail which devastates crop and family income. Farming is risky business; hard work. Harvest time is intense; long hours; a competition against the possibility of bad weather; the triumph of satisfaction once the crop has been bountiful and safely gathered in.

Then, the travelers turned off the interstate onto a country road going north, dust flying behind their vehicle. An airplane high in the sky seemed incongruent with a dramatic lack of movement on the ground where there was only swaying wheat, nearly immobile cattle in a roadside pasture, a tractor raising dust in a field in the distant west.

In contrast, travels with Mel flooded Ann's mind; scenes of cities where human hustle was everywhere, while here in the geographic center of the continental U.S., stillness of earth and sky prevailed.

Their vehicle slowed, turned east into a lengthy driveway where a farmhouse and buildings at the end of lane appeared; neat, organized, well-kept. This was their destination.

Lenore's cousin Raymond and his wife Rita had either been waiting in rockers in the shade of their large covered east porch, or come out of the house onto the porch and then were at the side of the SUV. Raymond and Rita were a few years younger than Lenore. There were hugs, introductions, inquiries about the trip. Raymond took two larger pieces of luggage into the house while Rita took the two small bags.

Their air-conditioned home was comfortable; neat and clean, reflecting housekeeping skills. Then, the group of four sat at a table in the kitchen with a snack of homemade cookies, cantaloupe and iced tea. Ann noticed a crucifix on the wall of the very clean kitchen.

The snack was refreshing, coupled with conversation about family, friends, acquaintances, situations past and present, all unknown to Ann who listened to language accents, inflections, phrases, and watched mannerisms, for she had never before been inside the house of a working farm. Yet, this was not a farm with pigs and chickens, Lenore told her. These farmers have wheat, cattle, and a small oil well on acreage a few miles away.

Talk shifted to Volga-German Catholic churches in the area, dating from 1885, though one now is in ruin from fire, but all are part of Lenore's video-camera pilgrimage. Raymond brought to the table a map of the county; better than the map Lenore had been working with.

Rita cleared the table, and took Ann through her nicely furnished immaculate home with pictures of children and grandchildren. They exchanged information about each other; especially how Ann had come to know Lenore. Rita commented that the local people tend to know each other's families for generations.

Raymond and Lenore continued working on the church itinerary, whether to start with what church. How to make best use of the time available. The afternoon passed without hurry.

Rita told of a dark bank of clouds forming in the southwest, and pushed aside a sheer curtain to confirm what she already knew, while remarking for Ann's benefit, "Rain now is not good for the wheat."

Lenore told Raymond she'd like to walk to their grandparents' farmhouse site, not quite a mile away as the crow flies. Yes, she wanted to walk, after sitting hours in the SUV. Raymond cautiously told her an earlier weather report predicted possible severe weather late in the afternoon. He suggested, "It's not a good idea to walk there and get caught in a storm before we can get back here to the house."

And so, Raymond, Lenore and Ann piled into his pickup truck. He had a straw hat for himself and for each woman, saying, "You'll want a little shade," as the truck was going out the driveway onto the main road going north for a short distance before turning back east onto a private road where they traveled a bit before stopping at a cattle gate on the left, which Raymond got out of the truck and opened while Lenore scooted into the driver's seat and drove the truck through. Raymond walked the gate closed, fastened it, and was then back in the truck. Ann saw a low pile of rubble not far ahead, and a trail of vehicle tracks which led to it.

"It's barren," Lenore gently narrated as the truck crept to the site. "Not a building, not a trace of the barn, pig pen, chicken coops, granary, other sheds, fences . . . except for remains of the house knocked into the basement. Everything is gone." Ann could hear emotion in Lenore's voice. Raymond stopped the truck, the three got out, put on the large straw hats as the sun was bright. He took a hoe with him from the back of the truck. "In case of a snake," he informed them.

The rubble pile was commonplace to Raymond, but not to Lenore who had not been there since the house was bulldozed years earlier so it would not slowly go to ruin or be vandalized after there was no longer anyone to live in it. This house had been in Lenore's dream. There, she regarded it as representing her psychological-spiritual frame of reference; her inner being; her core approach to life.

Lenore slowly walked the perimeter of the demolished heap — once a small stone house, intimately familiar in her youth. She had shared with Ann memories of home-made ice cream on Sundays on the small screened-in porch in the summer; the sound of her grandfather's violin and uncle's chording on the piano in the tiny parlor.

The house had no indoor plumbing. A windmill and pump provided water. There was a toilet some distance west of the house. A cellar outside the back door kept potatoes and other foods such as jars of canned foods.

Eight children had been raised in this small space, a fortress against the ever-blowing wind whatever the season. Three sons and five daughters shared two small bedrooms upstairs reached by tight spiral stairs in a corner. Chamber pots were used at night.

The outside east walk-in basement dug into the earth on three sides, kept a milk-separator and a fire pit necessary to make soap, but now the basement was a casket for the broken corpse of a house that had sheltered the family. It had been a harsh life; milking cows in the barn no matter how bitterly cold.

Religious duty, German traditions, and the weather governed their lives. In the early years (before automobile) horse and buggy took the family to church some miles away unless weather made the trip unsafe.

On this day, the site of Lenore's maternal ancestral home was quiet, except for the wind which spoke a kind of loneliness to Ann as she watched Lenore turn to face different directions, look here and there in the rubble, to re-experience this small spot on earth intimately meaningful to Lenore.

Ann looked about her. The farm was on a high place, a perfect lookout spot. Spontaneously, Ann's rich imagination envisioned a muscular male Native American mounted on a large horse, surveying areas to the east and south. This land, this earth was once his domain. And how was it before him? Seas covered the area, a pamphlet from Lenore's envelope in the SUV had informed Ann. She could feel the ancient and archaic; a sense of long, long ago; the eternal, eternity.

Raymond walked to Lenore and pointed out two large limestone slab stones each worn down in the middle, shaped by the family's stepping feet. Lenore nodded, remembering where they had lain.

This small limestone house, once neatly laid block on block jutting into the sky, now returned broken and jumbled to earth. The wreckage was a natural home for snakes, Ann vividly imagined as she watched Raymond lean on the hoe as he talked with Lenore. Ann had nervously watched the afternoon sky increasingly darken in the southwest and increase in ominous appearance. Ann was relieved when Raymond suggested they drive back to his house.

The three of them were back in the pickup, gate opened and closed like before, driving to the house as gusts of wind whirled dust in the air. Lighting flashed, thunder rumbled, torrents of rain began smashing the windshield, the wind was fierce as they were momentarily drenched running to the porch where Rita met them at the back door.

Chapter Forty-Six

Storm Cellar

Raymond shouted above the storm noise, "Follow me," and rushed to the end of the porch, lifted up the cellar door, while Rita led the way with a large flashlight lighting the steps which were quickly, carefully navigated to the cellar floor, a pitch-dark space except for the flashlight, and then Raymond was inside and latched the slanted cellar door. Safe. They were safe in the earth here in tornado alley, Ann reflected. She and Mel had talked about tornado alley where hot and cold air masses meet and whirl and destroy wherever they choose.

Raymond turned on a larger lantern and there was enough light to look about the brick cellar with a ceiling curving down to the floor. There were two unfolded aluminum lawn chairs; the kind with plastic woven strips. Rita opened two more chairs for Ann and Lenore.

No one spoke. They listened as wind roared and rain pounded the cellar door. Ann remembered rain was not good for the wheat this close to harvest. "The weather is boss," Raymond said in the truck on the way back to the house. It was a tense game of waiting. The beating rain was so loud, Lenore asked, "Hail?" Raymond and Rita shook their heads, "no."

Ann saw Raymond and Rita take jewelry from the arm of the chair on which they sat. Then Ann realized, not jewelry, rather, two glass-beaded prayer-beads. She knew Catholics had a name for the prayer-beads.

Finally, the wind died down, the rain was lighter. They waited a bit more before Raymond cautiously opened the cellar door, "The house is still here." Then opening the cellar door wider, his head turned up to the sky, "looks like the storm has moved on." On the top step, scanning the premises he announced, "Everything looks OK."

They climbed the cellar steps. "I put the porch furniture in the house," Rita informed. The sky was clearing in the west and southwest, but the eastern sky was a bank of frightening churning greenish black clouds fiercely intensified by the sun in the west shining on the eastern tempest.

"I'm going to check on the wheat," Raymond informed. Lenore wanted to go with him. Rita said she'd finish the evening meal while suggesting Ann go see the aftermath of the storm. Three of them left in the truck and drove a fair distance to different wheat fields, checking rain gauges attached to fences. Amidst the wheat fields and pastures with cows Ann asked, "What do cows and horses do during a tornado?"

Raymond said they seek shelter, under trees, in a barn, if available. Sometimes cows and horses are injured or killed in tornadoes. At each rain gauge stop, Raymond methodically read the gauge, wrote down the amount, emptied the gauge, got back in the truck and reported the amount of rain to his visitors.

Raymond explained the occasional stone post corner. "Years ago, for the first settlers there were no trees here to put wire on to make fences so the old-timers cut limestone into fence posts. The stone posts are mostly gone now, replaced with metal fence posts but I've kept a few stone corner posts just for memory. There is a story that years ago, people going through these parts on the train saw the stone posts a few feet apart in a row and thought they were grave markers; that we buried our people like that; in a cemetery alongside the railroad tracks." He was amused by the story; an obviously old story. Lenore said she heard the story as a child, and the two enjoyed this moment of mutual memory.

Raymond guessed this storm was not a tornado, but a strong, straight wind. Back at the house, Rita confirmed Raymond's assessment of the storm being a straight wind from what she heard on TV. Rita mentioned how late they were eating. She liked meals to be on time, she said. No rancor, just a comment. After the usual blessing, they enjoyed home grown green beans, fried chicken, mashed potatoes and gravy, tossed salad of lettuce with garden tomatoes and cucumbers. For dessert, vanilla ice cream atop homemade peach pie.

Snack lunch had been late, too, Ann told herself, feeling they were ruining their hosts' schedule, but did not say this aloud. Instead, Ann had questions about the cellar. Raymond suggested they go into the cellar again after the meal so Ann could take pictures to show Mel. Rita insisted she tidy-up after the meal while Raymond give the guests a guided tour of the cellar. He explained there are manufactured cellars now, but this one came with the house. Maybe a hundred years old, he guessed.

Raymond pointed out the axe and crow bar were there "in case you need to hack your way out the cellar door." There was bottled water; a plastic container with crackers and power bars; a tall plastic bucket with lid, a bathroom if needed, but "we've never had to stay down here long enough for that."

Ann noticed a crucifix on the wall as Raymond said, "We pray the rosary when we're down here; can't do anything anyway. It helps wait out the storm." Ann surmised the hosts would have prayed the rosary during the storm had she not been there.

She noticed what looked like a small braided or woven reed or straw, hanging in the corner. It seemed like a talisman of some sort. Raymond explained it was braided palm from Palm Sunday, the Sunday before Easter. Ann silently wondered, "Where is God in a storm?"

Chapter Forty-Seven

Jesus' Extraordinary Powers

At bedtime, in the neat guest bedroom with twin beds, the guests already showered, ready for sleep after a day that seemed like several days, Ann had a question for Lenore before they slept. Where did Lenore think God was in a storm?

Lenore differentiated between nature and God. Nature is part of this planet; weather systems and such, for example hot and cold air currents meet over middle America and can create tornadoes. Yet Lenore did not leave out the possibility that prayer may influence any and all planetary, earthly conditions. Jesus is said to have talked to a storm, told it to calm down and it did.

Lenore continued: "There's a lot about Jesus that humans either can regard as hyperbole, fabrication, exaggeration, or, there's a lot about human soul capacity, that is puny and undeveloped or at least underdeveloped, which is why we can't do what he did. His early disciples are recorded as having extraordinary powers. And today documented healings, evidence of non-ordinary happenings, are still part of the sainthood process in the Catholic church.

"Jesus asked people not to tell about some of his healings. I suspect he knew his power began in his soul, and Jesus was wanting to teach people about the soul, the sickness and health of the soul, and how soul affects everything." Lenore believed he recognized all kinds of human things and accomplishments but development of soul is the prize.

Lenore concluded, "Jesus said we would do greater things than he did, but I haven't seen this happening, though I feel overall the world is getting better in ways. Dennis and I talked about this in our desire that his rheumatic heart be healed. We prayed for this to happen. It didn't. Yet we had over thirty years together. So, I feel there an element of healing present or some kind of sustaining grace."

And then, Lenore suggested a dawn walk to the homestead site as the sun rises. Ann told herself she hoped Lenore overslept, and mentioned the mud from tonight's storm to further discourage such a plan. Lenore wanted an earthy, primal experience. Driving here she said she'd had the urge for years to go into a pasture and scream like Edvard Munch's painting *The Scream*. Lenore said Raymond discouraged a dawn walk earlier today when she said she wanted to cut through pastures for an earthy experience to the home site. He told her, "The barbed wire fences are strung tight. You'll have three fences between here and the homestead. It will be impossible for you to get through the barbed wire without ripping clothes, scratching or cutting yourself."

Ann saw Lenore's pushing-the-envelope trait, which is why she could be a psychiatrist. She had the guts to follow people into the enormities of their life. Ann would never be able to do that. But along with Lenore's gutsy approach Ann also noticed Lenore's simplicity when Lenore reconfigured their church route tomorrow after talking with Raymond. Lenore had a childlike quality at the table when she crossed herself and said grace with her cousins. Ann was learning about Lenore.

Lenore slept past dawn the next morning and so did Ann. However, once awake, Lenore quickly readied herself for the day, and Ann did so also, more slowly. Ann found her friend out in the yard with Raymond in the still early morning sky, fresh smell of wet earth from last night's rain, the cooing of doves. Ann noticed Lenore walk to a nearby fence and test the taut barbed wire to confirm, to fact-check. Raymond was correct: they couldn't have gotten through the fence unscathed. Lenore thanked him for taking care of his old cousin and her friend, to which he replied, "None of us are spring chickens anymore." Ann didn't know what a spring chicken was, but assumed it must be a young chicken.

A part of Ann wanted to compare herself to Lenore, looking for her own deficiencies, but quickly silenced the tyrannical old habit, remembering her therapist found Ann courageous, fearless, willing to walk through her personal morass. Ann realigned her thinking, realizing Lenore tried to help her patients, and likewise, Ann was trying to help the pregnant young women at the maternity center.

At the table in Rita's kitchen, after the usual prayer, there was a lovely breakfast, including homemade cinnamon rolls. They talked about the storm. Raymond believed the storm likely did not damage the wheat. There was talk about the churches they would see today. There was no lingering at the meal. Ann found herself worrying about disrupting Raymond and Rita's schedule and how relieved they'd be when the guests were gone. Ann stopped these thoughts remembering that Lenore was their cousin. The hosts might be enjoying the visitors; a break in their routine. And then the two friends were in the SUV, beginning the pilgrimage of the churches.

Chapter Forty-Eight

Prairie Churches

It was idyllic to see the spire of a church rising into the sky from some distance before entering a village. Overall, what could one say about the churches seen throughout that day? Ann viewed them as shrines of faith, monuments to hard work, ingenuity, cohesive communities, with priests, "Maybe Capuchin Franciscan Friars supervising the constructions," Lenore speculated. "At least the Capuchins came to have an enduring presence here."

In the churches Ann saw aspiration, inspiration, tradition and deep European roots reminiscent of what she'd seen in European cathedrals. She and Mel had been to Assisi in Italy, home of St. Francis; they'd toured the Basilica in Assisi.

Lenore marveled aloud, "Eight hundred years ago, when St. Francis was alive, the New World was not yet discovered by Europeans, whereas the American Civil War had already been fought by the time my ancestors settled on these plains of fertile earth."

Rita and Raymond said Lenore and Ann would not be able to see all the churches in one day and they were correct. Though the churches were not great distances apart, the women looked at each leisurely, took pictures, spoke with people when possible, and digested the architecture, the beauty, absorbed the serenity, the history, the effort of erecting these buildings that spiral toward the sky, some amazingly Gothic, all of them speaking a story of religious conviction, religious tradition. Hope in hard times. And they spent time in the cemeteries.

To Ann, interiors of the prairie churches seemed wombs of beauty with stained glass windows, other art, stations of the cross, an organ, choir loft. This was a protected place for exalted awareness, a home for the story (myth) of Christianity cultivated over centuries and brought to rural folk living in these isolated places. Pageantry, ritual, theology, and ancient historical roots were tied together for these people who worked the land. Bringing such creative imagination to the stark prairie spoke of tenacity, steadfast determination, strong will to provide a world of symbolism and mystical motivation despite whatever other intentions were also present. The churches were a statement about the religious impulse in Lenore's ancestors.

The women had lunch in the SUV, a lunch Rita packed generously in an ice chest with enough food for two meals. After lunch, Lenore telephoned Rita to tell they would also eat their evening meal in the vehicle to give them a longer day for touring.

As they drove around in the villages and towns, absorbing life today, Lenore told Ann about the traditions of *unsere leute*, "our people," Lenore translated. She told of memories from her childhood about different village's attitudes, identities and prejudices against another village, despite their German commonalities and the one-hundred-year Volga experience which kept them uniquely bonded.

Lenore told of the fun of a wedding dance, *hochzeit*, literally "high time," she explained, a time of celebration when chores and duties were temporarily laid aside; when the day began with a Nuptial Mass and ended in the evening with a live band and dancing that began with a grand march and continued until midnight. "Great celebration," she said, remembering the polkas and waltzes. Young and old. Everyone had a great time.

Lenore remembered a card game, *Durock*, which young and old played; simple enough for children to learn the basics and subtle enough for adults to refine the tactics of winning. In one small town, Lenore and

Ann had a conversation with an older woman who spoke "broken English," English with a still-strong German accent. They saw cemeteries with homemade iron cross grave markers, welded together in simple designs; occasionally ornate.

Lenore reminisced, "We were called *Roosians* by people who found our language and customs strange. First of all, we weren't Russian. And then, the derisive word, the way it was said, was mean, belittling. It cut deep and left scars in our souls."

Lenore was absorbed in the history of her people, their heritage, her heritage: biological roots, psychological roots, ethical roots, spiritual roots. She said rootlessness can leave a void in people. Healthy traditions teach people how to cope, to manage life. "I have seen patients who simply didn't have the kind of rootedness I had. They are adrift, tossed about by whims and cultural fads of the moment."

Yet she wasn't naively sentimental about tradition and heritage, and said they can stifle as well. "But overall, knowing where you come from gives one the advantage of being able to examine and select your own ways of handling everyday choices."

The first day of visiting the churches was indeed a pilgrimage of soul for Lenore. Ann noticed an unspoken ponderous mood seemed to grip Lenore for noticeable stretches of time as they drove from village to village. Sensing Ann could feel her mood, Lenore sometimes filled the times of disquiet with impersonal talk about the landscape, farming practices, the peaceful and beautiful sky today contrasted with yesterday's frightening clouds, and a moderate wind today after yesterday's fierce frenzy.

"A noticeable wind blows almost every day," Lenore observed again. "The sky and wind together enable one to feel small, vulnerable, alone, forsaken; the need for the Sacred is natural, automatic. However, this forlornness can also breed depression."

When the women arrived back at the cousins' farm, the sun was low in the western sky. Raymond had prepared his truck for their sunset watching at the homestead ruins. He demonstrated fold-up lightweight metal steps in the back of the truck, easily lifted out, placed on the ground, so they could climb the steps into the tail gate of the truck bed and safely watch twilight without increasing Ann's fear of snakes. She was grateful for his solution and thanked him profusely, probably embarrassing this very practical man.

Lenore thought out loud about both human ingenuity and nature's originality, "After spending the day with churches, sundown will be experienced in the cathedral of nature from the bed of a truck."

Chapter Forty-Nine

Birdsong Chorus

At the homesite rubble Lenore parked the truck facing south, "In case we need a quick getaway when the snakes gang up on us," she said, mocking Ann's fears. Ann laughed. Boldly, Lenore got out of the truck, walked to the back, lowered the tailgate, slid the steps out and placed them on the ground and Ann found herself on the bed of the truck, boots still on. Lenore closed the tailgate saying she wanted to experience nightfall walking on earth. This did not seem safe to Ann who insisted Lenore wear the boots, tossed them to the ground, and checked to be sure Lenore had a flashlight. Lenore leaned against the truck, slipped on the big boots, tossed her shoes onto the truck bed. Ann watched her brave friend walk into gathering dusk while Ann checked her cell phone to be sure she had Raymond and Rita's number.

Ann absorbed the glorious colors of sunset until the sun went plop below the horizon. She knew it was the earth that moved to create the sun's disappearance. Then there was the glow of twilight. She realized how seldom she had watched this panoramic phenomenon in her lifetime, for her childhood residence over retail stores faced east. The morning sky was more familiar to her.

Dusk became darkness. Ann could see lights of towns in the distance. Darkness was not absolute for there was the half-moon's light. She had a front row seat this evening in the safety of the truck bed. She was filled with endless vistas with no trees or hills to obstruct in every direction. This day had been full of country roads, rural landscape. Last night's experience of the storm cellar was still with her. Now she could barely see Lenore though her bold friend was not far from the truck.

Ann lowered herself onto the truck bed, putting her head on a folded mat she found there and reclined her body. Safely alone, she was mesmerized by what the naked eye sees in the night sky with no city lights to dim the glimmerings, knowing the sublime lights are but a tiny fraction of the galaxies seen through telescopes. Grandeur beyond words. She was lost in unimaginable splendor. All was silent. Even the wind seemed still. There was only quiet.

And then birds in a lone nearby tree began to sing. Their voices rose in triumph, decreased in gentle harmony, and swelled again and again, as if prompted by a conductor, the chorus continued at length. Such spectacular magnificence, and it seemed as if the birds knew she was listening. It felt as if something majestic and miraculous was taking place. Only after some time did the entrancing birdsong stop. Ann lay quietly in wonder. What had just happened?

After more than a bit she heard Lenore, "It's me." Footsteps approached, Ann lowered the ladder saying, "Can you believe the winged chorus!" Lenore enthusiastically agreed, "The music was beautiful. I said I wanted to scream in a pasture like Edvard Munch's painting *The Scream*, but the birds came and serenaded instead. Dear God, that was fine!"

Just then an animal howled in the distance. Lenore whispered, "a coyote." The coyote continued and then fell silent. They waited for more, but the night remained quiet. Lenore in a semi-whisper, "Was that great!" Ann giggled softly, "Two grandmothers, a chorus of birds and a coyote in a nighttime Kansas pasture."

They then remembered the birds had also been singing mightily as they were leaving the Montel home in Clarksdale to begin this ancestral pilgrimage, and with that memory each woman felt encouraged that perhaps the universe was watching, aware, with them.

Chapter Fifty

Devilish Obstacles

Back in the cab of the truck, overly-cautious Ann had put on the snake protection boots, for she would once again open and close the pasture gate, which she did in grand style and poetically announced as she re-seated herself: "I am a pioneer to the core, having completed my chore."

Lenore started slowly driving down the country lane, stretching time for the two to digest, to encapsulate their evening's experience in these few minutes before arriving at Raymond and Rita's door. Together they wondered what could account for the glorious bird serenade from a lone tree.

The moment the truck was at the farmhouse, Raymond and Rita were outside to greet the women for Raymond noticed the truck was moving so slowly, were they having trouble with the vehicle? Raymond had tracked them closely. No, they were simply talking, digesting their experience, nearly forgetting they were moving in the truck.

It was a beautiful evening, Rita suggested everyone sit on the west porch where the women gave more details about their twilight experience of birds and coyote. To see if she could entice another howl Lenore sang a la-la-la trill into the air, but there was no coyote howl. Buddy the farm dog, lying on the porch in the midst of the group, lifted his head and moved it about slightly, ears perked, as if listening to Lenore's singing. There was silence waiting to see if a coyote might respond. Since none did, Raymond howled instead. Buddy jumped up, looked at Raymond, and jumped off the porch as everyone laughed.

When asked where Buddy had been when the humans were in the storm cellar, Raymond and Rita simply said Buddy, who is an 'outside' dog, knows how to take care of himself. Wherever he'd been during the storm, he had greeted the group as they emerged from the cellar.

Rita complimented, "You have a good voice, Lenore." Lenore bowed in her chair, "This may be the beginning of a new career for me." Then she got serious, "It is so lovely for us to be together. I'd imagine most people never experience a bird symphony, howling coyote and a howling human the same evening. This has been memorable."

Lenore talked about the day's churches, ancestry, the loving generosity of breakfast, lunch and supper, her cousins' hospitality. Her sentimental words changed the tenor of the group. Raymond and Rita were perhaps embarrassed by Lenore's gushy talk. Everyone was quiet until Rita asked Lenore, "What causes depression? What is depression?"

Lenore was slow to answer. "Every person's story is different. Every person's circumstances, their living situation is different. I can't give easy answers, but I'll use the word 'obstacle.' I'd say in each life there are obstacles, inside and outside the person, which block, obstruct, impede, keep the person from living their potential. Depression is a reaction to crippling obstacles which cause us to feel defeated, hopeless, despairing. That's my simple answer."

Rita explained her questions, "We have a nosey neighbor who tells me mental problems are from the devil." Raymond, perhaps defending his wife, said, "That neighbor's a little crazy herself, if you ask me." He quickly added, "But she can be good-hearted, too."

Lenore maneuvered carefully. "Strangely, one meaning of the word Satan is *to obstruct*. Obstructions are obstacles. If obstructions have their way with us we can become psychologically paralyzed. Depression is a kind of mental/emotional paralysis. There are physical, even inherited tendencies that can be a factor in depression."

Ann didn't know whether Lenore's answer satisfied Rita, but it resonated with Ann and her time of depression, for she had chunks of paralysis in her personality prior to going into therapy. She had to encounter many internal devilish obstacles (demons) blocking her ability to feel confident or joyful; to embrace life or feel embraced by it. These soul-robbing obstructions and obstacles had their way with her much of her life and still do so at times, except now she recognizes them in her thoughts and feelings and they no longer keep her in their clutches and rob her of the enjoyment of being alive. As for genetic factors in Ann's depression, these remained a mystery, since she knew nothing about family beyond her parents.

The evening ended when Raymond said his watch told him it was past eleven o'clock. In the bedroom Lenore told Ann that one of Raymond's and Rita's sons suffered bouts of depression. Therefore, the nosey neighbor's comment was particularly prickly and personal. Ann felt Lenore's explanation of depression was more than adequate tonight, and she marveled inwardly that she was on such a personal trip with this smart, fearless woman. And yes, dear, long-time friend Beth had been correct about this being a meaningful trip for Ann. Even more than Ann knew.

Chapter Fifty-One

Brain-Hemispheres & Churches

Morning came later for Lenore and Ann than for farm folk who likely never slept-in. The smell of coffee greeted them, and breakfast was on the table within minutes once the house guests were in the kitchen. Ann admired and felt affection for these two generous hosts and regretted the possibility of never seeing them again and told them so; an unusual gesture for her. And she added, "But I never knew I'd be fortunate enough to be with you even once." She was amazed at her boldness in expressing her feelings. Perhaps the mystery chorus last night in the pasture brought added healing to her personality, she puzzled within herself.

The guests and their hosts lingered at the breakfast table where there was talk of politics, current events, the global economy. The farm hosts were well-informed. They watched the same TV programs as people in metropolitan areas. Private people themselves, they were not intrusive, but gently asked more about Ann's husband Mel; her daughters' families.

Ann told them Mel was planning to retire soon, making the prospect more definite than it was, for Mel loved his work. Architecture has been his life. Running a business is what he did. Ann had been telephoning him about her Kansas adventures, especially the storm cellar. She had not yet mentioned last night's mystery chorus to him, as she wanted to describe it in person

Ann would be with the Montel family tonight; then tomorrow she was to meet Julia's parents in Kansas City before going to the airport, and she would be home with Mel tomorrow night. She felt gratitude for this extraordinary time in rural Kansas, an unusual opportunity for her to taste life in a new way.

After more chatter and extended good-byes in the driveway of the farm, Lenore and Ann traveled to the interstate this breezy, pleasant Kansas morning with quiet landscape and vaulted sky intact. The two women were quiet the first few miles.

And then Ann asked, "Did you get what you wanted from the pilgrimage?" Immediately Lenore said "yes," and began to elaborate. "This trip was me. The homesite, as in my dream about it, embodies inherited generational habits and traits still alive in me. The churches are the huge Catholic part of me. The wind and cellar, sunrise, sunset, last night in the pasture, birds singing, coyote howling, the whole of nature, earth and sky; these are vital; a compelling daily frame of reference which shapes me. The rest of me comes from choices, decisions, education, marriage, parenting, friends, career, ongoing experiences. This is basically everybody's story, don't you agree?"

Ann responded, "Yes, I suppose so." *Unless you know so little of your family story, like me.* She decided not to go there. She wanted to know more from Lenore, in the little time they had together today traveling back to Clarksdale. "Could last night in the pasture have changed me? I was able to express gratitude to Raymond and Rita more easily than usual. And strangely, since last night with the birds and stars I have this strong inkling, actually a conviction, that I am soon going to learn something about my ancestry. This is very real to me. Can last night in the truck bed have changed me?"

Lenore picked up the topic, "Only in recent years have brain researchers found how malleable the brain is. Increasingly it is understood that the brain not only directs behavior, but also is affected by internal events like thinking, as well as by external happenings. Was last night enough to change your brain, and thus your attitude or ability in some way? When we speak of life-changing events, perhaps we are really saying brain-changing events. I thought a good bit about neuroplasticity of the brain and also split-brain information as we toured the churches."

Lenore's mention of split-brain information excited Ann, for as an artist she was intrigued with the specialties of each hemisphere of the brain. She believed she more easily engaged right-brain traits whereas Mel as an architect, functioned more fully with both sides of the brain. She didn't like to overplay this brain-hemisphere stuff, but felt there was something to it.

Lenore changed to a different kind of split within her ancestors, "As we were visiting the churches it occurred to me that my ancestors on this land perhaps had a cruel divide within themselves. The boundless sky of the prairie which can allude to eternity; to infinity beyond finite limitations, is the same sky that brings storm clouds, wind and fear that sent us to the cellar night before last, which is the same sky that brought unspeakable beauty to us in the pasture last night. So too, a wheat crop that brings financial stability to a family is itself a fragile uncertainty in danger of being wiped-out by the weather at any point before harvest. The churches that point skyward with endless, open possibility, had rules that dictated down to earth daily behavior. I wonder if my ancestors were unknowingly torn between opposite possibilities: a certain kind of religious certainty on one hand and brutal practical necessity and uncertainty in everyday life on the other hand. I wonder if they walked around split inside themselves, compartmentalized. Or did they simply know how to live with paradox. Life is filled with paradox."

"Were they more split than we are today between science and religion?" Ann asked.

Lenore reflected, "I doubt it." And then she talked about neurotheology and split-brain research and wondered what the two of them might have learned about what was going on in their brains last night in the pasture if they'd been hooked-up to brain-imaging machines.

Ann commented that Lenore's information-packed mind reminded her of Matti, which led to them discussing Julia. Lenore said, "I am triple-tied to Julia. First, I liked her as soon as I met her as a young psychiatric nurse at the hospital. We seemed to click. Second, I have a bond to my high school biology teacher mentor who opened doors for me, when I thanked her for all she'd done for me, she told me helping someone find their way would be the greatest thanks ever. I wanted to be a mentor to Julia. Third, Julia became my protégé after the fact of Matti and Matti's computer came into her life. To Julia, the computer represented Matti's arrogant intellectualism covering up the truth of abandoning her child, so I took the computer to extract content for Julia.

"I never mention the computer to Julia and she never mentions it either. I find some of Matti's work remarkably insightful; even profound. I feel Julia will someday be ready for Matti's writings."

Ann did not comment. She didn't desire more talk about Julia and Matti, but wanted something else from Lenore and asked her, "Tell me why your ancestors' churches make you feel they lived with a left-brain dominated religion. I see right-brain symbolism in the stained-glass windows, statues, paintings, architecture."

Lenore picked-up the topic, "I quite agree that right-brain, non-language, candles, statues and such do speak thousands of words in the ambience, the atmosphere, the sacred space they create. However, church is also about language: bible readings, sermons, prayers. Language is produced and understood in two areas of the left-brain hemisphere, labeled Broca's and Wernicke's areas. If a stroke damages one of these areas, you are going to have problems with language.

"The churches we saw appear to leave a legacy of right-brainness, true. However, there is more to the story. I grew up pre-Vatican II, when the teachings were rational, left-brain lessons translated down to the lay people as duties and obligations. Holy Days of Obligation, for instance. Why couldn't they have been Holy Days of Celebration, or Holy Days of Appreciation, Holy Days of Revelation, Holy Days of Deification. Obligation meant being required, obliged to go to church, attend Mass. Holy Days of Obligation seems dutybound more than inspirational.

"The pre-Vatican II formula was basically that religion consisted of faith, reason, and proper action. Something like that. What was missing was metaphoric, figurative understanding that hit home personally, psychologically. We can't explain this dilemma away by simply saying the field of psychology as we have it today hadn't yet developed.

"People early in church history had soul-understanding of what Christ brought to humanity. Clement of Alexandria and Origen within a short time after Christ walked the earth talked a great deal about the soul, which in Greek is *psyche*, and as you know, is the root of our words psychology, psychiatry, psychotherapy.

"If I had to define the difference between mind and soul, I would label the left-brain as mind and the right-brain as soul. Western Christianity in the days of our more recent ancestors, especially the last five hundred years or so, has been increasingly left-brain. Right-brain mystical experience came to be viewed suspiciously, even frowned upon.

"I believe *the* lesson to be learned today by everyone in religion and outside of religion is how to use both sides of the brain: the analytical and the intuitive. Neither brain hemisphere by itself is sufficient to live well. Each person must become conscious of their own brain-habits. This is *the* lesson for our time. We each must learn to read our own personalities, our own situations, circumstances, conundrums, in light of what is increasingly known about brain-hemisphere differences.

Lenore's enthusiasm continued: "I suggest the book *My Stroke of Insight* by a female neuroanatomist Jill Bolte Taylor who had a left-brain stroke at the age of 37, from which it took eight years of rehab for her to recover. Basically, as her left-brain functions stopped working, she became aware of right-brain activity; which was a blissful kind of experience. There's a TED talk video on this."

As Ann was getting pen and note pad out of her purse to jot down the information, Lenore told of other books.[1] What impressed Ann most

---

[1] Mario Beauregard and Denyse O'Leary *The Spiritual Brain: A Neuroscientist's Case for the Existence of the Soul* (Toronto, Ontario, Canada: Harper Perennial, 2007).

Iain McGilchrist, *The Master and his Emissary: The Divided Brain and the Making of the Western World,* (New Haven CT: Yale University Press, 2009, 2019). Also a website video, *The Divided Brain.*

Andrew Newberg, Eugene D'Aquili, Vince Rause, *Why God Won't Go Away: Brain Science & The Biology Of Belief* (New York: Ballantine Books, 2001).

Andrew Newberg, Mark Robert Waldman, *How God Changes Your Brain: Breakthrough Findings from a Leading Neuroscientist* (New York: Ballantine Books, 2009).

Jill Bolte Taylor, *My Stroke of Insight: A Brain Scientist's Personal Journey* (London: Hodder & Stoughton Ltd., 2008). For Taylor's online video, simply enter her name and look for the video.

was Lenore saying praying has been found to reconfigure the brain; to change the actual physiology of the brain. Lenore also pointed out that the language of mysticism and sexual orgasm is much the same: bliss, rapture, ecstasy. Some brain researchers suggest mystical experience may have arisen from the neural circuitry that evolved for mating and sexual experience, though mystical experience and sexual experience are experienced in two different areas of the brain.

Then, Lenore observed: "What fascinates me about Gabby's term *allusion confusion,* is not the basic idea, for that is the crux of psychodynamic personality theory in Freud, Jung, and others, but her extraordinary label itself: allusion confusion. Her term captures the essence of moods, desires, impulses, images, that *allude* to, hint at, give clues about, a profound story going on in the personality; the pains and potentials of the personality."

Ann understood what Lenore was saying, and knowing their time together was limited, she didn't want to go over familiar territory, and therefore changed the subject.

Chapter Fifty-Two

Psychic Residue

Ann returned to the neuroanatomist's left-brain stroke. Lenore explained that the woman scientist Jill Bolte Taylor explains in her book how, as brain chatter in her left brain language centers shut down, her right hemisphere began to experience Nirvana, ecstasy, Oneness, compassion, like what mystics of the ages talked about. Taylor describes what in Christianity is labeled apophatic prayer, a kind of 'resting in God,' whereas an example of kataphatic experience is mentally picturing gospel stories in the *Spiritual Exercises* of St. Ignatius of Loyola.

"Mental-imaging is well-known in psychotherapeutic circles, in Buddhism, etc. Julia once said she was going to try mental-imaging to dissipate her anger towards Matti. Don't know if she has, but we know she has gone to the sandpile and created helpful images. I remember Julia's brutal humor when she posed the question, 'Am I going to have to imagine Matti and Cal copulating, conceiving me?' Julia's humor can be raw."

Somehow Ann didn't want to go back to the Julia, Matti, Cal story. Instead, she found herself engaged with the sky, the land, and not wanting to forget the extraordinary chorus in the pasture last night.

Lenore used the word *panentheism*, which is that God and the world are interrelated. God is in the world and the world is in God.

Lenore began to talk about the ideas of the French Jesuit Pierre Teilhard de Chardin, a geologist and paleontologist who was part of the team that discovered the fossil remains of Peking man, or *Sinanthropus*, in 1929. Teilhard found rocks, soil, minerals, metals, the earth and all matter to be holy, sacred, numinous, spiritual.

Lenore told how she and Dennis designed their home to be open to nature. She mentioned earlier she wanted Ann to see the house before she dropped her off at Julia's. She continued telling that Teilhard's view of all creation including human potential, is evolving towards a point he called Omega, which he identified as the development of maximum complexity and consciousness which Christ inaugurated in his sojourn on earth, bringing all creation to its apex.

Lenore then switched to the work of English biochemist Rupert Sheldrake about the effects of energy fields on the human condition: "My understanding of Sheldrake's work is that everyone who has lived creates and leaves energy, which I call psychic residue. He speaks of morphic resonance, morphic fields. A simple example of morphic resonance is that the first person who learned to ride a bicycle created a change in the human condition which made it easier for others to ride a bicycle."

And then Lenore came to what Sheldrake's work meant for her: "I extrapolate Sheldrake's work to explain what Jesus did for humanity: Earthly Jesus' connection with God was of unfathomable, cosmic proportions. Upon his death the energy residue he left was and is of universal proportions. Therefore, the residue of Christ, his Holy Spirit, continues as a breakthrough reality, the messiah, the anointed one, a universal mentor and mediator, a cosmic companion. Humans have not yet lived-up to what he made available for us, though the opportunity still exists. His Holy Spirit is each person's potential soul mate, in today's jargon."

Ann remembered one springtime afternoon during her deepest depression, she was seduced out of bed and morbid sleep by the beauty of the day, kneeling in the yard pulling weeds out of a flowerbed, when she sensed Presence, and had an uncommon awareness that Jesus knew her name the day he died. "It was as real as anything I've ever experienced and remains so today." Ann had never told anyone about that day. Jesus, with his cosmic consciousness, knew her when he was on the cross. In the visual image that day, from the cross he gently said her name, "Ann." She decided not to tell Lenore of that extraordinary experience. She marveled that Jesus the cosmic Christ came to her before she was all that interested in him.

Lenore was saying, "Teilhard served as a stretcher bearer in World War I. And in a church close to the battlefront he experienced a powerful vision while looking at a picture of Christ, in which he saw nature mystically. Though trained in science, nature to him was not inert, but gloriously alive. St. Francis of Assisi, centuries earlier, knew nature as sacred sustenance, sacred life and living."

Being with Lenore reminded Ann of Gabby. In Gabby and Lenore did Ann experience Catholicism at its best? She saw a hint of this numinous quality in the rosaries and the braided palm branch in the storm cellar two nights ago. These spiritual artifacts fit with her love of stained-glass windows in the cathedrals of Europe and in the churches of Lenore's ancestors. From what she knew about brain hemisphere differences, these artifacts seemed right-brain in human nature, in understanding. A dedicated left-brain person might say her attraction to these artifacts is a "superstitious" side of her. If she treated the "things" (rosary, braided palm, stained glass) as magical, then yes, it may be superstition is at work. If, however, these "things" embody the mystery of the sacred, well then, she found a different dynamic at work.

Lenore's ancestral pilgrimage had been for Ann an experience of deep calling. From the primitive depth of the protective storm cellar to the heights of the bird chorus in the pasture experience rising into the night sky's unfathomable beauty; also influenced by the ancestral depths she sensed in the churches of Lenore's people, their history, their land, the rubble on the homestead and its meaning for Lenore; the stabbing depth of Ann's longing for her unknown family-history intensified by the hospitality of Lenore's cousins, the connectedness between them. This was a journey of deep calling.

Chapter Fifty-Three

The Sacred Brain of Jesus

Lenore spoke again of Teilhard de Chardin and his troubles with church authorities. How some of his writings were censured or condemned, "I believe he was too far ahead of his time. In his view, the development of human potential individually and collectively is part of reaching Omega point, which it seems to me is like *theosis*, divinization, deification in Eastern Orthodox theology, where it is believed humans can know God through energies, creation, though we are not able to know the absolute essence of God.

"Psychologist Abraham Maslow recognized that humans have what he labeled *peak experiences*, and a pioneer in studying consciousness, Charles Tart, gave us the phrase *altered states of consciousness*. In our fast-paced world of human-made objects, perhaps our brain gets desensitized to the energy nature exudes, its mystical quality, the numinosity inherent in our natural surroundings."

And then Lenore had more to say about the brain, "The ancestral church that burned-down was named The Sacred Heart of Jesus. The heart was seat of the emotions to ancient people, and indeed, the heart registers emotions which heart monitors show today. As a child I assumed the heart was the place of immense goodness, because of pictures of the Sacred Heart of Jesus. There continues still today a devotion to The Sacred Heart of Jesus, which is not just a cliché, but an abundant way to think of Christ.

"Now with neuroscience and what is being learned about the brain, I think about the *sacred brain* of Jesus; his evolved consciousness; how his neurons, the electro-chemical functionings of his brain were in-synch with wisdom, love, healing, peace, everything we connect with God. The "spiritual-not-religious" today may be ready for brain-talk about Jesus."

Lenore fell quiet. Ann realized Lenore was pondering ideas for she saw her do this repeatedly when they were in the ancestral churches, or driving on the country roads. After her quiet Lenore had rich things to say. This time she began: "A group of monks in Greek Orthodox Christianity developed a prayer practice which likely reprograms the brain, the personality. These monks are known as *hesychasts*. Their prayer practice is called *hesychasm*, which means 'quiet' and is described in a small book *The Way of a Pilgrim*, which tells of a Russian Orthodox pilgrim who repeats continuously, 'Lord Jesus Christ, Son of the Living God, have mercy on me a sinner,' until the words become synchronized with not only his breath, but also his heart beat, for the prayer is then reciting itself without effort on his part.

"Because heart beats are discernible outside the body, the heart was more real in ages past than the brain encased in the skull. But now that pictures of brain activity during prayer are available, I believe something wonderful is on the horizon.

"Mind-altering drugs change brain states, moods, uneasiness, disease, distress. I wager Jesus had a fully functioning brain. He was a metaphoric genius with parables; he intuitively knew what was going on inside another person; he could outwit adversaries who argued with him; he could heal and teach. When he said he and The Father were one, I believe we can translate that into saying his brain, his neural functioning, his consciousness was connected with the God of the universe, as was his heart.

"Why did he have such a clear brain? Well, the Catholic Church has taught that Mary was born without sin, which I believe means she was free from the usual flaws we inherit culturally and generationally. I don't know why this might have been so. It may simply be a way of saying she was an exceptionally clear conduit of grace. Maybe she had psycho-spiritually healthy ancestors."

Lenore returned to the *hesychasts*. "The *hesychast* prayer can be shortened to simply repeating "Jesus" or other combinations of the original phrase. Repetition creates prayer at a subliminal level, as if it is praying itself while we go about our daily activities. This prayer likely quiets overactive left-brain language centers."

Then Lenore asked herself a question, "Is it good to frequently acknowledge being a sinner, as in the Jesus prayer? In Alcoholics Anonymous a person says 'I'm an alcoholic' not to increase guilt and shame, but because truth is liberating even when it's not pretty. To me, the "sinner" in the Jesus prayer covers the whole range of human flaws including being limited, incomplete, underdeveloped, undeveloped in countless ways, leading to too little wisdom, too little hope, too little compassion. Sins of omission and sins of commission is one way to say it."

Ann had a question for Lenore, "Is there a change you'd like to see in Christian belief today." Lenore didn't hesitate, "Yes. The usual explanation given for why Jesus died for our sins seems outworn or insufficient to me, wherein it is claimed that God the Father sacrificed his only begotten son to make reparation for our sins. Either I've never understood this correctly, or there's something not quite right with it. To me, this explanation makes God the Father seem like a small-minded despot who needs and demands the first finally fully evolved human to die for the rest of us wretches, and aims to make us feel guilty and ashamed.

"I believe more enlightened statements are needed, better translations of the original and/or re-thinking the basic idea at its core. The world doesn't need punitive pettiness when something more profound is surely available."

Chapter Fifty-Four

Catholic Mass, Neurological Resonance

Lenore continued, "Eastern Christianity's salvation theology has always maintained that what Jesus brought to humanity is a pathway for each individual to become Christ-like. I find this a wholesome explanation of what Christ did for us. And Western Christianity says this, too, but not loud enough, or not clearly enough, it seems to me. Too much emphasis on salvation rather than maturation. Being saved from the fires of hell instead of fulfilling our potential, making our creative contribution. I have certainly seen in patients living an unfulfilled life that such can be its own hell.

"Now that split-brain research is showing metaphor is both created and understood largely in the right-hemisphere, perhaps we will stop mistaking figurative expressions for left-brain literal statements. While the left-side of the brain helps us survive in practical ways, the right-side of the brain is diffuse, cosmic, symbolic, metaphoric, spiritual. Using both sides of the brain might change religious ideas like the salvation theology I do not appreciate, do not understand as profound, wholesome, real or practical."

Ann asked, "So, do you think your ancestors had more or less of the presence of God in their lives than people do today? Their churches show that someone cared a lot about religion."

Carefully trying to explain herself, Lenore said, "My ancestors' religion, it seems to me, was stuck in a religious format several hundred years old—a format which developed in response to the Protestant Reformation after Martin Luther is said to have nailed his protests to a church door in Germany in 1517.

"At that time, voices within the Catholic Church had already been calling for reform, and transformation within the church became stronger as the Protestant Reformation developed. Ignatius of Loyola, who formed the Jesuits, Teresa of Avila and John of the Cross were reformers of the inner world, the soul. However, the Protestant Reformation ignited not only reform within the Catholic Church, but also reactionary control; a time of nailing things down.

"Thus, I see my ancestors' Catholicism as largely left-brain rational, instructional, belief-based religion housed in right-brain mystical, symbolic buildings from 12th century Gothic architecture. I also realized on this trip that the Catholic Mass potentially touches both brain hemispheres: the left-brain story of Christ, scripture and teaching alongside right-brain candles, vestments, ritual; a whole-brain experience, fostering a kind of *neurological resonance*, in today's brain science terminology.

"I believe today the individual personality is increasingly a legitimate focus of religion. To me, Teilhard de Chardin included this in his holistic view of the world: that everyone has a part to play as creation moves towards the Omega point. My patients today by-and-large respond positively to the idea that their life has unique purpose, though they often cannot or will not engage in trying to find that purpose."

Lenore switched to the story of Job. "Job's intact life fell apart and he tried to understand what had gone awry. His friends tell him he must be to blame. Job felt he wasn't to blame. Then, the human effort of Job and his friends is put in proper perspective when God asks Job if he was around when day and night were formed, whether he has journeyed to the sources of the sea, etc. I find the story of Job shows that human knowing in the here and now is, indeed, limited. Which is why faith is necessary. I've heard it said that faith endures when understanding fails. But even faith can be arrogant. There is this deep-seated tendency of humans to think we know more than we do."

Ann added, "However, I am just now getting over feeling that others nearly always know more than I do. I have not found it easy to be confident, let alone overly confident."

Lenore attempted to reassure, "We all stand on shaky ground. I find comfort in what Clement of Alexandria wrote: 'The more we know ourself, the more we know God.' I believe he was indicating that deep prayer shows us not *what* God is, but rather *that* God is, and this increases our confidence about everything, including ourself."

Ann asked Lenore how she pulls psychology and religion apart if they both deal with the personality. Lenore said prayer is the difference. In psychology one studies the dynamics, traits, qualities, aspects of personality, without emphasis on prayer. Whereas in religion prayer, Spirit, ritual, and such may gloss over personality. "However, psychology and religion together have more to offer than either alone. Crying out in the depths of one's being to what is Ultimate in distress or joy is prayer; the impulse for what is Infinite. A personality that does not, cannot, or will not do this is limited in knowing the height and depth, breadth and width of itself; its innate desire for transcendence."

Ann spontaneously prayed in distress, but knew she needed to learn more about praying in times of good fortune, such as this fortunate trip which was about to get even better.

Chapter Fifty-Five

Adoration

The two grandmother pilgrims were quiet as the neat countryside whizzed by. Actually, they were whizzing by the countryside, Ann corrected herself. Did the pasture chorus last night under sky-filled splendor increase her experience *that* God is? Yes, she told herself, and observed changing clouds on this pleasant June day; her tie to the sky forever strengthened by this trip. For an earthling, the sky is always everywhere; not so oceans, mountains, forests, desert. In this sense, the sky is godlike: Everywhere.

Ann was thinking about Lenore: the professional, who easily joined her cousins in prayer at mealtime, in an almost childlike way. The rosary, braided palm branches, churches they saw, the Catholic tradition Lenore inherited and embraced while looking at it with clear eyes. Ann wondered whether Lenore asked why God allowed her ancestors who had much faith, to have such hard lives. Why did these longsuffering people keep their faith in such a God? Why did they spend time, effort, money, building the extraordinary churches when God could have given them better situations in nicer climates? Did Lenore ask these questions?

Ann was silently posing these questions about Lenore's family which were indirectly old questions about her own relatives. What did her people suffer? Were they religious? Did they build mystical churches, dig storm cellars? What were their personality traits? She had a strong feeling she would one day know about her relatives. Somehow, birdsong which began the ancestral journey in the Montel driveway in Clarksdale, and completed it in the lone tree in the pasture, seemed to suggest a near-certainty she would learn about her family. She felt this.

Meanwhile, Lenore returned to the spiritual-not-religious today who want to know more about themselves. She spoke of Jesuit, Karl Rahner, German theologian, who died in 1984, and his comment that the Christian of the future will be a mystic. Not long before his death he was asked what he meant by his "mystic" statement. Rahner said he meant that in the future Christians would experience God in their personality, at its deepest core. He said it was unimportant whether one labels this profoundly personal, genuine experience of God "mystical." Rahner said his statement was opposing the idea that one can be indoctrinated about God from outside the person. He said a person desiring to be a convinced Christian wants to experience God in their personality. Rahner essentially reiterated what Clement of Alexandria voiced centuries earlier that one's experiential depths begin and end in Spirit."

Lenore had obviously thought about this a good bit, as she continued to talk about all institutional power today being questioned: the federal government, financial institutions, Catholic hierarchy having been devalued because of the pedophile scandals. She suggested humanity is in the process of growing up, maturing, no longer bowing so low to human power whether individual or institutional. She cautioned: "Because of social media, increasing mass media, we must become ever-smarter about the power of the collective mindset in culture."

Lenore announced they would soon be in Clarksdale. Ann's mental apparatus scrambled to get a wrap-up statement from Lenore about their trip. Nothing came to mind, so Ann asked her to say more about something she said earlier that Dennis believed she psychologized religion.

Lenore began, "He felt at times I was a novice playing with matters best left to scholars in religion. I know I stretched his world with my "sacred" psychological insights, because sometimes he repeated my ideas not realizing he was quoting me. Our personalities complemented each other.

"Marrying Dennis, my Volga German trait of endurance was essential. I knew from the beginning I could embrace the needed sacrifices to marry a man with a damaged heart; a man who may not live long; a man who would find it difficult to let me pick up the slack when his ever-present fatigue overtook him. We were uncommonly joined together: he needed a quiet life, which matched my need to read and study after spending myself with patients. Dennis and I were good for each other, grateful for each other, knowing our time together would likely be shortened by his health problems. But in every marriage, the end will come; if only we can remember that." She had said that before, and again it struck deep inside Ann.

Lenore began to sum up the trip, "The powerful dreams about my grandparents' farmhouse made me want to make this trip. Thank you so very much for coming with me. Somehow, you are the perfect person. And thanks to Mel for encouraging you."

Lenore explained how this trip was part of her own ongoing healing. That the left-brain practicality of her Germanic background plus scientific/medical background together made her dominated by left-brain processing, and how seeing the churches, and enriched by Ann's observations, she realized church architecture and art were right-brain influences which make it easy for her to *increasingly* appreciate right-brain function and the role it plays in correcting a lopsided bias in Western Culture for rationality, and scientific, empirical, five-sense knowing.

Ann shared with Lenore her sense that the architecture and art of the churches helped her people in their struggles just as art and symbol help all of us; humanity throughout the ages. On this pilgrimage Ann remembered the theatrical production of the play *Equus* where the word "adore" impressed her and caused her to wonder what there is to adore in this life. And then there is the word "adoration." Is it a meaningless word, or does it express an emotion, a feeling, an interior state of being? And when does adoration happen? Adoration was part of last night's sky experience.

Last night in the pasture, abandonment, letting go, merging with immensity without boundaries, limitless expanse led to adoration even before the bird chorus arrived. Lenore told Ann about the Catholic term, "perpetual adoration" where people adore God in Jesus Christ, in the symbolic presence of a Eucharistic host in a special holder called a monstrance. During a time of perpetual adoration parishioners volunteer for a specific time in church so that there is continuous (24-hour) adoration in Christ for a specified amount of time, a week, a month." This was beyond what Ann could fathom.

Lenore's fertile mind circled back to brain-hemispheres and what she said earlier about AA's Serenity Prayer. "This popular prayer written by Protestant theologian Reinhold Niebuhr, is a prayer for personal peace, not happiness, not fame or finances, or even an easy way out of a tough situation."

Lenore explained phrase by phrase:

God grant me the serenity to accept the things I cannot change; (right-brain, open-ended, receptivity and possibility)
courage to change the things I can; (left-brain, practical, problem-solving attitudes)
and wisdom to know the difference. (discernment which emerges from using both sides of the brain).

Lenore summarized, "The Serenity Prayer is profoundly practical. It does not let us off the hook, avoiding what we can do. And so we pray for the grace to act upon and react to our current situation while remaining grounded, knowing our egoistic limitations, incompleteness, and powerlessness. Like St. Paul, we are strongest when we know we are weak."

Ann made a mental note to share Lenore's explication of the *Serenity Prayer* with Beth, whose favorite prayer seemed to be the *Serenity Prayer*.

Chapter Fifty-Six

Purple Notebook

Just now, Clarksdale was visible in the distance and before long they were driving on Clarksdale's tidy streets. The pace was busy but unhurried downtown. In residential areas, well-maintained lawns and houses were intact. Ann saw the town with different eyes than before they went on the pilgrimage. Clarksdale was an urban area compared to the interstate, the fields and pastures where they'd been. She felt a familiarity with the town, with Julia's everyday life, a connection she didn't have before.

They drove south through Clarksdale towards the edge of town, and turned into a driveway nearly hidden by cedar trees. The driveway wound gently upward. Now, some distance from the road, in a yard of trees and ivy she saw a distinctive shaped house with a thatched-looking roof (metal), and an amazing front-door mandorla edifice. It looked like a medieval hut or chapel. Lenore stopped the SUV at the front door in the circle driveway. The air was fresh, the sun bright and friendly between the shade of many trees and a carpet of ivy. Lenore unlocked the heavy wooden door that looked classically medieval.

Ann knew the symbolic significance of the mandorla, an ancient symbol, older than Christianity. The mandorla (which means almond in

Italian) is the almond shape which occurs when two circles overlap. The significance of the mandorla is that it represents the coming together of two entities. Adopted by Christianity, it is often used in church windows and doors, where it can symbolize the coming together of the human and divine, just as Jesus the Christ is regarded as fully human, fully divine.

Ann explained to Lenore she knew about the mandorla through her graduate studies. She quietly also knew, because of architect Mel, the increased financial cost of building such an unusual house (an octagon) with its metal roof.

As if Lenore was reading Ann's mind, she said, "We spent the family fortune on this place. The children were out of college when we built it. We had fourteen years together here. Dennis created the basic design, which was refined by an architect. Commercial construction materials were used. Dennis knew people in the construction business."

The first glance inside was straight through the house to the out-of-doors on the other side, where water gently flowed, out of a low-level native stone wall, and disappeared below stones, recycling back again while plants enhanced the gentle wall of water.

The center of the house was flooded with light from a skylight, which was a large octagonal periscope-looking protrusion into the sky that bathed every part of the house with light when interior doors were open.

It was not a large home, with two bedrooms and two baths. Later, Ann learned there was another bedroom and bath downstairs. On the main floor, immediately to the left of the entry way was the guest bedroom and bathroom, then curving to the south, there was a library area without doors.

The library was enchanting; here Ann felt the influence of Dennis and his impact in Lenore's life. There were philosophy and theology books; an impressive array. This was his avocation, Lenore explained. Over against the other wall were her books. A few on psychiatry and psychology. Why so few, Ann wondered. Again, Lenore must have known Ann's thoughts and said when she retired she donated most of her professional books to the hospital library. Ann could well imagine Lenore and Dennis spending time together in their separate worlds of books and interests.

Before leaving the library Lenore opened several of Dennis's books which showed his under-linings, and occasional words written in the margins. She observed, "He studied books; did not merely read them. Even if old and infirm I could probably never sell this house, for I want these books to remain on the shelves just as he left them; arranged as carefully as the pharmaceuticals at his work."

They left the library and were again in the open den with its low, igloo-type fireplace, and several well-placed, large exotic potted plants enhancing the area. The exterior curved glassed wall included glass doors leading outside onto the inviting patio with stone floor, trickling stone water wall and ivy. The slightly treed yard beyond the patio was uneven, a bit elevated and easily seen above low shrubbery planted around the patio to curtail the onslaught of the south wind on the patio. Ceiling beams of the patio roof were entwined with ivy growing in unstoned soil areas round the patio. It was a sweet patio.

Back inside the house there was the dining area, kitchen, and completing the curve of the house, the master bedroom and bath. This modest-sized house with its vaulted wooded ceiling culminating in the rooftop periscope was spacious for it had no more stucco-textured interior walls than necessary. An iron-railing led to the lower area which included a tornado shelter. The staircase to the lower level also led to the over-sized two-car garage dug into the hill on which the house was built. Dennis and Lenore said they would have a chair lift installed if they got too old to navigate the steps.

The house sat on six acres in the middle of lightly treed gentle hills, high enough to see parts of Clarksdale through the cedar trees. Sunrise and sunset, critically important to Dennis, were easily visible throughout the unusual house. Ann felt his personality in the architecture of this house just as Mel's architecture lived in their house. She was momentarily overwrought by the sheer magnitude of the power of architecture learned through Mel. She brushed aside this emotional burst of love and lightheartedly said instead, "Who washes all these windows?"

Lenore pointed to herself, then laughed and explained the windows were washed by others, and described the joy of sparkling, just-washed windows several times a year. Ann commented that even the dining room table top was glass, whereupon Lenore pointed to the glass low table in front of the sofa.

Lenore had cleverly moved Ann's attention to that low table, for on it was an imposing book which Ann walked to investigate, gently rubbing her fingers on its cover. The over-sized thick leather book of luscious purple was illuminated with medieval-type designs burned into the leather forming a two-inch frame around the edges front and back. Grooves of intricate etching were painstakingly painted with a cacophony of bright colors interwoven with gold and silver. It was exquisite. Ann thought of the hands that tooled and painted, the artistry that conceived this exquisite creation.

Ann sat down on the couch and gently brought the intriguing book to her lap, noticing it was a binder, a notebook, not a bound book. Lenore watched as Ann opened the book and found the title page in large script on elegant parchment paper: **From Matti's Computer**

Ann's eyes filled with tears. She took a tissue from her pocket to wipe away the tears, wanting nothing to blemish this treasure. And there it was, page after page of Matti's ideas laser-jet printed onto exquisite paper.

Chapter Fifty-Seven

Matti's Writing

FROM MATTI'S COMPUTER
Replenish

- Replenish what? Hermeneutic habits.
- Which means? Having a robust way of interpreting.
- Interpreting what? Experience.
- Experience is? What passes through one's being.
- Requiring what? Exponential processing.
- Exponential? In more than one way.

I am writing about the multi-faceted fourfold habit of looking at physical, psychological, moral, spiritual aspects of being alive. I am writing about deciphering allusion with metaphor. Allusion is not illusion. Illusion is about deception, whereas allusion deals with hints and clues.

Metaphors Are Tiny Allegories – Allegory is Extended Metaphor

Aristotle wrote in his *Poetics*: "To be a master of metaphor is the one thing that cannot be learnt from others, and it is also a sign of genius." Perhaps an even greater earmark of genius is an individual's ability to use metaphor to identify the core of his or her cravings, impulses, moods, desires, yearnings and longings.

Gabby shared her early insights with me and the two of us together uncovered details on the topic of metaphoric discernment. The definition of metaphor means *to carry beyond or across* in Greek. Indeed, metaphors carry us beyond or across our current way of understanding to new awareness, insight and discernment. Gabby came to be in touch with two facets of metaphor: (1) descriptive metaphor (2) metaphoric discernment.

(1) Descriptive metaphor expresses what has already been discerned. (2) Metaphoric discernment is the discerning capacity itself; a hermeneutic tool, primary and basic intuitive knowing of truth.

Here are some of Gabby's examples of ***descriptive metaphor***: "You are driving me up a wall" doesn't meaning I am literally, physically climbing a wall, but that my feelings of irritation or annoyance towards you at the moment makes me want to climb a wall if I could to get away from you. "You can bank on something" is likely not referring to a financial bank or a bank (pile) of dirt, but referring to something trustworthy, dependable. "That hit the nail on the head" means what you said resonates with me, not that you're literally, physically, working with a hammer and nail. "Food for thought" indicates something which promotes thinking, not food from the kitchen. "It looks like I'm going to have to walk every step of the way by myself" isn't about physically walking, but about having to do something alone, without help. If I call you a "pansy," I'm not saying you're a flower, but that you can't stand the heat, just as pansies wilt in heat for they are cool weather plants. If I say you are "barking up the wrong tree," it doesn't mean I think you're a dog, but that you're wrong about something. If you tell me "a forty-year-old man is still tied to his mother's apron strings," I know you are saying he is overly dependent on his mother, not that the strings of an apron she is wearing are tied to his clothing or body.

Descriptive metaphor is alive and well in U.S. culture today. However, metaphoric discernment is anemic, leaving an inadequate hermeneutic for discerning the vast range of human experience.

Here are Gabby examples of **metaphoric discernment** gathered from the classes she taught on sleep-time dreams:

Losing your car in a dream may indicate losing your drive. Being in your car which is being driven by someone else may show you are being driven. Being lost in a dream may depict not being able to find your place, your way, in who you are or what you want to do with your life, having no sense of direction. On a more positive note, one can also be lost in thought, lost in wonderment, or lost in the moment. Travel in a dream may show where someone is emotionally, mentally coming from, or where the person is headed or moving psycho-spiritually.

Falling dreams can be about almost anything. There is a plethora of falling references from everyday speech. For instance: falling in or out of love, falling from grace, falling for a salesman's pitch, falling into depression, feeling that a performance fell flat, or that everything is falling into place.

Flying dreams may suggest being in a good mood, flying high, or having flights of fancy, maybe rising above a situation, feeling free as a bird, no longer held down by gravity, gravitas, seriousness. If a flying dream is disturbing then it might be saying one needs to be more grounded, more down to earth, more realistic.

House dreams can be about our frame of reference, or the framework or constructs which currently house our feelings, ways of understanding, our mental and emotional states.

Being followed, chased, or someone breaking into our house are usually frightening dreams. It's quite feasible that a thought, feeling, intuition which is unknown to us is trying to catch up with or break into our mind, our current frame of reference, and it is natural to fear the unknown.

This kind of metaphoric activity can help uncover what is going on in one's waking phantasies (moods, cravings, impulses, longings and yearnings) to keep *allusion confusion* (addiction and compulsion) away. Metaphorical discernment unravels symbols so they don't devolve into allusion confusion—bodily or behavioral symptoms. The words symbol and symptom share a common root.

Reading the Bible
Allegorically/Metaphorically/Figuratively/Exponentially/
Symbolically

Hermeneutics was important in the early days of Christianity because the question of how to interpret the Bible needed an answer. One scholar claims the "practice of understanding scripture figuratively became the unanimous tradition of the Church in its first fifteen hundred years."[2]

In other words, for the first 1500 years of Christianity scripture was most often interpreted exponentially, which means in more than one way. The word exponent is popularly thought of only as a mathematical function; actually, it comes from Latin *exponere*, which means to put forth, to expound, to interpret.

Thus, in medieval allegorical exegesis a verse of scripture was interpreted in several ways; at times there had been as many as seven ways of interpreting scripture and as few as three. However, four *senses* became the standard. This means, a verse of scripture could be read, interpreted, explicated, understood, in four ways:

1. in a literal/historical traditionally understood factual sense
2. in an allegorical/metaphorical/hidden/figurative sense which includes: explicating the New Testament depiction of Christ with terms and images drawn from the Old Testament; realizing that a word may have more than one meaning; recognizing that some people extract more meanings from scripture than others
3. in a tropological/moral ethical sense
4. in an anagogical/spiritual mystical sense

---

[2] Henri de Lubac, *Medieval Exegesis: The Four Senses of Scripture*, vol. 1, translated by Mark Sebanc, foreword by Robert Louis Wilken, (Grand Rapids MI: William B. Eerdmans Publishing Company, originally published 1959, English translation 1998), pp. ix-x.

Gabby and I have thought a great deal about #2 above, for it is this sense we are striving to expand to include what is known about the personality today. The field of psychology as we know it did not exist at the time the bible was read in this fourfold way. However, there was the activity of finding Jesus pre-figured in the Old Testament. An example of this kind of Christian-figural interpretation is speaking of Jesus as the Lamb of God (Paschal Lamb) which comes from the Jewish slaughtering of an animal at Passover. This way of comprehending Jesus continues today. The phrase Lamb of God is still used as one way to refer to Jesus.

I want to make it clear that what Gabby and I have been working on is not focused on the Christian-figural schema. Rather, our emphasis is on scripture as allegorical/psychological *theoria/theosis*, divine therapy, soul healing.

Well now, since neither soul or personality has qualities such as being pink, red, or chartreuse, or weighing a pound or two. The concepts soul and personality are important though not quantifiable in usual ways of quantification. The ancient Hebrews had a comparable word, *nephesh*, which is usually transliterated as soul. Likely, no language exists without a word for soul or deep personality.

Needing an adequate reading of scripture the medieval fourfold method looked at it from four angles, perspectives, viewpoints, which revealed four lessons. In the gospel story example which follows, we make psychology the allegorical lesson.

However, before talking about the gospel example, the words of C.S. Lewis (1898-1963) are helpful. He was an Irish/English medievalist, novelist, essayist, poet, academic, literary critic, lay theologian, who understood the connection between metaphor and what goes on in a human. He said allegory [extended metaphor] is a natural expression of moral "inner conflict" and it can be argued that modern psychoanalysis itself is a species of allegory.[3]

What does Lewis mean that psychoanalysis is a kind of allegory? He seems to be saying metaphor is essential if one wants to be in touch with

---

[3] C.S. Lewis, *The Allegory of Love: A Study in Medieval Tradition* (New York NY: Oxford University Press, 1958), pp. 60-61.

and talk about inmost, shadowy, phantasy[4] aspects of personality, which emerge spontaneously, uninvited, and have a mind of their own, whether beneficial or destructive. Depth psychology today understands this. Does popular culture?

Here now, is our example of how fourfold exegesis might work when it includes today's psychological understanding:

The story in Mt 14:24, when Peter becomes frightened and sinks in the water while walking towards Jesus, can be considered a concrete event, something that really happened, is literally, historically or at least traditionally true, and the text being used is authentic. If someone cannot accept this as a literal happening, the story can still instruct.

There is also a psychological lesson. Peter was caught between faith and fear. The lesson for Christians is that like Peter, one may drown in fears, frets and worries if not keeping focused on Jesus. This category was the allegorical, hidden sense, a figurative, lesson (which we suggest today can be used for personal, psychological lessons).

And there is a moral element in the story. Morality and ethics deal with choices and consequences. When Jesus put out his hand at once and held Peter, Peter did not refuse his hand and continue to wrestle on his own. Peter allowed Jesus to rescue him. Peter made a choice. As a consequence, Peter didn't drown. This illustrates a moral lesson in the story.

And lastly, the story is a universal lesson/story. It shows Jesus, cosmic, universal essence, saving each person, one by one, from being inundated, overwhelmed, sinking into and drowning in one's own personal abyss by walking towards Jesus, no matter how slippery or unstable our situation is. This spiritual lesson is the anagogical (spiritual) level of understanding.

---

[4] The spelling distinction between fantasy and phantasy is explained in a ground-breaking paper by Susan Isaacs (1885-1948), a British psychoanalyst, child-development theorist, educator. The paper is "The Nature and Function of Phantasy," *International Journal of Psychoanalysis* XXIX, pp. 73-97, 1948. In Old French *fantasie*, in Latin and Greek, *phantasia*. The differentiation Isaacs makes: fantasy is conscious, willful activity like daydreaming, and can be positive or negative. Phantasy is unconscious spontaneous phenomena like sleeptime dreaming, or waking spontaneous thoughts, emotions, cravings, impulses, that come to us unbidden and seem to have a will and life of their own, whether positive or negative.

In the next section we show how, in Europe in the 1500s, categories #2 and #4 began to die after centuries of fading, which means psychological and mystical right-hemisphere brain ways of interacting with the bible were marginalized. And importantly, category #1 also changed from the literal/historical into the literal/scientific-physical. What basically remained of the medieval fourfold hermeneutic were categories #1 and #3, left-hemisphere brain processing. This means instruction and explanation became elevated while allegorical, psycho-spiritual possibility dwindled. This was a hermeneutic shift, a hermeneutic shrinking.

How and Why Metaphoric Discernment Died

By the 1500s, cultural trends in Europe were converging which shrunk the fourfold way of looking at the bible. Eventually, a hermeneutic shift took place in all areas of European culture which was devolving into a more and more reductive mindset. Below are sketchy details of widespread hermeneutic happenings at the time the New World was being explored. Some of these happenings squeezed out metaphorical discernment as a way to understand experience.

1. **Empiricism.** Science was on the rise, as shown by the dates when prominent contributors to the development of the empirical method lived: Nicolaus Copernicus (1473-1543), Andreas Vesalius (1514-1564), Francis Bacon (1561-1626), Galileo Galilei (1564-1642), Johann Kepler (1571-1630). Scientific methodology required objectivity, clarity and precision; a kind of black and white mindset which could identify extraneous variables that interfered with the work of quantifying, verifying, replicating.

   Metaphoric, symbolic skills had no place in the nuts and bolts of scientific methodology. The "subjective" personality was demoted; considered almost an obstacle to scientific "objectivity." Figurative language allows one to describe what the personality experiences. For example, I may be feeling "high" today, or I'm feeling "paralyzed" at the moment, or yesterday was a real "downer." "High," "paralyzed," and "downer," all *allude* to emotions. Allusion is about hints and clues.

Allusion shouldn't be confused with illusion. Illusion has to do with deception, or trickery. Allusion is about referring to, suggesting, insinuating what is abstract, ethereal, perhaps non-quantifiable but absolutely real—emotions, inspirations, intuitive-knowing. In the 1500s in Europe the art of allusion lost ground. Scientific methodology devalued the subjective personality and figurative language. And then, figurative understanding would be abandoned even more.

2. Literalism. Protestant reform movements wanted more direct, historical, literal exegesis to replace allegorical interpretation of scripture, which was often claimed to promote Catholic dogma. The Reformers were not the first to favor a more literal kind of exegesis. By the 1500s, *allegoresis* (bible exegesis with allegory) was beginning to be regarded as empty speculation, frivolous guessing, and sometimes this may well have been the case. Eventually, metaphor and symbol were largely dismissed.

Already mentioned, the definition of metaphor means *to carry beyond or across* in Greek. Indeed, metaphors carry us beyond or across our current way of understanding to new awareness, insight and discernment. Metaphors use the five-sense world to tell us about psycho-spiritual realities (Jesus' parables are an example of this). Multiple metaphors used together become an allegory. Thus, a metaphor is a tiny allegory. Metaphor and allegory at their core are the same.

The word symbol means *to throw together*. This means several meanings are thrown together in one event, one person, or one thing. For example, the cross in Christianity is a symbol; it carries multiple meanings: Jesus died on a cross which was a common way to execute people at the time; a cross is a geometric design formed by drawing a vertical line and a horizontal line which intersect at the center; the cross of Jesus symbolizes the central event in history, a time when the height and depth, breadth and width of human history were gathered together in struggle and triumph; the cross of Jesus symbolizes our daily life/death crucifixions of turmoil, tension, stress. His cross symbolizes all kinds of dying that are a prelude to resurrection, transformation, metamorphosis. The cross can signify surrender, powerlessness, dying to egoistic self-sufficiency. The cross is a rich symbol.

We can think of ourselves as a symbol. We are a composite, configuration, combination, mosaic, of ancestry, environment, choices, inclinations, talents, etc. We are spiritual, psychological, ethical and physical creatures. We are multi-faceted mystery even to ourselves; largely unknown by ourselves, yet capable of self-knowledge. We can be confused about ourselves; misread and mislive our desires, wishes, yearnings, longings, cravings and impulses. Then, biological and behavioral *symptoms* appear.

Symptoms contain hints and clues about symbols. The word symptom means *to fall together*, as if we unknowingly *fall* into a confused physical, psychological or spiritual state because we don't know how to understand a symbol that needs decoding. Quite simply, undiscerned symbols can become symptoms.

Though a cultural perspective away from *allegoresis* was not absolutely new in the hermeneutic shift of sixteenth century Europe, Johannes Gutenberg's development of the printing press in 1440 made the non-metaphoric, non-symbolic religious sentiments of the 1500s uniquely forceful, for the written bible was now widespread, and a new kind of literalism had emerged.

The literal sense of Scripture in original allegorical exegesis was about being careful that the biblical text being studied was true to what was traditionally considered historically valid in the body of biblical literature.

Today's literalism, emerging in 16th century Europe, is a mindset that says each word has only one meaning and that meaning is about physical five-sense reality. This kind of literalism is compatible with empiricism, which quantifies, replicates and verifies the physical, the material. Both are five-sense based. Five-sense reality is privileged. Everything else is non-sense, which came to mean frivolous, silly in the word nonsense, or immaterial (irrelevant) which is simply not-material. The hermeneutic habit of Western Europe and the New

World was biased towards a "no non-sense materialism" and the educational theory of a Frenchman fell in line with empiricism and literalism.

3. Plainism. The educational system of Frenchman, Peter Ramus (1515-1572), spread throughout Western Europe and to the New World. This teaching stressed expressing ideas with as much plainness and simplicity as possible.[5] In Puritan New England, Richard Mather and other leaders were disciples of Ramus-style thinking and speaking, which meant symbolism and metaphor were marginalized in earliest U.S. history. The harshness of pioneer life also promoted simple physical survival above all else.

Richard Mather, along with all the other founders of New England, was a disciple of Petrus Ramus, a practitioner of the plain style.[6] In general, the founders [of New England] adhered to the logical system of Ramus.[7]

And then, alongside empiricism, literalism, plainism, there was rationalism. Centuries earlier Aristotle declared man a rational animal. St. Anselm of Canterbury and later St. Thomas Aquinas used logic in their work. Next, there was Rene Descartes.

4. Rationalism. French philosopher Rene Descartes (1596-1650), helped solidify trust in systematic logical deduction which was a long time coming in Europe. In earlier centuries, emphasis on the rational aspect had waxed and waned, but eventually the idea that "intellect" itself, through systematic rigor can arrive at knowledge and understanding, became a dominant perspective.

Scholasticism of Thomas Aquinas (1224-1275) used the logic of Aristotle to arrive at knowledge. However, in Aquinas's day allegory/metaphor was still alive, but as rationalism/scholasticism

---

[5] Walter Ong, *Ramus: Method and the Decay of Dialogue* (Cambridge MA: Harvard University Press, 1958).

[6] Perry Miller, *The New England Mind: From Colony to Province* (Cambridge MA: Harvard University Press 1953), p. 12.

[7] Perry Miller, *Roger Williams: His Contribution to the American Tradition* (New York: Atheneum, 1965), p. 437.

grew, figurative language came to be considered problematic as a way to knowledge. By the time Descartes came on the scene, metaphor and symbol were largely out of favor. Descartes's philosophy elevated rational thinking to the pinnacle of importance glimpsed in his famous phrase, "I think, therefore I am."

Therefore, rationalism took its place alongside empiricism, literalism, and plainism, to de-value and disqualify other ways of knowing in everyday life (such as intuitive metaphoric discernment). The rational bias would continue to grow stronger.

5. **The Enlightenment.** In the 1700s an intellectual movement, The Enlightenment, spread from France throughout Europe elevating rational-empirical knowing while increasing the stranglehold on allegorical-analogical considerations. Twin dogmas empiricism and rationalism became the linchpins of modernity. On the upside, the Enlightenment helped moderate superstitious, dogmatic, ways of understanding. This was its aim and purpose, and its accomplishment in many ways. The downside of the Enlightenment is that it squelched what was not empirically-rationally based, which is much of the human personality.

6. **Vienna Circle**. The Vienna Circle in the 1920s and 30s, was a group of philosophers, scientists, and mathematicians gathering around the University of Vienna in Austria who championed logical positivism which limited understanding to rational-empirical ways of knowing. Reductive hermeneutic habits were once again reinforced. However, this doesn't mean we can't expand them.

Metaphorical Discernment in Alcoholics Anonymous

Beth's enthusiasm for Alcoholics Anonymous sparked interest in why the program works for many. Amazingly, the underpinnings of AA are mirrored in our revised version of abandoned allegorical exegesis. However, regrettably, AA is post-addiction treatment, where healthy thirst for Spirit has already been smothered in allusion confusion by drinking alcoholic spirits to help deal with life's struggles. What if discerning one's need for Spirit could instead become a hermeneutic habit *before* a web of entanglement begins in addiction or compulsion.

As mentioned earlier, allegorical interpretation of the bible began to disappear in the 1500s in Europe. In 1935, Alcoholics Anonymous came into being with an exponential (layered, multi-faceted) paradigm which has glimmerings of old fourfold exegesis. AA embodies a new fourfold edifice, as if what was abandoned long ago has reappeared to help struggling humanity today.

Below, the Twelve Steps and other philosophical underpinnings of AA are matched with physical, psychological, moral, spiritual concerns modified from the original exegesis format.

Alcoholism as Spiritual Thirst

I. Anagogical (spiritual) matters are directly addressed in seven of the Steps of the Twelve Step Program.

Step Two: Came to believe that a Power greater than ourselves could restore us to sanity.

Step Three: Made a decision to turn our will and our lives over to the care of God *as we understood Him.*

Step Five: Admitted to God, to ourselves, and to another human being the exact nature of our wrongs.

Step Six: Were entirely ready to have God remove all these defects of character.

Step Seven: Humbly asked Him to remove our shortcomings.

Step Eleven: Sought through prayer and meditation to improve our conscious contact with God *as we understood Him,* praying only for knowledge of His will for us and the power to carry that out.

Step Twelve: Having had a spiritual awakening as the result of these steps, we tried to carry this message to alcoholics, and to practice these principles in all our affairs.

II. Tropological (moral) considerations are in four Steps.

Step Four: Made a searching and fearless moral inventory of ourselves.

Step Eight: Made a list of all persons we had harmed, and became willing to make amends to them all.

Step Nine: Made direct amends to such people wherever possible, except when to do so would injure them or others.

Step Ten: Continued to take personal inventory and when we were wrong promptly admitted it.

And thus, eleven of the twelve steps deal with spiritual and moral issues, which leaves unmentioned, Step One: We admitted we were powerless over alcohol—that our lives had become unmanageable.

III. Allegorical (psychological) factors are assumed in Step One and articulated throughout AA literature which talks about personality traits, dispositions, attitudes, temperaments, and characteristics.

IV. Literal (physical) level is parallel to AA's interpretation of alcoholism as disease: an allergy, a biological/genetic propensity or predisposition for an unusual reaction to alcohol—a bodily disease with alcohol. Family history and somatic factors are a significant part of the AA interpretation of alcoholism as a disease which is certainly treatable, manageable, although AA believes there is no cure.

AA in its Twelve Steps, literature and practice, interprets alcoholism from physical, psychological, moral, and spiritual perspectives. AA works because it has an adequate understanding of the dynamics of addiction. AA is a grassroots return of what began to be repressed five-hundred years ago by adequately (intuitively) recovering the subjective human personality (the soul).

Ann Dramm asked a thought-provoking, clarifying question: "How different would AA be if just one of its four perspectives was eliminated?" The answer is obvious: so much would be lost the AA paradigm would disintegrate. AA works because it includes spiritual, moral, psychological and physical factors.

I emphatically warn! At best, metaphoric discernment fosters discovery about one's own deep personality. At worst, metaphoric discernment promotes self-righteous diagnoses of other individuals' personalities and situations. Remember this. Metaphoric discernment can be personally insightful, or smug assessment of others. There are many virtues and vices of metaphoric discernment between these two extremes.

* * * *

Ann flipped through pages, asking, "Has Julia seen this amazing notebook?" Lenore replied, "Not yet. Perhaps I'll give it to her on her birthday." Ann was overwhelmed, reading familiar material, and some she'd never seen before. Lenore returned from another room with a copy of Matti's writings in a plastic notebook for Ann, saying, "I have kept a copy for you, for myself and am sending one to Beth. The insights of Gabby and Matti must not die but trickle out to others."

Chapter Fifty-Eight

Mel

Next morning, the Montel children were off at camp, Marc was at the store, Julia and Ann were ready to begin their trip to Kansas City where they would meet Julia's parents, then drive to the Kansas City airport and Ann's flight back to Connecticut.

Julia's cell phone rang. Marc was calling to say his mother collapsed shortly after arriving at the store and was just now being put into an ambulance to be taken to the hospital where Julia and Ann met Marc. Rose was admitted to the hospital, made comfortable, and diagnostic tests begun.

Later, too much later, Julia and Ann were back in Julia's car on their way to the Kansas City airport, reconciled to Ann not meeting Julia's parents. This was not to be the only trauma Ann would face that day after the flight home.

Arriving at the airport in Connecticut in the late afternoon, eldest daughter Rachel was there to pick her up instead of Mel, and Ann was given the news that Mel had suffered a heart attack a short while ago, but was doing OK. Younger daughter Sarah was at the hospital with him.

The story was that Mel left the office early, getting something to eat at a restaurant, not wanting to feel rushed on the way to the airport to pick-up Ann, when he started feeling horrible, but was able to drive to the nearest emergency room, which was thankfully nearby, where he drove to the emergency entrance, laid his arms and head on the car horn, so that hospital personnel came running. He was now in stable condition.

Rachel's words were surreal to Ann as they drove to the hospital. Mel had had a heart attack. Ann was in a stupor; in shock. Two medical emergencies in one day; Rose and now Mel. Sarah was with Mel as he waved with his fingers when he saw Ann at his bedside in CCU. She kissed his cheek, careful not to disturb the oxygen tube, gently rubbed his forehead, joined her hand to his. He smiled slightly, lifted a finger pointing to Ann, as if asking about her. She answered, "I'm fine. The flight was fine. I'll tell you everything when you've rested."

Scarcely moving his hand he pointed to a chair. He wanted Ann to sit. Sarah pulled the chair to his bedside and Ann sat down, placing his hand in hers. Familiar hands together for so many years. The room became quiet with only oxygen and other medical devices making noises. Mel appeared to drift off to sleep.

Ann whispered, asking Rachel and Sarah if they needed to go back to work or home with children, who will soon learn about their grandfather, or perhaps they already knew. A nurse came in, checking tubes and medical devices as Sarah asked when they could speak with a doctor.

Ann internally scolded herself, *I shouldn't have gone to Clarksdale. But Mel encouraged me. Forget that. He is always selfless. Of course he encouraged me, but I should have known better. What if he dies?*

Mel survived the severe heart attack. On medical advice, he retired from his firm; the baby he had birthed and grown large. Daughter Rachel took over his position. Mel had to learn how to rest, be quiet, putter in their large yard the rest of the summer. This was not easy for a man whose work was his life. As summer was fading, Ann could tell he was not looking forward to winter, short days, being indoors.

As cooler weather arrived he went with Ann on errands, while he stayed in the car, He had cabin fever and had to get out before winter would make that difficult. When trees began to change color he suggested small trips around town to enjoy the breathtaking colors as well as look at buildings he'd had a hand in designing. Ann, too, enjoyed seeing both the buildings born in his brain and the vibrant colors of nature.

The two of them sat together in the various rooms he'd designed in the home he reconfigured for them, and together they absorbed the Fall artwork of transforming leaves. These weeks together were peaceful, tender. Rachel, Sarah and their families came by for short visits. The family experienced beautiful closeness.

Mel wanted to go into the countryside before the Fall phantasmagoria faded completely. One day on a car venture in the country, Mel began having chest pains. He took the pills he had with him, Ann drove him to the nearest hospital where everything was done to save him—but nothing worked.

After the traditional Jewish funeral and burial, at home Ann wore Mel's cardigans, sleeves rolled up into bulk, for the comfort the sweaters gave her, wrapping her in his achingly familiar presence. She was transfixed in grief and found it impossible to articulate the loss. Rachel and Sarah were worried their mother might slip into depression. Ann received support from many who knew Mel professionally and shared stories of his integrity, his talent. Everyone who knew Mel knew he would have been miserable living long-term not immersed in hands-on architecture. Ann knew this, too.

However much family and friends sustained Ann, winter months were bleak in their once-cozy home. The house was too large. Thoughts of its future maintenance overwhelmed her. The maternity center became an ever greater source of solace, and staff were increasingly important as Ann spent more time there, but her home was too much for her to handle.

And then, Ann learned that Rose Montel in Clarksdale died. Diagnosed with pancreatic cancer, in her final weeks Rose lived down the hall from Stefan in the skilled nursing section of Golden Acres. Julia told Ann that Stefan's behavior improved somewhat after his mother's diagnosis. He seemed pleased that his mother was also in Golden Acres. He was mindful of the rest she needed, did spend time with her, and was in better spirits than Julia had ever seen him. He had a morbid interest in who would die first, himself or his mother. Julia said after Rose's death, Stefan became as irritating as ever.

Chapter Fifty-Nine

Aunt Gloria

Some months after Mel's death, on a late Monday morning the telephone rang, and Ann heard an older female voice ask, "Is this Ann Dramm?" And then, "I may be your aunt." Ann sat down in the nearest chair to steady herself, overwhelmed that an unknown relative may be contacting her. Or was someone scamming this new widow?

Ann listened as the voice said she was the sister of Peter Hoyt. "My name is Gloria Hoyt. Is your father's name Peter Hoyt?"

Some part of Ann heard the woman say she was nine years younger than her brother Peter — she was now 81, and asked, "Is Peter alive? He would be 90." Ann heard herself say her father died at age 64. The telephone voice, as if speaking to itself, said quietly, "Oh, my, he's gone . . . if only I'd found him. Did he marry Vivian? Is Vivian your mother?"

Ann answered like a robot, "My mother's name was Vivian. She died a few months before my father."

The voice asked, "Did Peter mention our parents, Harold and Anna?" *I am named after my father's mother, my grandmother?* The thought pierced Ann's being. The voice continued, "When the name Ann Hoyt was found online, I suspected you were who I was looking for."

The thought of people searching for Ann made her feel creepy, but she kept listening as the voice persisted, "As I grew older the heartbreak and loss increased and I desperately wanted to find my brother and relieve the pain, and though I paid people to help find him, they always hit a dead end, until the right person found Ann Hoyt, graduated from high school in Bridgeport, CT, is this you?"

Ann's brain was clogged with suspicion. *Anyone can search on the internet for anybody* she concluded and asked, "Why are you searching for your brother?"

The voice didn't hesitate, "There was a terrible disagreement between my brother and my father and it destroyed our family. We never again heard from Peter. I was nine years old at the time. My mother died two years later of a heart attack, which I believe was from a broken heart, and my father died eighteen months after that from cancer. I lost both parents before my fourteenth birthday."

The voice seemed sincere, decent, yet Ann decided to stop the conversation, thinking, *I do not know this woman.* Ann boldly interrupted, "It's been interesting talking with you, but I have no way of knowing if I am the person you are looking for, as I have no information about my father's family."

The voice graciously replied, "Of course. I realize you don't know me, or whether anything I've said is accurate. I understand. Thank you for talking with me. Sorry to have bothered you."

"Indeed," Ann concluded with a formal but friendly tone, relieved to end the conversation. She checked caller ID and found the call was from an Albany, NY area code.

Days later, certified mail from a law firm in Albany arrived. Inside the envelope an attorney's letter corroborated Gloria's identity and her believed relationship to Peter, Ann's father. Enclosed was a faded, water damaged snapshot of four people: a young girl with a veil, dressed in white, allegedly Gloria. An older boy, allegedly Ann's father, and parents allegedly Ann's grandparents. Even with a magnifying glass, it was impossible for Ann to discern if the young man in the picture looked like her father. The photo was taken at a distance. And this was a copy.

Daughter Sarah checked the credentials of the law firm, found it to be of sound reputation, and by return mail Ann indicated willingness to meet Gloria Hoyt at a law firm in Stamford. Both Sarah and Rachel offered to accompany Ann the day of the meeting. Ann declined their thoughtfulness, convinced she needed to do this by herself.

The day of the momentous meeting arrived. It was nearly Spring but seemed more like winter, for it was an unseasonably chilly day with even a few snow flurries flitting about. Ann felt concern for an 81-year-old woman named Gloria arriving in weather like this after a flight or car ride from Albany. Ann parked her car and walked a short distance to the attorney's office. Feeling somewhat depleted having scarcely slept last night, she was especially chilled and pulled her neck scarf up over the bottom of her face as the sparse snowflakes danced in the wind and anxiety whirled inside her.

In a lovely room with comfortable chairs a woman with the law firm introduced Gloria and Ann, as Gloria remained seated, saying, "Are you as stressed as I am?" Disarmed by Gloria's informal comment, Ann replied clumsily, "Yes, I'm somewhat undone." Gloria softly said, "Oh my, I'm sorry,"

The lawyer showed Ann and Gloria a buzzer on the low round table in front of them which they were to press if there was anything they wanted or needed. She closed the door behind her and the two possible relatives were on their own.

Chapter Sixty

Family Wound

Gloria, with white hair, blue eyes, clear skin, arthritic hands, may or may not resemble Ann's father, who Ann never saw as old as this stranger. Then Gloria asked, "Do you have siblings? Are you are married? Have children? Grandchildren?"

Ann gave details. Gloria expressed sadness over Mel's death, asked a few more questions about Ann's life, and began a soliloquy.

"My story is basically this. I lost my parents before I was fourteen. They died, but I've never known what happened to Peter, my only sibling. Death is like having a tooth pulled, but not knowing if someone is dead or alive is like a non-stop toothache. Before I die, I want this old, old pain in me to stop. I want to know what happened to Peter.

"One Sunday afternoon in June, in Steelton, PA, our town where daddy worked in the steel mill and mother was a housewife, my daddy and my brother had an argument that didn't reverse itself like their arguments had before. As an adult I came to realize daddy wanted his son to be tough, physically strong, ultra-masculine like himself, whereas Peter was artistic, gentle, sensitive. Peter was nine years older than me. Aunt Jenny told me my mother had miscarriages between the births of Peter and me.

"In Steelton generation after generation worked in the steel mills. I don't think daddy wanted that for Peter, but felt my brother needed to be strong in case that's what he had to do. Daddy had an eighth-grade education. He was proud of Peter graduating from high school.

"Daddy worked hard at the mill, and kept our house in top shape. There wasn't money for big changes, but daddy knew how to keep things working and looking decent in our house and yard. Mother sewed with her sister, Aunt Jenny, who was an exceptional seamstress. Mother was her helper. Daddy had a difficult life. Trying to understand him in my adult years, I've had to come to appreciate how brutal his life was and how well he coped under the circumstances. But I was terribly angry at him for years.

"Daddy's parents, along with his brother and sister, all perished in a nighttime fire that burned down their farm house while they slept. Daddy was nineteen at the time, living in Steelton, already working in the mill helping support his farm family. They perished because he wasn't home to get them out, he said. He believed if he'd been there he could have saved them.

"He also believed if he hadn't missed Mass sometimes after he moved to Steelton, the farm house might not have burned down. But his work schedule at the mill was grueling; he had to sleep when he could even if that was on Sunday. We heard this often. He was a dutiful Catholic through and through.

"On that tragic Sunday afternoon when Peter left forever, daddy and Peter were arguing again about Peter marrying Vivian, who was not Catholic, and sin upon sin, her parents were divorced, both remarried, and 'Vivian was probably needing a home, a meal ticket,' daddy said. Peter's marriage plans were in every way wrong in daddy's eyes.

"Peter, whom daddy loved dearly, was putting his immortal soul in danger if he married this girl who'd been at our house only once for a short afternoon. As an adult I realized it wasn't about the person Vivian. It was about religion; daddy's fearful religious attitude."

Gloria told the story: "Daddy and Peter were shouting at each other that Sunday afternoon. Daddy said Peter should listen to his father who knew how bad life can get, who was no stranger to catastrophe, like losing his whole family in a scorching blaze. Peter said he wasn't a kid. He knew what he was doing. If daddy knew what losing family was like, he should know he wouldn't want it to happen again, Peter threatened.

"Finally, daddy said he would "disown" Peter if he married Vivian. I was yet to learn precisely what that word meant, but hearing it for the first time I felt a devastating impact of something awful. Amidst Mother's tears, and mine, because I saw her crying, Peter walked out the door that Sunday afternoon and we never saw him again, though we didn't know that day it was a forever thing. I know mother wrote to him repeatedly at the rooming house where he was living in a nearby town, but the letters came back. He'd moved and we didn't know where. Our house turned into a morgue.

"Life in Steelton was harsh. Aunt Jenny and family lived next door. Her husband Edwin lost his life in the mill when I was too young to remember. Their daughter Carrie seemed OK at birth but turned out to be crippled: cerebral palsy. After Edwin was gone, daddy helped Aunt Jenny, as overworked as he was, with what needed fixing around her house. She was more a tailor than a regular seamstress and mother did most of the ordinary sewing while Aunt Jenny did the tailoring jobs. Aunt Jenny was lucky to have a home job so she could be with Carrie.

"Peter was kind to Carrie who was near my age. He often read to both of us. And Peter took care of those horrible chickens, gathered their eggs, which he delivered to regular customers in the neighborhood, and saved the money which after graduation he used to go to a job in Harrisburg. After he moved, the chickens were mine and I hated taking care of them; the hens flying at me from nests as I gathered the eggs. After daddy got sick, we sold the chickens. He gave me the money to keep for a rainy day, he said.

"After both mother and daddy died, Aunt Jenny and Carrie moved into our house with me, as our house was bigger than theirs. Aunt Jenny rented out her house, and we always kept a female boarder in our house, which helped us survive through the years. Along with Aunt Jenny's sewing, the three of us had more financial security than many in Steelton. Aunt Jenny repeatedly told me to remember that half of my parents' house belonged to me and half to Peter. We both thought Peter would come back into our lives."

Chapter Sixty-One

Aunt Jenny, Carrie

"Aunt Jenny prayed at every meal for everyone we knew, living and dead, especially Peter. Even during the years I was angry with God, I prayed for Peter. He was named Peter after St. Peter, the Rock on which the church was built. My name is Gloria because of the Latin, *Gloria in excelsis Deo,* Glory to God in the highest. My father insisted on both names, Peter and Gloria. He was a religious man. Mother's Catholicism was more mellow, balanced, deeper. But she hadn't had the tragedy in daddy's life; she didn't have his fears.

"Aunt Jenny also had deep, soothing faith. For all of Aunt Jenny's hard knocks, she was always thanking God for the three of us having each other, food, a house, geraniums that bloomed indoors during the winter, another tailoring job, and she never forgot to pray for those less fortunate. Memories of geranium blossoms in winter remained with me; their brightness helped immensely on dreary days, during dreary times.

"Not long after daddy died, I stopped going to Mass. Aunt Jenny and I took turns staying with Carrie on Sunday, as she couldn't walk, or control her hands, or even sit straight. Her body twisted more as the years went by; she was never left alone. However, when it was my turn to go to Mass, I didn't go. If the weather was decent, I walked in the direction of the church but took a detour for a long walk and then came home at the right time. In bad weather, I walked into the church, sat at the back, and forced myself to think about a book I was reading or made my imagination go someplace else, like fantasizing about what it would be like when Peter was back with us. I disliked God and everything related to **HIM**. He was a troublemaker.

"After high school graduation I told Aunt Jenny I didn't want to go to church anymore. She understood and didn't make a fuss, but then Aunt Jenny didn't make fusses. I stayed home with Carrie so Aunt Jenny could escape the house, for she rarely went out, as I made the few errands around town.

"One Sunday when I was a senior in high school, I was in the last pew, and almost against my will I heard part of a bible reading:

It was you who created my inmost self
And put me together in my mother's womb
For all these mysteries I thank you
For the wonder of myself, for the wonder of your works.

You know me through and through
From having watched my bones take shape
When I was being formed in secret
Knitted together in the limbo of the womb. (Psalm 139: 13-15)

"I found it in the bible at home and read this to Carrie and Aunt Jenny. It was not easy for Carrie to make her wishes known, for a spasm overtook her when she tried to talk; almost none of Carrie's body worked right, though her intelligence was intact. However, with great effort she indicated she wanted me to read the bible words again, and then again. To the end of her life she never stopped wanting to hear those words.

"Carrie knew lack of oxygen at birth caused her condition. She once used the word "unusual" to describe her life. She died in her mid-twenties when her crippled distorted body forced one organ to push against another so her internal organs couldn't function properly, which the doctors had predicted. When Peter left, a great love in Carrie's life had gone away. I always knew I'd leave Steelton.

"Not long after Carrie died, Aunt Jenny died from heart problems, like mother died from heart problems after Peter left. Aunt Jenny was older than mother. She told me she was an old-maid before Edwin came into her life. She was a remarkably resourceful woman, selling her house next door when she realized Carrie was dying. Thus, Carrie's medical bills and funeral expenses and her own were paid for. She didn't leave much money, but no debts either.

"By the age of twenty-four, I was free to leave Steelton. I was ready for a job where I could use the shorthand I never stopped practicing after the Gregg shorthand class I took in high school. After that class, I did shorthand in all classes, recording every word anybody said. When a customer came for a garment fitting with Aunt Jenny I scratched out their conversation. Then, I would read their chatting back to Carrie, exaggerating the voices, the intonations, making them sound sassy and silly, which amused Carrie. It was a game for us and excellent training for me. When we got a radio, I practiced my shorthand while listening to it.

"I first saw the marvels of shorthand from our female boarders, all secretarial types for the bosses at the steel mills, which is why I originally took the shorthand class and then later I became hooked on the idea of shorthand being my ticket to earning my own living someday, someplace other than Steelton."

Chapter Sixty-Two

Locking the Door

"After Aunt Jenny's death, the house sold quickly. Neighbors and others anticipated her death and had an eye on buying the house knowing I would not stay in Steelton. Through the years I told anyone who would listen that I intended to leave, but always said it in a way not to offend Aunt Jenny or Carrie. I loved them fiercely, for they were my world after Peter left and death took mother and daddy.

"Closing the house the last time, I took a train to Albany NY. Nearby Harrisburg was where people usually went to find work because of being the state capital, but my dream was to leave the area, the state, so I went to neighboring New York, where in Albany, I expected many government jobs waiting for a self-proclaimed shorthand whiz. Before I left Steelton I stopped-by the high school and thanked Mrs. Garner for believing in me and told her my plans. As always, she expressed high hopes for my future and the encouragement felt good.

"As the train left Steelton, I had cash in my purse to get started in Albany, knowing that money from the sale of the house was waiting for me in a bank in Albany, sent there by the bank in Steelton. The future felt secure. I would search for Peter from Albany. I was tearful; leaving behind the graves of mother, daddy, aunt Jenny, Carrie, and the scene where Peter left. I now would no longer expect him to walk up the front steps. He wouldn't know where to find me though I told the people who bought the house I would send them my address when I had one, should Peter ever send a letter.

"Leaving Steelton made Peter more gone than before. I was determined to keep his half of the money from the sale of the house in a savings account where it would draw interest. Giving the money to him would be an added joy when we met again. And he might be in Albany! This thought cheered me considerably. I was young and optimistic.

"But leaving the house seared into me like a blast furnace. The house held my life and much death. I walked into every room, wept, and told the room good-bye. The wall paper was what mother and daddy put there. I speculated that Peter and I were the only people in the whole world who could remember the wall paper in each room. This thought increased my overwhelming nostalgia for the house I hadn't yet left. Strangely, I wanted to emotionally burn inside as if to cauterize my many aching wounds, my massive heartache.

"The house sold with the furniture in it, even the books and magazines. That hurt. The chicken coop and fence were by then overgrown with tangled vines which were greening again. There was no trace of where the garden had been. Memories of Peter, mother and daddy kept flooding in as I slowly said good-bye to everything the house meant to me those last weeks before I left. It was early spring. The night before I left, I cried myself to sleep.

"Locking the door for the last time, I said good-bye to the pots of red geraniums on the front porch, which had survived another winter indoors on the floor by big windows because Aunt Jenny taught me they need as much sun as they can get and do best when kept on the floor where the room temperature is coolest.

"After Aunt Jenny brought the plants in for the winter, every day she raised fully the shades on the south side double windows in Carrie's room, the parlor, for Carrie and the plants. Oh, the joy the bright blossoms brought Carrie. A bright floor lamp was kept on all day for her during grey days of winter, which likely helped the plants as well. A few more sewing stitches would pay for the added electricity, Aunt Jenny said.

"My aunt gave her entire being to the life which was hers. Long work days were bearable, I believe, because she greatly enjoyed sewing, creating garments. She knew fabrics and loved them. Thousands of hours she spent at the sewing machine, and a vivid memory is her body bent over the dining room table cutting out another garment.

"I learned to cook but never well. We did always have fine meals served on time, as Carrie looked forward to meals and Aunt Jenny knew that. In Albany I would have only myself to be concerned with, I assumed. I would work hard and life would go well. These were some of my thoughts as I said good-bye to the geraniums on the porch that spring day."

Chapter Sixty-Three

Pete and Vi

Ann found Gloria an interesting story teller in the cozy lawyers' office on that most unbelievable day, when Gloria looked pointedly at Ann and said, "I've talked far too much and need to use the restroom but do you feel your father is my brother; that I am your aunt?"

Gloria's abrupt change startled Ann. "Probably," is all Ann offered back while she was feverishly thinking: what Gloria said seemed true, which explained why Ann's parents showed no interest in religion, since religion had torn the family apart. Yet it seemed inconceivable that Peter was estranged from his parents and sister for the rest of his life. That was almost too much to believe.

Yet, the "warehouse" of Ann's youth likely reflected the emotional clutter of Ann's parents. Since her own therapy, Ann thought in terms of outward symptoms mirroring deep emotions; the chaos of her parents' living quarters reflecting their psychological chaos.

Ann mentally rehearsed in Gloria's restroom absence: this woman of average height; a thin person whose dark grey slacks were topped by a light blue-gray pullover sweater atop a white blouse with a white collar accenting her white hair cut in a natural bob. The sweater and her light blue eyes complemented each other. An attractive woman, looking younger than her 81 years, except for her hands with gnarled joints.

Ann remembered the family photos she had brought with her, one of them a professional photo with Pete and Vi at Ann's wedding many years ago. This she gave to Gloria upon her return from the ladies' room. Gloria adjusted her eye glasses, moved the picture closer and further away, hoping for better focus and peak lighting. Ann wished she'd brought a magnifying glass. She pushed the buzzer on the table and a magnifying glass was brought to Gloria whose face was serious and intense; as she asked questions. The most recent snapshots were when Vi and Pete were living in Grand Suite with Ann and Mel, but by then Ann's parents were ill.

Ann's wedding photo let Gloria know how Peter looked as a healthy, fully mature man, and she looked at the picture again and again.

Gloria asked, "Were your parents happy together? Did your father ever speak of mother, daddy, me?" Ann regretfully replied, "Not that I recall. The few times I remember asking him about his growing up he would say something like, 'That was a long time ago,' or 'I don't remember.' And I never knew my father to be untruthful so I believed him. When I asked mother, her comment would be poetic, 'What you are wanting to know is buried in the far distant past, misted over by time.' Her lyrical words satisfied me. Together we lived a life of disordered closeness."

"By disordered you mean physically messy?" Gloria wanted to be sure.

Ann clarified, "Yes, physically disheveled. There was no abuse of any kind or neglect. Our home was not mean or awful. It was chronic slipshod mayhem because of it being the joint work studio of two hardworking creative people who I now know had unresolved issues in their lives."

"As to whether they were happy together, I'd say *yes*," and Ann told how Pete and Vi in their last months, sitting side by side in their wheelchairs, hooked their fingers together. "They worked, smoked, drank endless cups of coffee together, became ill together, she of emphysema and he of lung cancer, and died within a short time of each other. I'd say they found each other interesting; they were deeply bonded; were maybe almost too alike.

"My father sketched me as quickly as anything, making funny caricatures, which I found in my bedroom closet when we cleaned out the warehouse, and I still have them; my greatest treasures from childhood. Someday you'll see them. My mother performed her skits while I was her audience. Sometimes I sang with her as she played the accordion. Music, books, magazines, museum posters, travel posters, papers, art supplies filled our unusual residence. My parents were Pete and Vi to me, for as long as I can remember; never mommy, daddy, or anything like that."

Gloria calmly observed, "Perhaps they could not bear the pain of those words." Ann's therapist had made the same observation.

Gloria took her cell phone from her pants pocket to check the time, as she told Ann of the college student Ryan, who accompanied her on the flight that day, and was now studying in an adjacent room. She shared, "I first resisted having a cell phone, but now find it indispensable. Resisting a changing world doesn't work, I learned the hard way."

Chapter Sixty-Four

Giles Gaylord

Gloria told of being disheartened upon arriving in Albany with her shorthand skills only to find that a stenotype machine outstripped what she could do with shorthand. So, she went to school in the evenings to learn the machine. She lived frugally, determined to keep Peter's house money for him. Her financial plan was working until Giles came along when she was 28, and working as a court reporter.

Giles Gaylord, single and exciting, in his early thirties, co-owner of a restaurant, was attracted to Gloria as he served on a jury for a trial in the court room where she was recording testimony on her now familiar stenotype machine. He was attracted to the court reporter who took no notice of him, busy doing her job. After the trial was concluded, he one day arranged a 'coincidental' meeting at the door he knew she exited, and introduced himself as she was leaving work.

By this time, she was no longer a naïve Steelton girl, for court room dramas had stretched her understanding of the world. But with no experience in the ways of romance, she was easily caught in the web Giles spun. His doting attention filled many gaps in her life. The old pains of loss began to take second place to the thrill of being with Giles. After a few months, the two were married at the court house and moved into an apartment.

She continued to work hard with the stenotype machine, and Giles spent long hours at the restaurant; their time together was uncommonly precious to her, and so it was wrenching when Giles began working longer and longer hours. He came home later and later at night, cleaning up, readying the restaurant for the next day, doing the books.

Disturbing as this was, Gloria looked forward to Sunday, for the restaurant was closed on Sunday. But as his partner did less and less, Giles began to spend Sunday evenings at the restaurant preparing for the coming week, and needed to hire additional employees. Gloria understood the need to buy-out his unreliable partner.

What began as a slight drain of money from Gloria's salary, began to dip into money she had in savings, and buying-out the partner required the bulk of Peter's house money, which would be easily repaid once Giles had full control of the restaurant.

The awful truth broke Gloria's heart. Giles was a gambler. Long nights of poker in the back room of the restaurant swallowed up his money, her money, Peter's money. The deception tore Gloria into pieces of unbelievable sadness and despair. The divorce put her in debt. She had to start over. Peter's money was gone.

At that time, she yearned for the masculine strength of her father, who, despite his faults would have protected her from a wolf like Giles. And she ached for her mother's soothing comfort. Grief for her parents consumed her grim days and nights. Worry clung to her; exhaustion was a constant companion. Amongst the few possessions brought from Steelton was her mother's white rosary which she began taking to bed, reciting the prayers, relaxing, and falling asleep, helping her face another day. However, she became and remained a chronic worrier, especially about money.

Gloria told how she took college classes to help insure a financial future for herself, met friends who remained friends to the present time. Eventually, she re-found religion, began going to Mass, and remembered that after Peter left her father often said, "'I should have prayed. That's what I needed to do. I should have prayed instead.'" Gloria wiped away a tear. Ann wondered if such emotional recall was healthy for someone Gloria's age.

Chapter Sixty-
Five

Vivian's Pregnancy

More chatter, and Gloria said they needed to have their picture taken together. Ann pressed the buzzer on the low table so office staff would come take photos. Gloria telephoned her escort Ryan, studying in an adjacent room, to come meet Ann. Gloria clearly had her wits about her and gave the impression of an alert, take-charge woman, at her age or any age; someone who has been in charge of her own life. She asked about the pictures Ann brought, "May I take a picture or two with me, until we meet again."

Gloria chose Ann's marriage photo and several others, and commented, "Family pictures were in an upstairs trunk and an unknown leak in the roof ruined everything in that trunk before Aunt Jenny discovered it. The snapshot the law firm sent you was the best of those rescued."

Before Ryan appeared, Gloria had more questions: "Did Peter attend college or a trade school?" Realizing again how little firm knowledge Ann had about her parents she said, "I don't think so; I've always believed he was self-taught."

Gloria muttered to herself, "He deserved college." Then asked, "Was he ever in the military?" Ann did have that piece of information, "No, he couldn't pass the physical; was in an auto accident, broke his left leg in several places and always limped." These words obviously pained Gloria.

Strong, wholesome-looking college student Ryan appeared. Gloria introduced him as her escort for the day. They chatted as coats, scarves, gloves were brought to them. The receptionist accompanied the threesome to the elevator. In the lobby there were hugs. Gloria and Ann kissed each other on the cheek. Gloria had her arm through Ryan's arm, and used her cane with the other hand, as they made their way outside to the waiting cab.

Ann walked to the parking garage, and paid special attention finding her car knowing she was on emotional overload and needed to be alert. She easily exited the parking garage and entered the expressway towards home. She was full of everything; filled to the brim. She told herself to keep focused on driving.

Off the freeway and onto residential streets she allowed more thoughts of Gloria and wished Mel was here to share this adventure, for her lack of family history was always a mystery to him. Ann pulled into the driveway and Rachel's car was already there. While getting out of her car, Sarah's car pulled into the driveway behind Ann. They walked together under architect Mel's overhang at the side door of the house. They opened the door of the house greeted by its warmth, the smell of food. Rachel had brought food from a deli and was warming it.

Telling her daughters what Gloria shared, it was clear to Ann's girls that Ann was in Vivian's womb the Sunday of the terrible argument between Peter and his father, and thus, Vi's pregnancy was Peter's urgency to marry. Vivian's pregnancy was the cause of Peter's stressful stubbornness when he was arguing with his father. Perhaps Gloria had arrived at the same calculation today, though she didn't say so. The thought of Vi's pregnancy hadn't occurred to Ann as her head was too filled with Gloria's stories.

Chapter Sixty-Six

Cremains

Early next morning, Ann was at her computer to send an e-mail to aunt Gloria thanking her for yesterday, when she found an e-mail sent last night when Gloria returned home, typed by a caregiver at her assisted living facility with Gloria's words: "Today was the beginning of the end of the ache for me. Quite a lot has happened for this old body to absorb. More later."

But there would be no more words from Gloria, for she died two days later. Travel, the chilly weather, and the stress or relief of meeting Ann were perhaps too much for her. Or maybe Gloria died at the "right time," Ann told herself.

Gloria's cremains were sent to Ann, who with daughters Rachel, Sarah and their families took the ashes to Steelton along with those of Ann's parents, to be interred in the Catholic cemetery next to Ann's paternal grandparents. The cremains of Gloria, Vivian and Peter were put to rest.

Gloria's stories changed Ann, who remembered the premonition in the Kansas pasture alive with birdsong and stars, coupled with the

Montel driveway birdsong, that she would soon learn something about her ancestry. This had come to pass.

However, life without Mel was a strangeness that didn't stop. Ann yearned for the familiar, the dependable sameness of his presence, his steady energy that completed daily living. Their home was too large for Ann to handle. The very idea of maintaining it drained her.

Well-meaning people gave Ann advice: don't make big changes in your life after your spouse dies; give yourself time to adapt. She found she couldn't take that advice, for the many rooms of the house increased loneliness, and kept reminding her of Mel's designs, plans, renovations to their original starter home. She had trouble sleeping without his reassuring presence beside her.

Her upper-level art room of glass no longer felt welcoming. She must sell the house and move. No, she must move and then sell the house. She couldn't wait. Which is what she did. Her daughters understood and helped her. With their help, plus the energy and expertise of a remarkable real estate agent, who was also to become her friend, Ann was settled in a high-rise condo before the house sold.

Ann wondered about the future. She now knew the paternal part of her ancestral story. She was still dealing with the loss of Mel. She'd walked through her own depression, lived through the deaths of Matti and Gabby, found satisfaction volunteering at the maternity facility, met Julia as well as Julia's biological father, Cal.

What might the future hold? Ann was yet to meet and impact the life of Dee Kendrick, who was drinking coffee in her own backyard when this book began. Dee's remarkable story is told in the novel *What Might We Know*.

ACKNOWLEDGMENTS

Special thanks to Maureen Lumley, PhD, who connected the author with Jennifer Leigh Selig, PhD., publisher of Empress Publications.